DATE DUE

Also by Cat Sebastian

The Seducing the Sedgwicks Series
It Takes Two to Tumble
A Gentleman Never Keeps Score

The Regency Impostors Series
Unmasked by the Marquess

COMING SOON
A Duke in Disguise

The Turner Series
The Soldier's Scoundrel
The Lawrence Browne Affair
The Ruin of a Rake

A GENTLEMAN NEVER KEEPS SCORE

A Seducing the Sedgwicks Novel

CAT SEBASTIAN

AVONIMPULSE
An Imprint of HarperCollinsPublishers

A GENTLEMAN NEVER KEEPS SCORE. Copyright © 2018 by Cat Sebastian. All rights reserved. Printed in the United States of America. No part of this book may be used or reproduced in any manner whatsoever without written permission except in the case of brief quotations embodied in critical articles and reviews. For information, address HarperCollins Publishers, 195 Broadway, New York, NY 10007.

Digital Edition JULY 2018 ISBN: 978-0-06-282063-1
Print Edition ISBN: 978-0-06-282158-4

Cover art by Fredericka Ribes
Cover photographs (left to right); © Jenn LeBlanc 2015 (man); © Mary Chronis, VJ Dunraven Productions & PeriodImages.com (man); © wtamas / Shutterstock (face); © Jana Mackova / Shutterstock (background)

Avon Impulse and the Avon Impulse logo are registered trademarks of HarperCollins Publishers in the United States of America.
Avon and HarperCollins are registered trademarks of HarperCollins Publishers in the United States of America and other countries.

FIRST EDITION

18 19 20 21 22   HDC   10 9 8 7 6 5 4 3 2 1

For my children, who are very patient with my failure to write anything about dragons

ACKNOWLEDGMENTS

As always, this book wouldn't have been possible without the support and hard work of the entire Avon team, especially my editor, Elle Keck. I hope all writers have cheerleaders and advocates as tireless as my agent, Deidre Knight, and my beta reader/friend/plot-hole-wrangler, Margrethe Martin. I'm indebted to Tasha Harrison for reading an early version of this book and providing the sort of feedback that is pure gold to a flailing writer.

CHAPTER ONE

1817

Hartley wrinkled his nose. "Why are you wearing that?" he asked his brother. Will's coat had quite plainly been tailored for a different person, if it had been tailored at all, which was an open question. Loose threads and threadbare patches renounced any claim the wearer might have to gentility. It had likely been a depressing garment from the start, but now it was the stuff of tragedy.

"This?" Will asked, looking down at his chest. "It's a coat. I know we're a bit carefree at the moment," he said, gesturing to the empty bottle of wine that stood on the table between them. "But you do know what a coat is."

"That's not a coat," Hartley sniffed. "It's melancholy, in sartorial form."

"It's really very comfortable," Will spoke earnestly, as if this quality could possibly matter in a garment.

"I'll give you five shillings if you let me burn it."

Will clutched the coat close to his body as if Hartley

might try to pull it off his shoulders. "The real question is why *you* are wearing *that*," he said.

Hartley examined his own attire. Slate gray waistcoat with mother of pearl buttons; shirt and cravat of snowy white linen, well starched; dove gray kerseymere pantaloons; black coat of Italian wool. He let his gaze linger with satisfaction on his top boots, snug to the point of impracticality and buffed to a highly satisfactory shine by his valet. The overall effect was flawless, utterly correct, and à la mode while still being understated. "I'm dressed impeccably," he pronounced. Not a boast, just the unvarnished truth.

"Exactly. To sit at home with me."

"Was there someplace you wanted to go?" Hartley spoke with as much dignity as he could muster after half a bottle of claret. "Don't let me keep you."

Will shook his head and leaned back against the sofa. "That wasn't my point. You've been holed up in this house for two months."

"Untrue. I walk every day in the park," he said. It was neither here nor there that he timed these walks to occur when the park would be deserted, sparing himself the embarrassment of sharing space with those who had cast him out. "Besides, I've suggested that we travel. We could go to Paris and then be in Italy before winter." He could picture a well-kept *pensionne*, an unlimited supply of heady Italian wine, and something like the promise of a blank slate, or at least oblivion.

Will examined the remnants of wine in his glass as if they were particularly interesting. "I've seen enough of the world. And I have obligations keeping me in England for the time being." He addressed these words to the glass, not looking at his brother.

Hartley hadn't been anywhere or seen anything, nor had he any real urge to do so, but it would be better than staring at these same four walls day in and day out. Unlike his brother, he hadn't even the faintest shadow of an obligation to any living creature, which surely ought to bring him some satisfaction. "The less said about your obligations, the better," he said coldly. Will only gave him a disappointed frown. Hartley cleared his throat. "If not five shillings, then perhaps a guinea? You could buy two ugly coats for that much."

That got him a laugh, and Hartley let his mouth twitch slightly in return.

"Why don't you travel on your own?" Will asked. "Or with a friend?" His voice hit an odd register on *friend* and Hartley shot his brother a quelling look. "Or maybe you could move to a different part of the country? Somewhere you could have a fresh start."

"I don't want a fresh start," Hartley snapped.

Will was kind enough not to mention that a moment ago, Hartley had been willing to get on the next packet sailing for Calais. But that would have been for Will; Hartley might loosen the stranglehold he had on the tattered remains of his life if only he could tell himself it was necessary for one of his brothers. But to leave of his own accord felt like defeat. He was still here—still alive, still in this house, still where people had to reckon with his existence. He wasn't going to let himself get erased on top of everything else.

"If I ever take up crime," Will said after a few moments of almost companionable silence, "it'll be arson. And I'll start with this house."

Hartley pretended not to understand. "Please take up something more profitable than arson."

"As if you don't have insurance. Sell it. Let it. Stay at a hotel. Stay with me. Pitch a tent among the cows in Green Park for all I care. But you can't carry on living here." He looked around the room, as if taking in for the first time the crimson velvet drapes and deep mahogany bookcases. His gaze lingered on a few blank spots on the wall, where the paper hadn't faded to the mellow green of the rest of the room. The staff at this house had always been vigilant about drawing the curtains when the sun shone through the tall windows, but even so, some light had leaked into this room over the years, and Hartley knew why it hadn't reached those few rectangles. "I don't believe in ghosts, but this place is haunted. You must see ghosts everywhere. And, Hartley, it's ruining you. You're twenty-three and you're living in a mausoleum."

"You say that as if you're eighty. Perhaps we ought to talk about how you aren't living life to its fullest either, dear brother." Will lived in a hovel and spent his days writing dismal little things for magazines that forgot to pay him. It was nothing short of a miracle that he managed to keep body and soul together. When Hartley thought of the things he had done and the dubious choices he had made, all to give his brothers a chance at having the safe, secure life of gentlemen, and what a mess they had all made of it, he could scream.

Will shook his head. "But I'm content, and you aren't."

He finished the wine in his glass. "You can't go on living here," he repeated.

"Of course I can. It's well situated and lavishly furnished. I couldn't ask for a more suitable home. I'm grateful that it was left to me by my doting godfather." He was rather proud that he kept his voice entirely free of irony.

"Hartley."

"I have Lady Mary Carstairs to the right and Mr. Justice Burke to the left. It's a very good street."

"Hartley," Will repeated.

The house was utterly silent around them except for the swinging pendulum of the longcase clock in the corner. The servants had gone to bed, Hartley having given instructions that they needn't wait up for him.

"Perhaps next time you'll join me at my lodgings for a drink," Will said, rising to his feet and taking his hat off the table. "Or we can meet for a pint at your local." *Anywhere but here* was Will's unspoken meaning.

Hartley threw back his wine and stood somewhat unsteadily. "Does it bother you to think of why he left me this house?" he asked, looking up at his brother. Even as the words left his mouth he knew he was being pathetic, looking in the wrong place for proof that he hadn't ruined all their lives. "Is that why you don't want to be here?"

Will touched his shoulder. It had been so long since anyone had touched Hartley—even his valet had learned to dress him with only the most glancing and impersonal contact—that he was momentarily taken aback.

"Hartley, the question is whether it bothers *you*."

This was precisely the sort of arrant nonsense that Will *would* say. Hartley stepped away and let his brother's hand fall to his side.

There was something about an empty pub that never felt right to Sam. Some places were meant to be filled with the warmth of bodies and the buzz of voices; silent, they were haunted by the people who ought to have been there. While there was some relief in seeing the last customer out the door and spending a quiet hour polishing pewter tankards to a satisfying shine and wiping any sticky traces of spilled beer off the bar, Sam was certain the Bell was at its best when it was crowded and a bit chaotic.

He had only started his ritual of rubbing down the bar with lemon oil when the door swung open. Any of the Bell's regulars would have known it was closed, so Sam turned toward the door, ready for a minor emergency: somebody in need of a hot meal, a clean bed, or a couple shillings to pay the rent. Or maybe they just needed the kind of safety only a looming former prizefighter could provide. Sam was happy to be able to give that kind of safety. Life in London was hard, harder still if you were poor, black, and out on the streets past ten at night.

But it was only Kate. "It's late for you to be about," he said, putting down his chamois in order to pull her a mug of ale. There was only one reason for Kate to be out this late, and the lines around her eyes and the disordered state of her hair corroborated that she had been at another lying in. She said it happened every autumn, this rush of new lives, but Sam couldn't remember her being so thoroughly run off her feet in years past.

"Fourteen hours," she said, sitting heavily on a stool at the bar. Her voice was hoarse. "Then another two trying to get the babe to nurse." Even as Kate spoke, Sam heard a scratching of paws along the flagstone floors of the taproom. Every other minute of the day, Sam was sure the dog was as deaf as a stone. But all Kate had to do was whisper and the mongrel materialized at her side. Kate had rescued—stolen, not to put too fine a point on it—the dog from a rat pit near on ten years ago, and it had been following her around ever since.

"Have you eaten?" Sam asked, already reaching under the bar for a dish.

"Not since yesterday."

Sam had put aside a slice of pork pie for his own supper, but he could have some bread and butter later on. He slid the pie across the bar to Kate, and she thanked him by giving him a tired salute with her mug. Sam poured himself a pint and they drank in companionable silence for a few minutes. After a few years behind the bar, Sam knew the look of someone who needed to talk. He also knew that a person was more likely to speak if he kept busy, so in between sips of his ale he silently set about cleaning the tankards.

"Nick asked me to marry him again," Kate said. No surprise there. Sam's brother had been fond of Kate since they were all children together. They both might have thought Sam was a blind man, but he saw Kate coming and going from Nick's rooms upstairs at all hours of the night and day.

"What did you tell him this time?"

"I reminded him that we're both too busy to get married."

That was a poor excuse. It was true that they were busy. Nick was up every day at dawn, cooking the meals they sold at the Bell. And after years of working alongside her mother, Kate was midwife to what seemed like every black woman in London. To Sam's mind, that was an even better reason for them to get married—two busy people who enjoyed one another's company would surely be best served by shortening the distance between themselves, but he wasn't fool enough to tell Kate how to live her life.

"Did my brother pretend to believe you or no?" Sam asked without looking up from the tankard he was polishing.

Out of the corner of his eye he saw her crack a smile. "He did, bless him."

Sam never ceased to be amazed by Nick's inherent decency; as far as Sam knew, his brother had never done any living thing the least harm. Nick had been born good, while Sam had to learn it secondhand. And, as foreigners often spoke with traces of their old tongue, sometimes Sam feared he would never lose traces of that old blood-soaked accent. "Want to tell me the real reason you don't want to make an honest man out of him?"

"You'll think I'm daft."

"Already do."

"Here, give me one of those." She took a rag and began attacking a tankard as if it had done her wrong. She knew her way around behind a bar, Kate did. She had been a barmaid at the Bell back when her father still owned it, long before

Sam had bought the place. They had been a good team. They still were: Kate brought people into the world, Nick fed them, and Sam poured their drinks and gave them a place to be warm and safe.

Sam went to fetch the broom, and when he came back he found Kate paused, rag midair. "It's about the painting," she said.

"What painting?" He instinctively checked the wood-work for peeling paint that needed to be retouched. That would be an expense that had to wait. This week he had already paid half a crown to the chimney man to do something about the smoke that billowed through the room whenever the wind blew from the north, and then another two shil-lings to the glazier to mend a window some neighborhood ruffian lobbed a rock through.

"The dirty one I sat for."

Oh, *that* painting. "That was, what, five years ago?" In her youth, Kate had been a bit on the unruly side. She had been helping an opera girl bring on her monthlies when the gentleman who had gotten the girl in trouble took a fancy to Kate. He had offered her a princely sum to let him paint her in the altogether. Kate agreed, having been a bit pressed for cash due to her father making a habit of losing money on bad wagers and strong drink. "What made you think of it now?"

"Closer to seven years. I don't like the idea of there being a picture out there of Nick's wife stark naked." She hoisted herself up onto the bar, her legs dangling off the edge as they had when she was a kid.

"But Nick already knows. Hell, he's known about that

painting since he tried to persuade you not to do it. If it bothered him, he wouldn't have asked you to marry him."

She twisted the cloth in her hands. "That's why it's bothering me."

Sam raised his eyebrows. "Because he doesn't care?"

"No!" Smiling, she flung the rag at his head, but he caught it. "Because I remember what he said. 'How are you going to get a decent husband with your bosoms out there for all the world to see,'" she said in a passable imitation of Nick's serious-minded way of speaking.

"He was a kid when he said those things." And if Sam knew his brother, he'd apologized a thousand times over for having said them in the first place. "Besides, wasn't it a lord who wanted the painting? What are the odds of someone who knows you and Nick happening on a painting in a lord's house?"

"Could be someone who comes in to clean his windows or empty his chamber pots. And anyone who knows me would recognize it straight away."

That was true enough. Kate had a mass of black curls and a welter of dark brown freckles on her light brown skin. Sam frowned. "Still, I don't know there's much to do about it." He brought his tankard to his mouth.

Kate looked up at him, her dark eyes dead serious. "I want to get it back."

Sam nearly choked on his ale. But he knew better than to try to persuade Kate away from a bad idea. "Do you even know where it is?"

"The old pervert probably still has it. Like as not in a room with a pile of other dirty paintings for gents to gawk at."

The thought made his stomach clench in anger. "But you aren't sure."

"One way to find out." She shrugged.

He had a sinking feeling that she didn't mean writing a polite letter inquiring as to whether the man still had the painting and offering to purchase it for a fair price.

"Tell me you don't mean to shimmy up drain pipes." When she didn't answer, he pulled a chair off the table and straddled it, resting his chin on his forearms. "Because I can tell you my brother wouldn't fancy having to visit you at Bow Street. And neither would I."

Her brow furrowed, so he thought he might be getting through to her. "I suppose I could pay someone. Mrs. Newton's son, maybe."

"Telling Johnny Newton there's a dirty picture of yourself might not be your most discreet option."

"There has to be something I can do." She had a desperate look in her eye that made him worry she might do something foolish to get this painting back. He wanted to remonstrate, to tell her that she ought to stay safe, to mind all the written and unwritten rules about what a black person could do in this country. These days Sam himself followed every rule, no matter how trifling, and stayed well clear of anything that even looked like it might carry a hint of a problem. His license was paid, his pints were poured generously, and he made sure there was nothing for the building's owner to complain about. He never let himself lose sight of the fact that if anything ever went wrong, someone would be only too happy to pin it onto a black man. That had been a lesson he'd learned too well and too often, God help him.

That didn't make it fair, though. Nick and Kate ought to have a future, a life, all the good things they deserved, without it being ruined by rich men. The idea of a dirty old man having a painting of Kate when she had been too poor to turn down honest money—it didn't sit right with him. Kate shouldn't have that hanging over her for the rest of her life. Sam worked so hard to make sure the people in this community were safe and fed and had the best chance even though the deck was stacked against them; it was grossly unfair that Kate and Nick might have that taken from them. He knew exactly what kind of things people did with themselves when they were desperate. That was another lesson he had learned the hard way.

"What if I took care of it for you?" he heard himself asking.

Kate opened her eyes wide.

"I'd just find out about it," he said hastily. "See if maybe there's a kid in the kitchens who knows anything about naked paintings." He'd slip them a couple pennies to do a bit of poking around. Nothing wrong with that. "It's at least worth a try. What was the man's name? Sir Bastard somebody?"

"Were you sampling the new ale tonight?" she asked. "I want to tell you to be careful, and that you don't need to do this, but you know that already." She slid off the bar. "His name is Easterbrook, and he lives in a grand house on Brook Street."

Maybe if he could tell Kate that her painting wasn't hanging up for all the world to see, she wouldn't go about getting herself arrested. He could breathe easy for another day, knowing that he had kept his family safe.

CHAPTER TWO

William had been completely off the mark when he accused Hartley of never leaving his house. Here he was, strolling through Hyde Park just as he had always done, even if it was an hour past sunset and he wasn't likely to run into anyone he knew except a park warden telling him the park was closed. He was very nearly getting used to spending entire days not seeing anyone other than members of his dwindling staff.

It was the servants' day off, and while in most households that usually meant a girl stayed in the kitchen to make sure the fire didn't burn the house down, and a footman stayed upstairs to answer the door, Hartley had decided the footman and kitchen maid might as well enjoy whatever frolics the rest of the staff got up to. The fire could be safely banked and the front door could be bolted. It wasn't as if Hartley was expecting callers who would be put out if the door wasn't properly answered.

Other than Will, who could hardly be considered a proper guest, Hartley hadn't had any visitors at all in the two months since Martin Easterbrook, his godfather's only son, came of age, inherited his father's papers, and learned the truth about Hartley's relationship with Martin's father. Martin mustn't have wasted any time spreading the tale about town, because one day Hartley was a darling of society and the next he was a pariah. He had heard a single whisper: "there are letters," and knew his fate was sealed.

Even at sixteen, Hartley had known enough not to put anything on paper that would incriminate him. But he had sadly underestimated the ability of jaded London aristocrats to put the tawdriest possible spin on a set of facts. Hartley couldn't remember exactly what he had written, but he knew he had discussed spending time at Sir Humphrey Easterbrook's country house, knew he had asked for presents and advancement for his brothers. But those ill-advised letters might not have been enough to ruin him if Easterbrook hadn't left Hartley the townhouse.

Before Martin Easterbrook had opened his mouth, society had been content to assume that Sir Humphrey left his beloved godson the house on Brook Street out of affection, a gesture to smooth Hartley's way into the best society. But now they knew that it had been quid pro quo, knew, moreover, that in leaving the house and a legacy to Hartley he had impoverished his own son and heir. Impoverishing one's title was likely quite as bad as sodomy as far as the *ton* was concerned.

Since then, there hadn't been a single invitation, not even to the sort of dull dinner or musicale he never would have bothered attending a year ago. Acquaintances cut him dead or crossed to the opposite side of the street when they saw him. Hartley supposed he ought to be grateful that this comprehensive shunning was his only punishment, because if Martin had produced evidence, or if any witnesses had come forward, Hartley could easily have been pilloried or hanged. Being utterly alone in the world was a seaside holiday by comparison.

It was all for show, of course. Hartley understood that. Some of the people who had formerly welcomed him into their homes must have known all along that he wasn't precisely a ladies' man. Some men of his inclinations looked and acted like everybody else, but Hartley never quite managed it, and had long since stopped trying. Whatever it was that gave him away, whether it was a habit of speech or a set of mannerisms that identified him as a man who preferred men, it was so intrinsic to who he was and how he lived that he couldn't get rid of it.

It was dark now, and a chill was settling in that felt more like November than September. Hartley turned up the collar of his topcoat and tucked his hands into his pockets. His thin kid gloves did nothing to keep his hands warm but the change of seasons came as a relief. Autumn meant an excuse to put another layer of clothes between his body and the world. It meant a reprieve from the tyranny of merrymaking that a run of decent weather seemed to inspire in his countrymen. Autumn meant a glorious few months spent indoors, complaining about fog and drinking warm beverages.

The recollection that he'd be experiencing these pleasures alone had a significant dampening effect. He had never had close friends in the highest echelons of London society; he wasn't any good at confidences or warmth or whatever it was people expected of friends. He was an entirely passable acquaintance: he made amusing conversation, wore the right clothes, and blended into good company in a way that made people forget he hadn't been born to it. With the faith of a child and the ignorance of a tourist, he had assumed that once being accepted into their company, he wouldn't be cast out.

He turned into the mews behind his house. The kitchen door was left unlocked so that when the servants returned later that night they'd be able to let themselves in. This might have been imprudent but for the fact that Hartley had sold off everything worth stealing years ago. His godfather had left him the house and its contents but nothing to live on. In order to scrape together enough capital to invest for a modest income, Hartley had needed to auction off nearly all the furnishings. Any housebreakers would be sadly out of luck.

The mews was quiet at this hour, and Hartley was able to make his way to his house without being seen. But as he approached the door, he saw a figure standing in the shadows. Hartley went still and let his eyes adjust to the darkness. It was a man, broad and tall, even though he looked like he was making an effort to disappear into the gloom. Beneath the brim of his hat, his skin was dark brown, nearly as dark as the wool of his coat. Hartley recognized him as the same man he had seen across the street the previous week. Evidently, he had been watching Hartley's house then, as he was now.

Hartley could not think of any good reasons why a man would be lurking outside his kitchen door. But he couldn't think of any bad reasons either. Surely a housebreaker wouldn't simply stand there. In all likelihood he was walking out with Hartley's parlor maid and was waiting for a chance to steal a moment with her. Hartley wished them well. Godspeed, young lovers.

Surely, though, if he was walking out with the maid, he'd already know that this was her day out. Perhaps he was a spurned lover, and if so, Hartley did not want him making trouble for any of his maids. He stepped out of the shadows toward the stranger.

"Come into the light so I can see you," he said, his voice rusty from disuse. That was the worst part of being an outcast—London teemed with people but there was nobody to talk to. The stranger startled, and Hartley congratulated himself on his superior skulking abilities. "I'm unarmed," he added, holding up his empty hands. "I thought I'd take the opportunity to suggest that if you're walking out with Janet, you ought to know that her favorite sweets are peppermint creams. And also that if you hurt her I'll have you murdered."

"I never heard of Janet," the man said.

"It had better not be Polly," said Hartley, bristling. "She's hardly grown."

"I have no idea—"

"Cook, then?" He would have thought Cook a good deal too old for that sort of thing, but one never knew. "Good for her," he said. "I reckon she'll murder you herself if you put a foot wrong."

"Are you drunk? Do you need help getting home?" There was a touch of—could it be concern?—in the stranger's voice.

Hartley stepped even closer. "If you're not here for one of the maids, does that mean you're here for me? How flattering," he drawled. "One usually has to go to such trouble to arrange this sort of thing, and here you are, delivered to my doorstep." That ought to scare the fellow off right enough.

But instead of turning on his heel and running away, the stranger sighed. "All right mate, let's get you home where you can sober up someplace safe. Can't have you making advances to people in dark corners. You'll get yourself killed."

"I—I beg your pardon," Hartley stammered.

The stranger paid him no heed. "This where you live? Let's go."

A strong arm came around Hartley's shoulders, steering him toward the kitchen door. His customary fear stole his words and made him powerless to protest, but it was accompanied by a bittersweet awareness that in another lifetime, he might have wanted this strong arm around him, bringing him to a safe place.

Hartley let himself be shepherded inside.

For several evenings now, Sam had watched servants come and go from the grand house, but they kept to themselves. None seemed to be the type who would spare a few kind words to a stranger, let alone negotiate a bit of friendly espionage. Now that he was inside the house, he'd see what he could find out, but first he was going to get this poor sod someplace safe. It was no more than he'd do for a slightly deluded patron of the Bell. Really, you couldn't go around

making approaches to people like that. It was tricky, finding
your way as a man who preferred men, unless you had somebody to help you out. There were places where men could
meet one another, but maybe this fellow was too young or
inexperienced to know about them. Sam might mention it
before leaving, maybe: *go to the King's Arms at the docks, try
not to get yourself killed*. Just a helpful word to the wise. With
any luck, the lad would tell him about the paintings out of
gratitude.

The kitchen was dark, and Sam had to fumble around a
bit before finding a lamp. Now he could see the lad. Pale hair,
neatly combed close to his head; dark clothes that, to Sam's
eye, looked very fine, and probably meant he was a valet
rather than a footman; almost delicate features arranged in
an expression that gave nothing away. Not drunk, then.

"What time does his lordship get home?" Sam asked.

The lad blinked, pale eyes flashing in confusion. "Pardon?"

"Your gentleman." Sam wanted to know how long he had
to get out of there.

"My gentleman," the lad repeated.

Sam wasn't going to say *master*. "The person who pays your
wages."

The lad looked at Sam long enough and with such per-
plexity that Sam started to wonder if he might be a bit tipsy
after all. "In about an hour," he said finally.

"If I leave you here, can I be sure you aren't going to
wander back outside and start propositioning strangers?
Look here. What you want is a tavern called the Cross Keys
near Limeburner Street." No way was he sending this wisp of

a lad to look for trouble at the docks. He assumed the Cross Keys was still a going concern; the place was pretty much an institution among men of his sort. Sam hadn't set foot in any of those places in years, though. It wasn't worth the risk. Avoiding establishments like the Cross Keys was another rule that he always followed.

"Ah. Thank you for the advice." The lad's voice was faint. It was also a bit too polished. Too fine, just like that coat of his. But Sam didn't really know what valets looked or sounded like. Maybe they all wore waistcoats with approximately eleven golden buttons. Maybe they all had watch fobs laden with sparkling rainbows of jewels.

"Ah, shit," Sam muttered, running a hand over his jaw. He had just accused a lord, or a lord's son, if there was even any bloody difference, of attempting to proposition him. "You're Easterbrook, then? I thought he was an old man." He tried to remember what else Kate had told him. "Unless you're the son. I won't tell anyone what happened." He stepped toward the door. "I ought to be—"

"I'm definitely not any Easterbrook whatsoever." His voice was crisp and clear now. No trace of confusion. "And if you thought the Easterbrooks were in residence then your information is so sadly out of date that you plainly have nothing to do with any of the servants in this house. This leaves me to wonder what business you could possibly have standing in the mews."

Sam froze. Outside, the lad—although he was plainly not a lad, but a gentleman, sod him—had sounded amused, as if he were getting a thrill out of chatting with strangers and threatening to murder them if they mistreated a house-maid. Now, he sounded dead serious. The lamplight fell on the man, revealing a face that was some years older than Sam had guessed from his slight form.

"We're going to the library and having a drink," the man said. "And if my servants come home while we're talking, we'll say you've come to collect for some worthy charity."

His servants. Any hope Sam had that this wasn't the master of the house evaporated. Oh God. Sam had known all along this was a terrible idea. He cleared his throat. "I'd best be leaving."

"And so you shall. But first we have matters to discuss. You were lurking in the alley outside my house, which probably ought to bother me, but for how you thought it was the Easterbrooks' house. People don't usually lurk for terribly noble motives, which leads me to believe you intended some harm to the Easterbrooks. If so, we may have something in common. We might enter into a mutually beneficial arrangement."

He was standing under the light now, and Sam could see him quite clearly. His features were refined, Sam might even say pretty, but the set of his mouth was positively malevolent. His eyes were the color of boiled gooseberries, pale and a bit sinister. He did not look like a man anybody in their right mind ought to enter into any kind of arrangement with.

But if he could perhaps bargain with this man for Kate's painting, that might be worth it. "Fine," he said, feeling like he had just made a deal with the devil at a crossroads.

Now that he had this stranger in his library, Hartley was having misgivings about the soundness of his plan.

First, this man was significantly larger than anyone needed to be. The Hepplewhite chair hardly contained him. Hartley had good reasons for not feeling particularly at ease around large men, but this man didn't seem threatening. He sat in that chair as if it were a church pew, his hat politely on his lap. Hartley started to lower himself into the matching chair beside his guest, but then thought better of it and perched on the edge of a table, enjoying a false but comforting sense of height.

Second, it was unwise to trust strangers with his secrets. But Hartley had no secrets anymore; he had nothing to lose. It occurred to him for the first time that he could perhaps take advantage of his situation. He might as well behave fearlessly, if it meant getting a bit of his own back.

He was aware that Will would say he ought to put his grievances to rest, that making peace with the wrongs that had been done him was the only way forward. And he had to concede that Will knew something about that topic. But Will was also kind and decent, and Hartley was neither; he was petty and vindictive, because those qualities were all the sword or shield he had.

He poured some brandy into two glasses and handed one to his guest. "The long and short of it is that I would like nothing more than to do a grand disservice to Martin Easterbrook. If you'd like to join forces with me, then I'm interested. If not, so be it. We can pretend tonight never happened."

"And if I don't want anything to do with you? If it turns out this Martin fellow is my best mate and I tell him you're set against him? What if I tell a gossip rag that you tried to approach me?" The man spoke with a rough London accent that was laced through with something else that Hartley couldn't identify.

"You're welcome to," Hartley said lightly. "My name is Hartley Sedgwick. Hartley with an *E*. Be sure to have the paper spell it correctly." He reached into his coat pocket and pulled out his card case with a flourish that was marred by the hinge being stiff from want of use. "For reference," he said, holding out a card between two fingers.

Something went wrong because the man palmed the card but then politely shook Hartley's hand. Hartley froze. The man wasn't wearing gloves and Hartley had removed his own—gentlemen didn't eat or drink with gloves on, and Hartley couldn't bring himself to abandon the rules he had worked so blasted hard to master. Hartley didn't much care for being touched, least of all being touched skin to skin. He felt like he was being flayed alive. Were other people's hands always so warm, or was this stranger about to succumb to the ague?

"Samuel Fox," the man said as he finally let go of Hartley's hand.

"A pleasure, Mr. Fox." Hartley tried to sound like someone who wasn't in danger of becoming unglued.

Mr. Fox took a sip of the brandy, and Hartley realized belatedly he ought to have offered ale or cider. Fox wore trousers that were worn at the knees and a coat that strained badly across his broad shoulders; his hands were rough with work. He was plainly not of the brandy-drinking classes, and to have presented him with the drink now seemed farcically affected.

"Who is Easterbrook to you?" Fox asked. "I thought this was his house."

"It was. It's mine now. Sir Humphrey Easterbrook was my godfather." Hartley's voice only caught a little on that designation. "He died a few years ago and left this house to me. Your turn," he said briskly. "What was Easterbrook to you?"

"He has—had—something that belongs to a friend of mine."

Hartley raised his eyebrows. "I'm not going to ask whether you intended to walk in and help yourself to—to what, may I ask?"

He took a sip of brandy as he watched Mr. Fox decide whether he could be trusted. Hartley wondered what it must be like to be able to judge trustworthiness on sight. No, he wondered what it must be like to even want to. It was much easier to simply not trust people at all. Hartley trusted Will. He also trusted his older brother, Ben, but that wasn't any great accomplishment because Ben was utterly incapable of malice. He supposed he also trusted his youngest two brothers, but they were far away so he didn't have to put it to the test.

"It's a painting," Fox said.

Hartley's glass dropped to the parquet, shattering into bloodred shards. He squeezed his eyes shut. He didn't want to see Fox, didn't want to see the mess he had made, didn't want to see the empty spaces on the walls. A second passed, and he willed his composure to freeze him over into something cold and solid and impenetrable. When he opened his eyes, he knew he had mastered himself, at least as far as it was possible for him to do so.

"Easy," Fox said. "It's only a glass. Daresay you have a dozen more like it."

"I don't give a damn about the glass." He tried so hard not to think of Easterbrook's paintings, so hard not to remember any of it, and now he could almost smell the linseed oil, see Easterbrook's leering approval. Fox had come to stand before him. "You'll ruin your boots," Hartley managed.

"Top-shelf brandy isn't the worst thing I'm like to step in tonight," he said. "Now, you only have a few drops on your trousers, no harm done."

Hartley watched in horror as Fox produced a handkerchief from his pocket, a worn and faded thing that was folded into a neat square. Fox bent and dabbed at the brandy a few inches from the hem of Hartley's trousers.

"You don't—Mr. Fox—that's quite unnecessary." From the coolly efficient hands of his valet, Hartley would have endured these ministrations. But Fox's hands were large and warm, motivated by kindness or pity rather than seeing a job to its end. It was too personal, the single layer of wool too flimsy to prevent Hartley's skin from feeling exposed. He wanted to curl into a protective ball. "Please stop," he managed.

Fox stepped away as quickly as if Hartley had pulled a

knife on him. His dark brown eyes looked concerned, damn him. Hartley didn't think he could maintain the already tenuous hold on his composure in the face of outright kindness. "The—" he forced himself to say it. "The painting that belongs to your friend. Am I right that it's not the sort of painting that would be shown in polite company?"

"Ah, no, it isn't."

"I don't have those." He gestured at the blank walls with their pale, haunting gaps. "I don't know what he did with his art collection." When Hartley inherited, there had been no art except for a few bland landscapes, so he decided the portraits must have been destroyed. That, he now realized, was the delusion of a child, a stupid and gullible child who wanted to believe he had a future. An entirely new wave of fear washed over him.

"He could have sold them, you mean?" Fox looked dismayed.

"If he did, I haven't heard of it. And I rather think I would have. He probably gave them to his son, but he and I don't keep in touch," he said dryly. "It would suit me to help you find out exactly where they are. It would suit me very well indeed." It would be the tiniest of revenges; hardly any revenge at all, since one couldn't hurt a dead man. But getting his hands on those paintings would be the only victory Hartley had managed in months, and it suddenly seemed entirely necessary.

CHAPTER THREE

Sam was busy pouring beer, polishing tankards, collecting coins, and making change. It was a rhythm he knew as well as the jab and feint of a fight. There wasn't an empty seat at the Bell, and some patrons had taken to standing in a cluster against the wall. That meant Nick, who ought to already be in bed so he could get up before dawn to do the marketing, was bringing around trays of drinks.

Nick dropped his empty tray on the bar. "That's it for now," he said.

"Ta. Looks like things are slowing down. You ought to go to bed. I can manage on my own until closing."

The door opened, bringing in a blast of cold air and a handful of new customers, and extinguishing any hope of Nick getting to bed at a reasonable hour. As they worked for a solid few minutes pouring drinks and taking money, Sam decided they needed to hire somebody, and soon.

"We really need another set of hands," Nick said after they had a minute to themselves, echoing Sam's thoughts. He gave Sam a friendly pat on the arm and headed to the back room. Sam took out a rag and started polishing the bar, not because it needed polishing but because he liked to keep his hands busy while he thought.

Their father, who had always treated the Bell as his personal parlor, regaling customers with stories of decades-old boxing matches, had happily pitched in when they were short staffed. But he had died that spring, and Sam hadn't seen his way to filling in the gaps his father had left. Occasionally one of his aunts or cousins came to help during the evening rush. But they needed somebody permanent who could help in the kitchen as well as the taproom.

It was a good problem to have, he told himself. He had bought the Bell as a way to help people—to provide food and money when people had nowhere else to turn, to help people find work. People needed a leg up, and Sam was determined to give it. He had been lucky, born with the build of a boxer and the benefit of his father's experience, luckier still not to have been killed or injured in the ring. He thought of his father's tremors, he thought of Kate's father's fits of rage, both common in boxers who had managed to survive too many blows to the head. Most of all, he thought of what had happened to the one man he had tried to train. Giving food, drink, and actual coin to people who needed it was the least he could do to make up for that disaster. Not that he could ever make up for it, not fully. But for as long as he could, he would use the Bell to give a helping hand to other people in their small— but growing, if the number of babies Kate was delivering was any indication—community of free black people in London.

Sam's gaze strayed to the table where his father had sat every evening. On the wall above there still hung prints of him in the ring and clipped lines from boxing papers describing his victories. Sam had never wanted to keep mementos of his own boxing days. He didn't want to think about it, really. When someone came into the Bell wanting to talk about boxing, he sent them to Kate, who had been ringside for almost her entire life. Back when Kate's father owned the Bell, there had been matches in the back room. Sam could still see bloodstains on the flagstone floors, even though Kate and Nick said he was imagining things. But he had shed some of that blood himself, and was pretty sure he remembered where it had spilled.

"Did you see a rat?" Kate was watching him with her head tilted. She must have come in while he was polishing the bar.

"What?" Oh God, rats were the last thing they needed. Rat catchers didn't come cheap.

"Or a fire? A masked bandit?" When he continued to stare blankly at her, she gently smacked the side of his face. "Because something must have happened to make you look like that."

"It's just what my face does. If you don't like it, go look at something else."

She raised her eyebrows and stepped away slowly, as if backing away from a hissing cat. But then she caught sight of Nick and her expression transformed to pure happiness. Sam watched as his brother slung an arm around her, then caught his eye and smiled. Seeing them together filled Sam with a bone-deep sense of rightness.

He felt a fresh wave of anger at the thought of the painting. He was fairly certain that if it somehow became public, Kate would be mortified for Nick's sake and Nick would be angry on Kate's behalf, but they'd get over it after a few days. The problem was that they wouldn't know if or when that might happen. Instead, that possibility would lurk in the future, spoiling their happiness, all because some rich old sod had taken a fancy to having the naked portrait of a girl who had been too poor to refuse.

Those words brought Davey to mind. Sam should never have taught Davey to box, so the fault was his no matter how you looked at it, no matter what Nick and Kate liked to say. But there was also a rich old man to blame for what happened to the lad. After that fight, Sam found out that the man who had backed Davey's opponent promised Davey five pounds if he let the first blow fell him. Davey had held his end of the bargain; he was unconscious before he hit the ground, dead before sunset. And all for five pounds, when winning the fight could have earned him a dozen times that amount. But Davey had needed the money badly enough to think a guaranteed five pounds was worth more than a chance at sixty. Fixed fights were far from rare, and Sam still regretted putting Davey into a situation that had effectively put a price on his friend's head. But there was enough blame to go around, and Sam reserved some for the man who had offered Davey the five pounds.

It wasn't fair. Nobody should have that kind of power over anyone, no matter how much money they had or if they had a title in front their name. And while Sam had ample evidence that life wasn't fair and never would be, and that rich folk had all the power they could possibly want and then some, he wanted to make things as right as possible for his family.

But as he polished a pewter mug to a silvery shine, he thought again of the brandy that gentleman had given him, long fine fingers curled around a glass that must have cost two shillings six. Men like Mr. Hartley Sedgwick didn't often appear in Sam's world. The regular customers of the Bell worked for a living. Some worked in nearby Fleet Street, some were servants or tradesmen; some were black, some were white, and a few came from the East. None had clean, smooth hands. There had been the young idiots who sometimes came to see his father, self-consciously ordering a pint of bitter and sitting uneasily on the edges of their seats while waiting for Hiram Fox to hold forth about the art of pugilism. Sam hadn't needed to talk to them; he poured their drinks, took their coin, and later swept out the cigarillo stubs they left on the floor. Fine gentlemen were blessedly irrelevant to Sam.

There was no reason for Sam to be thinking of Sedgwick at all, in fact. He wasn't even that handsome unless you had a liking for fragile-looking men with fussy clothes. But Sam couldn't forget what had happened when he had tried to blot the brandy off the other man's trousers. Sedgwick had gone still, as if frozen in place. There had been fear in his expression; Sam knew damned well what that looked like at close range. But he hadn't been afraid to bring Sam into his home, to shut the door on them during their bizarre conversation.

No, he wasn't afraid of Sam, but of being touched. And that made Sam feel something dangerously like sympathy for the fellow.

He wondered what Sedgwick's reasons were for wanting to do one over on Easterbrook's son. After the man had dropped his brandy, his hands had been as shaky as Sam's da's hands had been at the very end. Sam shook his head. He didn't want to think about whether Sedgwick's nervousness had to do with whatever the old bastard had done.

He would be meeting Mr. Hartley Sedgwick again the following Sunday, and if Sam was looking forward to it, he told himself it was purely for the importance of the task they were to complete, not because he had any interest at all in what lay behind those pale, inscrutable eyes.

Even when you were an outcast, there were some people who had no choice but to speak to you, and that, Hartley supposed, included one's solicitor.

He dressed with an even greater level of care than usual, or at least as carefully as he could without a valet. Briggs had given notice two days earlier. Rather than have his chin shaved by someone who didn't want to be there, Hartley had paid the man's wages and sent him on his way. He supposed he had been lucky to keep his valet this long after his disgrace; it would do nothing for the fellow's professional repute for his handiwork not to be seen in public. Hartley told himself it was nothing personal, that Briggs would have given notice if Hartley had been bedridden rather than ostracized. But now he looked back at all their dealings in the past months with the mortified suspicion that Briggs had despised him all along and had been brushing Hartley's coat and sewing on his buttons resentfully.

He chose a dark green waistcoat with lighter green embroidery, a bottle green coat, buff pantaloons, and top boots that he had polished with his own hands. His hair was inclined to disport itself in flyaway unruliness, but he had combed and pomaded it into submission. He was quite satisfied with his reflection in the cheval glass. Truth be told, he generally was satisfied with his reflection, but today he was especially pleased with the effect he had achieved: subdued, respectable, dignified.

Then the solicitor's clerk made him wait. Not in the sitting room that held the brandy decanter, the Axminster carpet, and the porcelain vase of hothouse flowers, but in an airless chamber that was little more than a glorified cupboard.

"I sent word to Mr. Philpott that I required an appointment today," Hartley told the clerk. He had sent two letters, and neither had been answered. In retrospect, that ought to have been his first indication that things were not going according to plan.

The clerk had only blinked at him.

After half an hour in the dingy little cell, he poked his head into the clerk's room to ask when the solicitor might get around to seeing him.

"Mr. Philpott is quite busy this afternoon," the clerk said with a proud sniff.

For God's sake, he paid Philpott, not the other way

around. If it were so important that Hartley's shocking presence be kept away from the sensitive eyes of his other clients, Philpott ought to have suggested a time to meet when Hartley could have been discreetly brought up through the back stairs. Hartley considered barging into Philpott's office; there would be something satisfyingly theatrical about that, but it was so ill bred. For a moment Hartley wondered what it would be like to throw out his notions of manners; they weren't doing him any good at the moment, etiquette being rather beside the point when one is all but marooned on an island. But his standards, like his house, were his. He had earned them, and they couldn't be taken away. He was a gentleman, and so he'd quietly wait.

After another half hour the clerk ushered him into the solicitor's office with obvious reluctance.

"How can I help you, Mr. Sedgwick?" Philpott's expression was pained. He was about forty, with thinning gray hair, a somber coat, and a belly that suggested a lifetime of good living. He looked exactly as a solicitor ought to look, which his clients no doubt found reassuring. His firm had been the Easterbrooks' solicitors for generations and had executed Sir Humphrey Easterbrook's will. Hartley had always been dimly aware that Philpott wasn't overly fond of him, but now the man regarded him as if expecting him to do something felonious or lewd at any moment. He didn't offer Hartley a seat.

"I'm inquiring about the status of the Easterbrook art collection." Hartley suppressed a cringe at the formality of his speech, knowing it was a primitive defense.

"Art collection?" Philpott's brows furrowed. "I heard you sold the landscapes that used to be in the grand salon." He said this with probably the same tone he'd use to accuse a man of whipping a dog.

"I refer to the paintings that hung in the library. I saw them when I was last a guest in the house, but that was some years before Sir Humphrey's death."

Realization dawned slowly, the solicitor's face reddening and his expression turning nauseated. "*Those,*" he nearly spat. "Sir Humphrey's will granted you ownership of the house on Brook Street and everything in it at the time of his death."

"Quite." Hartley was intimately familiar with the terms of his godfather's will. "The library walls were most certainly bare when I took possession. I assure you that paintings of naked women are not to my taste." Hartley knew he shouldn't be trying to antagonize the man, but it was most satisfying to watch him turn scarlet. "I suppose what I'm asking is whether he disposed of the paintings in a separate bequest." They certainly hadn't been mentioned in the body of the will; Hartley could not have failed to notice that. "Or perhaps he sold them prior to his death?" In the event that he had transferred the collection to another of his properties, possibly one that was entailed to his son, Hartley wanted to know about it.

"Mr. Sedgwick," the solicitor said, as if Hartley were a lax student and he a frustrated schoolmaster. "I was appointed to execute Sir Humphrey's will and administer the Easterbrook estate during his only son's minority. I cannot approve of how he disposed of his property. It goes against prudence and responsibility and . . . and . . . decency." He slapped his hand on his desk, causing a cloud of sand to rise off his blotter. "And for you to come to this office to speak of that filth, I simply will not stand it. No, sir. I will not. I have done what was required of me by Sir Humphrey's will, and now, if you have any other legal matters, I suggest you engage another solicitor. One who has different standards for his clientele."

Hartley wasn't exactly shocked. He had known all along that Philpott would have preferred Sir Humphrey's son and heir to the baronetcy to inherit the entirety of the Easterbrook estate. Instead, Sir Humphrey had overspent and gambled, leaving his son only an overmortgaged and entailed property, while granting Hartley his only valuable asset, the house on Brook Street.

What surprised him was the venom in the solicitor's voice. He expected grudging tolerance from Philpott, not outright contempt. After all, Hartley paid him an outrageous sum for his services.

"I see you've heard the gossip," Hartley said, picking a bit of lint off his sleeve.

Philpott's face went red. "I don't wish to discuss this."

"Neither do I, but Sir Humphrey's conduct and Martin's nasty tale-telling have made it so I have no choice." He wanted the solicitor to have no illusions about the characters of the men he apparently still esteemed higher than Hartley. "I'll leave presently. But first please tell me whether you know where Sir Humphrey's art collection is. If the paintings were indeed in the London townhouse at the time of Sir Humphrey's death, that affects my legacy."

"They were not present in the house when my clerk did an inventory a week after Sir Humphrey's death," the solicitor said grudgingly. "I know nothing more."

"Thank you kindly," Hartley said, rising to his feet and executing a perfectly proper bow.

He hailed a hackney. At least hackney drivers weren't above taking his money, and that had to be worth something. He thought about directing the driver to Will's lodgings, because it would be good to see someone who didn't despise him. But his brother's lodgings—God, his entire life—were dismal. Hartley didn't think he could stomach dreariness today.

Instead he went home, heard that the footman had given notice, and proceeded to make a list of places Sir Humphrey's paintings could be. Now with even the sorry remains of his old life crumbling around him, exacting this small bit of justice for himself seemed even more necessary.

Chapter Four

It was an hour past sunset, but there was no light in any of Sedgwick's windows when Sam approached. This was the servants' day out, he recalled, but surely that didn't mean gentlemen sat around in the dark. He could have spent the rest of the evening deciding between going to the front door (which, he reasoned, would be convenient for a gentleman without any servants to answer himself) or the kitchen door (which was where everybody who wasn't a toff went on a street like this one). In the end he flipped a coin and went to the mews behind the house.

He had to knock several times before he heard footsteps. Sedgwick opened the door, his slim figure a mere silhouette against the background of an even darker room. Sam caught a scent that had to be the man's perfume—perfume, indeed. It ought to have reminded him of how very irrelevant and out of place Mr. Hartley Sedgwick was to him, but instead he found himself taking a deep breath to fill his nostrils with the scent of . . . green woods. And fine candles. He liked it, more's the pity.

He realized he had been standing there in the doorway without saying anything for a full half minute. He cleared his throat. "It's Samuel Fox."

Mr. Hartley Sedgwick gave a laugh that sounded strained and nervous. "I know who you are. Come in."

They passed through the dark and chilly kitchens and up a set of stairs to the same room they had sat in the last time. It was the library, he supposed, although there weren't so many books. Sam had thought libraries were supposed to have thousands of volumes, piled right up to the rafters. And even though he couldn't fathom what any right-thinking person was supposed to do with so many books, he still felt this room to be a bit of a disappointment with its bare shelves. There was also a small table, a pair of hard chairs, and a sofa that had every sign of never having been sat on. Before the hearth lay a rug he supposed had cost a pretty penny even though it was ugly as sin, and in front of the windows hung dark red drapes that probably blocked out all the light during the day. It was not Sam's idea of a comfortable room, certainly not what he'd want for himself in the imaginary world where he had money for extra rooms. For all he knew, this house had an endless succession of far better and more comfortable chambers, and he was only allowed in the worst of the lot.

He sat in one of the chairs while Sedgwick prodded the fire with a brass-handled poker. He was in a getup every bit as fussy as the last time. Close-fitting coat, waistcoat glinting with silk thread, pantaloons clinging to his slight form. Sam could have spent a happy hour contemplating the sight of his pantaloons. Virtuously, he dragged his gaze back up to safer ground, landing at that waistcoat. Twelve buttons, six on each side. Not gold this time, but ivory or maybe bone. Whatever it was caught the firelight and made the lad look like he had twelve moons marching up and down the length of his chest. Except—Sam squinted—the waistcoat was buttoned wrong. One of the buttons had gotten into the wrong hole. The rest of the man's dress was flawless, and it was odd nobody had mentioned the button. Didn't gentlemen have people to sort out their buttons? Surely they had looking glasses. Hell, Sam had neither and still managed to get his buttons where they belonged, and if he had so much as a spot of soup on his shirt he heard about it from six people before noon. Something about the imperfection, juxtaposed with the plain finickiness of the fellow's grooming and attire, endeared him to Sam. His mouth quirked into an involuntary smile.

"So." Mr. Sedgwick finally ceased prodding the fire, which had been blazing quite sufficiently even before his efforts, and sat in the chair across from Sam. "I'm fairly certain the paintings are at Friars' Gate, which was Sir Humphrey Easterbrook's shooting box in Sussex. He used that house to host some of his more, ah, specialized house parties, and if he were to have sent the paintings anywhere, it may well have been there." He straightened his cuffs and smoothed the front of his waistcoat, as if accounting for all his buttons. When he reached for a stack of papers that rested on a nearby table, something went wrong and the papers fell to the ground. Sam moved quickly to catch them before they landed in the fire, taking care not to get too close to Sedgwick lest he frighten the man as he had the last time. He collected the pages nearest to him and let Sedgwick manage those closer to his own feet.

"Ah. Yes. Thank you," Sedgwick said when he once again had all the papers in his hand. With one hand he gripped the papers so tightly they wrinkled under his fingers, and with the other he fidgeted with the hem of his coat.

Sedgwick had suggested that Easterbrook used the place for rude parties, and Sam wondered whether Sedgwick had been there as a guest or something more complicated, but he held his tongue. Instead he asked, "Do you know the people who live there now?" If Sedgwick knew whoever occupied this house, then maybe they could resolve this with some plain speech and a bit of money. Sam had a bit laid by and figured getting rid of this painting would be a fine wedding present for Kate.

"It's likely unoccupied. The house is part of the entailed estate, so it can't have been sold. The owner—my godfather's son—is on the Continent. I suppose there may be a tenant, but I'll cross that bridge when I come to it."

Sam frowned. "Do you plan to break into the house and see for yourself whether the painting is there?"

"Well, yes, unless you have a better proposal." Sedgwick thumbed through his stack of papers and pulled out a single sheet. "This is the plan of Friars' Gate. It's been years since I visited, so the rendering isn't perfect, but it's the general lay of the land, at least. It ought to be of some use in figuring out the best way in."

Sam took the sheet of heavy cream-colored paper. The rooms were neat boxes, with windows and doors carefully sketched in. He had even drawn trees and shrubberies around the outside. Items were neatly labeled in the darkest indigo ink with an even, feathery hand. It was the finest thing Sam was like to lay his hands on this twelvemonth, and it was the map of a house he was meant to burgle in a quest for lewd paintings.

"You say this is a shooting box? What's that?"

"A small house gentlemen use for shooting parties. It's just a country house by another name." Sedgwick said this without any surprise at Sam's ignorance. Which was good, because Sam thought it was daft to call a house as large as the one sketched out before him—eight bedrooms upstairs, not counting servants' quarters—a box. He reminded himself that rich people, including the pretty one sitting across from him, were a puzzle he didn't want to solve. Even if they did have misbuttoned waistcoats.

Sam filled his lungs with air. "I can't be breaking into houses in the countryside. That's not on the table. If anyone sees me, they'll know I'm the only black man within miles. Even if I'm not, they'll tell themselves I am, because I'm a stranger. And the whole point of my finding out what happened to this painting is to make life easier for my family, which won't happen if I'm hanged for a thief. I'm grateful for your help but I can't take this kind of risk." Sam prepared himself to be dismissed.

Sedgwick didn't answer right away. Instead he nodded slowly. "I see," he said. "Quite right." He pursed his lips in a way that sent Sam's thoughts careening wildly away from fears of arrest. "Didn't think of that. I'll come up with something else, then." He got to his feet again and started pacing. "Drink? I have brandy but I also brought up some ale, if that's what you fancy."

"I'll have brandy, thank you." It was an odd thing to have somebody pour his drink for him, especially a man like this one. "I drink a lot of ale and beer. I keep a public house."

"Do you?" Sedgwick looked interested as he gracefully poured two glasses of brandy. "Where?"

"Near Fleet Street." Sam wasn't quite sure why he didn't just tell him that it was the Bell off Fetter Lane, but it felt safer not to, as if giving Sedgwick the Bell's name and address would make it easier for the man to slip unwanted into Sam's thoughts while he worked. Sam thanked him for the brandy and took a long sip, trying his best to keep his eyes on the liquid in his glass instead of on the man in front of him.

Hartley drained his glass, feeling the warmth of the brandy hit his stomach with acute relief. He had been on edge all day, partly because planning a felony was something new to sink his teeth into, and partly because he knew he was looking forward to seeing Sam Fox again. He had a healthy distrust of large men, but when Fox tried to keep him safe during their first meeting in the mews, it had sent Hartley's carefully constructed defenses toppling to the ground. Hartley had to bite back a smile whenever he thought of how Fox had so helpfully tried to tell him where he might look for men to keep him company. As if Hartley didn't know exactly where to go for that sort of thing. But Fox had been sweet about it, and sweetness wasn't something Hartley had come to expect from men, or really from anybody at all. That tiny bit of kindness had done something to ease Hartley's usual discomfort, but without the customary edge of fear, he was experiencing something close to attraction to the man.

No, not *close* to attraction. It was the real thing. Hartley took in the sight of Sam Fox, trousers straining over thickly muscled thighs, sleeves shoved back a bit to reveal strong forearms. And he was handsome. Lord, was he handsome. True, his nose had been broken a couple of times but it somehow suited him, as if everyone walking around with straight noses had resorted to something embarrassingly obvious. He wore his hair cropped so close to his scalp that Hartley wondered if he sometimes had his head shaved, and that suited him too. Everything about him, from his head to his boots, was utilitarian; not shabby so much as having the air of a body that was well lived in.

At that moment Fox glanced up and caught Hartley watching him, but his eyes didn't betray any distaste. Hartley did not want to dwell on the fact that he could no longer differentiate between the absence of distaste and actual interest. He suspected, based on Fox's knowledge of establishments such as the Cross Keys, that his tastes might not differ greatly from Hartley's own. That didn't mean he wanted anything to do with Hartley, however, and as Hartley wasn't going to bed with anybody, it wasn't worth thinking about.

Still, he smoothed back a lock of hair from his forehead as he caught the man's eye.

"So," he said, settling back into his chair, crossing his legs before him with only a little bit of exaggerated grace. "I'll slip into the house and take the painting myself." Strictly speaking, he didn't need Fox there, although if he correctly remembered childhood mischief, sneaking in and out of buildings was always easier with someone to hoist one up through high windows. Going it alone, on the other hand, would make it less awkward to accomplish some other petty acts of revenge while he was there. "But how will I know which is the painting of your friend?"

There was a slight pause before the man answered. "How many paintings of naked girls do you suppose there are?"

Hartley laughed, and he wasn't sure whether he was nervous or amused. "Enough so that I won't be able to carry them all out myself." Naked girls and at least one naked boy; Easterbrook's tastes were eclectic.

"Christ. What kind of bastard was this fellow?"

"Oh, a thoroughgoing one, I assure you. I could, I suppose, burn the canvases, but smoke coming out of the chimney of an empty house would draw rather more attention than I'd like. Or," he mused, tapping his fingers to his lips, "I could use a knife." That would be pleasantly violent. "Perhaps you could tell me what the painting looked like." Hartley tried to remember the details of some of the portraits, but it had been long ago, and he had always made such an effort to avoid looking at the walls. "Is there any chance she posed with a tiger rug? I vaguely recall one like that."

"Couldn't tell you. Never saw it. And I wouldn't like to ask my friend the details." He swirled the brandy in his glass, the tumbler dwarfed by his large hand. "She's black. Not as dark as me, but there'd be no mistaking her painting as one of a white girl, I don't think."

Hartley was not in the practice of being charitable, but he felt a sense of allegiance with Mr. Fox's friend. If life as an outcast was unsavory for a gentleman of means, then it would be downright dangerous for a woman of the class likely to be on intimate terms with Mr. Fox. "You'd imagine that would narrow down the field, but with Easterbrook it wouldn't. He liked to collect paintings of people who wouldn't otherwise pose for him." Hartley had never quite understood the man's motives in wanting lewd portraits of respectable shopkeepers' daughters, but chalked it up to Easterbrook being generally awful.

Fox nodded. "Before you go breaking into houses, don't you want to be sure the paintings weren't sold? Or given away?"

"I'm almost positive they haven't changed hands," Hartley assured him. "Or, if they were, not in England."

Fox's brow furrowed skeptically. "How can you be so sure?"

"I called on the agents who handle that sort of painting, and they hadn't bought anything from Easterbrook." That had been a bizarre series of errands, the strangest aspect being that the dealers in obscene art were the only people who had treated him better than a leper in weeks. It had been an odd reminder that there were shadowy corners of London where he might build a life for himself, if only he could make peace with having lost his old life. But he didn't want to make peace with the wrongs that had been done him. Today his thoughts were trained on revenge, and it was the closest thing to peace he had felt in a long while.

"Honestly," he continued, fiddling with a button on the underside of his sleeve, "if they were anywhere that people saw them, I'd have found out almost immediately." One of the paintings, albeit one that had been kept within a private cabinet in Easterbrook's bedchamber rather than the more public library, was of Hartley himself, and he hadn't changed so greatly since sixteen that he would be unrecognizable. If the paintings had changed hands, the whispers about him would have been very pointed indeed, and Philpott wouldn't have been confused when Hartley asked about the art collection. "If you, ah, understand my meaning."

Fox regarded him with warm brown eyes. "I don't, but I don't need to, do I?" There was no pity there, no contempt, only the understanding that Hartley had secrets, the understanding that a man was allowed his share of things that didn't bear talking about.

Hartley swallowed. "No, I suppose not." He considered telling Fox everything, letting him know exactly who he was getting mixed up with. He had no reason to believe that Fox would be repulsed by him even if he possessed all the sordid details of Hartley's past. But if Fox really wanted to know, he could find out easily enough without Hartley having to talk about it.

"All right then," Fox said, slapping his thighs in a way that suggested he thought it was high time that they be getting on with things. "I can't let you steal the painting for me. It's not fair for you to do all the dirty work. What do you get out of it?"

Hartley pressed his lips together into a mirthless smile. "Trust me that I'd get something out of it. You've only given me an idea that would likely have occurred to me sooner or later." For two months he had been thinking of revenge, and now he had a way to chase after it. Destroying the paintings would do Martin no harm, and nothing would ever again harm Sir Humphrey, but Hartley decided that destroying the paintings had the flavor of revenge, and revenge was a taste he was increasingly hungry for. "And I just realized I can bring mineral spirits. That'll nicely ruin the paintings without going to the trouble of burning them or the effort of slicing them apart. Or a pail of paint. See, I can manage this on my own quite nicely."

Fox looked skeptical. "You'll need a lookout."

Hartley waved his hand dismissively. "I'm not worried about being caught."

Fox didn't even twitch an eyebrow at this obvious lie, for which Hartley was grateful. "You ought to be."

"Be that as it may, I'm choosing not to." He had made plenty of bad decisions already; adding one more to the tally hardly seemed to matter. He got to his feet and walked to the window. The curtains were drawn, and it was too dark to see outside anyway. He smoothed his palms against the velvet of the curtains because it gave him something to do, something to feel other than the angry thudding of his heart. "It's my neck." The words came out snippier than he meant.

"All right, now. No worries." The words were low and soothing and they came from right behind him. Hartley turned so his back was against the window. Fox stood about two feet away, slightly farther than normal speaking distance, but he was so large that he seemed to loom over Hartley. As if sensing his fear, Fox took a step back and held up his hands in surrender.

"You don't need to do that," Hartley said.

"Maybe not. I reckon there are a lot of things I don't need to do. But I know what it looks like when a person is afraid, and it's not something I fancy seeing." There was something in the way he frowned that made Hartley think maybe Fox had his share of bad memories. And of course he did. Hartley knew he was hardly alone in misfortune, although lately his own troubles had consumed his thoughts like a nagging toothache—tiny, in the grand scheme of things, but really quite bad enough to be all one thought about.

"I'm not usually like this." Hartley's voice was a whisper.

Fox waited a moment before answering. "Like what?"

Jumpy as a cat? Snappish and clumsy and rude? Hartley didn't even know where to start. "I'm usually very genteel," he said with what he hoped was an obviously ironic sniff. "Sophisticated, even."

Fox's face broke into a wide grin, and Hartley realized it was the first time he had seen the man smile. One of his eye teeth was chipped and Hartley found he liked it. "Your waistcoat is buttoned wrong. Is that what the sophisticated gentlemen of London are doing this season?"

Hartley glanced down, squinted, and saw that Fox was

right. "Oh blast. I need spectacles." Or he needed another valet, but that was dashed unlikely. He bent his neck to see where he had gone wrong. Right at the top button. He was going to have to unbutton the whole thing and start over.

"Don't," Fox said, when Hartley had undone the top button.

"Pardon?"

"I really don't care what state your buttons are in. And, besides, it's—" He stopped abruptly, as if realizing that he shouldn't end the sentence in whatever way he had been planning, which only made Hartley absolutely need to know what he hadn't said.

"It's what?"

"Rather . . . adorable, if I'm honest."

Was Fox making an approach? If so, Hartley was on familiar—if uncomfortable—ground for the first time this evening. He cast his eyes down, then looked coyly up at the other man. "You can unbutton them yourself, if you like." Scripted lines in a bad play, and he was weary of it all. It was a fool's errand to try this again. It had been ages since he managed to go through with it; there had been a few moderately successful ventures after Easterbrook was through with him, when the pleasure had slightly outweighed the terror of the encounter. But in the three years since inheriting this house, he had hardly even wanted to try, and there was no reason to believe things would be different with Fox.

Fox didn't move any closer, though. Instead he frowned. "I didn't think you liked being touched."

Perhaps he hadn't been making an approach, which was

rather mortifying. But how had Fox figured out Hartley's problem? Probably when he had gone half off his head during last week's brandy spill. "I don't," he said, pitching his voice low and trying to imbue it with as much of an invitation as he could muster, "but you can do it anyway." That was what he had done in the span between Easterbrook's death and inheriting the house: one-sided encounters where he let things happen to him.

Fox let out a sigh. "No, mate, that's not what I want. I don't want you to let me touch you. There's no fun in it if I think you're just going along with it."

Hartley felt the words like a slap to the face even though Fox's tone was kind. Fox's gentle rejection was a stark reminder of everything Hartley had lost. He smiled tightly and thought of revenge.

CHAPTER FIVE

The sun rose on one of those perfectly crisp autumn days that made it hard to believe muck and fog were in the near future. Hartley considered staying in bed until the sun went away.

"You! Wake up!"

Hartley rolled over to see one of his few remaining servants looming over his bed. "Why?" he asked.

"The girls gave notice," Alf said. "Their mum won't let them come back. Said you're depraved."

Hartley rubbed his eyes. "That's not giving notice," he argued, sitting up. "That's just quitting." It was just past Michaelmas, one of the quarter days when servants typically came and went, so the departure of a few servants wouldn't have mattered if he had any hope of replacing them.

"Right," Alf said. "But where does that leave me?"

"Do you want to leave as well?" Then Hartley would be utterly alone in this house. "I'll pay your wages through the next quarter."

Alf rolled his eyes. "You don't need to worry about my delicate sensibilities, mate." When Hartley acquired Alf, the boy had been fifteen years old and loitering in an alleyway near the docks infamous for its supply of all manner of prostitutes. Hartley had gone there in one of his ill-fated attempts at liaison; Alf had said what was needful and named his price. Before matters went much further, Hartley saw that the boy was scarcely out of childhood, and offered him a pallet in the kitchen and work around the house.

"But I'm not doing your cooking," Alf went on. "So either you hire a proper cook or we're eating pie from that dodgy place in Moorfields you like so much."

"Pie it is, then," Hartley said, and flopped back down onto his pillow.

"Let this house, for the love of God. Cross my heart, there are hobgoblins in the attic. I can hear them when the wind blows," Alf said with the wide-eyed earnestness of someone who had been raised on such vulgar stories. "We can move to lodgings."

Hartley heard the *we* and turned his face into the pillow to hide a smile. "This is my house," he said. He had repeated that phrase a dozen times, to Alf, to himself, to Will. "I'm not letting it go. You'll need your wages increased, though," he said, "if you pick up some of the slack the girls left."

"Won't argue there." Alf shuffled his feet and looked as if he wanted to say something. "Here's what I don't understand. I'd have thought every maid in London would want to work for you," he said. "What with how they know you won't be after them."

"People think that if a man is so depraved as to go to bed with other men, then he won't stop at anything."

"Yeah but have they actually met you? Because all it takes is one glance to know you aren't going to be bothering any girls."

Hartley had a mad urge to fling the pillow at Alf, as he would have at one of his brothers who was determined to annoy him. Instead he bit the inside of his cheek to suppress a laugh. "There are people who cheerfully lie with both men and women," he pointed out gently, thinking not for the first time that Alf might find this reassuring.

"Not you, though. Listen, if we're staying here in this horrible old place, you need someone to make certain everything's done right and proper. Maybe sew on a button, that sort of thing. I'm fine with hauling and fixing, but you'll look like the rag man if you're left to me."

"I'm perfectly capable of taking care of myself. I didn't grow up with servants to wait on me." Then he saw the look of disappointment in Alf's face. "Unless, that is, you know somebody who would be well suited to that line of work."

"Well, somebody I used to know from, well, you know." Hartley assumed he meant the streets. Alf shuffled his feet in a way that reminded Hartley of one of his younger brothers confessing to stealing fruit from the neighbor's orchard. "If you wouldn't mind hiring a—"

"You know I wouldn't," Hartley said quickly, sitting up. "In fact, given how things are, you probably ought to ask your friend whether he minds working for someone with no reputation."

"Oh, she doesn't have any parents to fetch her away. Or, I suppose she does, but they turned her out so I don't reckon their opinion matters much."

"You say she's been working the streets?"

"And sleeping rough."

Hartley sighed. "Bring her round whenever you like. Offer her whatever we paid Polly." There was one other concern, though. If Alf was keeping in touch with friends from his old days, there was a chance he was still walking the streets himself. Hartley didn't want to see the boy hurt or arrested. But the lad had always been deeply ashamed and loath to talk about it. "Alf," Hartley said, carefully weighing his words. "Do I pay you enough, or do you find that you need to supplement your income?"

Alf might be entirely unschooled and unlettered but he was quick. "Nah, no worries. The gent who used to comb your hair left his muffler here, and I thought one of the lads might want it, so I brought it round to the docks. It's getting cold."

"Indeed." He noticed that Alf had no reservations about giving away other people's belongings, but it was true that Hartley hadn't had any intention of sending the muffler on to his former valet, even if he had known where to find the man.

Alf shuffled his feet again. "When I was there the other night, a few gents did think I was offering trade. They may have remembered me."

"More likely they assume anyone young and dressed like a guttersnipe isn't there to purchase anybody's company, so they came to the obvious conclusion that you were there for the other reason. Take care, Alf," he pleaded.

It was a terrible risk to even have Alf under his roof. Since the gossip had spread about town, Hartley sometimes thought there were constables watching his house, waiting for any excuse to bring him before a judge. They'd see Alf and force one of the lad's former customers to testify against him; they'd drum up evidence against Hartley and he'd be put in the pillory.

But Hartley couldn't turn Alf out, because the boy didn't have anywhere else to go. That had always been his downfall. Someone helpless needed aid, and he went out of his blasted way to assist them. Urchins needed a home, and Hartley opened his doors. Will needed a commission, and Hartley went to bed with the only rich man he knew. It wasn't self-sacrifice—that was for noble-minded decent sorts. Hartley didn't even like people, much less want to sacrifice his comfort for them. He didn't give money to worthy causes, he didn't go to church, and he was utterly confident that if Martin Easterbrook were on fire, he wouldn't so much as piss on him to put it out. He was motivated entirely by something like anger at injustice, although he hated to admit that to himself; anger was terribly gauche and injustice seemed a topic best confined to badly printed broadsides read by men who dressed like Will.

"You all right there, sir?" Alf asked. He always managed to tack on "sir" like he had only just managed not to say "you bloody great fool."

"Would you take it amiss if I stressed the need for discretion?"

"I'm pretty keen on discretion myself," Alf said, his eyebrows raised.

"Right. Of course you are." Nobody wanted to be put in the stocks. Preferring not to be hanged or pilloried wasn't some refined preference of Hartley's. All men in their world knew the price they would pay for a single misstep. "Perhaps stay away from places frequented by people who might mistake you for trade, Alf."

Nobody in his life would be safe from the taint of scandal if the worst happened. Perhaps it was for the best that there were precious few people in his life at all.

Wisps of fog were already gathering when Sam returned from walking his aunt home. She had come in to help for a couple of hours and Sam wasn't going to repay the favor by having her make her way through the dark foggy streets on her own. Countless horrors unfolded nightly on these streets, but they were a hell of a lot less likely to happen in the company of a large man.

Sam had been on his feet since morning and was looking forward to collapsing into his bed. It would be one of those nights when he barely managed to get his boots off before falling asleep. To walk his aunt home, he had circumvented the seedier and more raucous streets, but now that he was on his own, he took as direct a path as possible, walking straight through one of the more tumbledown neighborhoods near Grub Street.

When Sam first spotted the man on the other side of the lane, he thought it was a trick of the fog and the darkness, or maybe that his tired mind wasn't behaving reliably.

That his mind, however tired, would supply an image of Hartley Sedgwick, of all people, did him no credit. Perhaps his thoughts this week had been so populated with Sedgwick that his brain was now conjuring the man's vision out of thin air.

He squinted. That was no vision. It was Hartley Sedgwick, in the flesh. Even from across the street, even through gathering fog, Sam could see the man's watch chain glimmering in the moonlight. A man had to have a death wish to walk through a neighborhood like this with a bit of gold hanging out of his pocket. Stealing the watch would be child's play, but the sight of a chain like that would give a thief ideas about what else the man might have in his pockets and what riches a good beating might produce.

Swearing under his breath, he crossed the street. "Mr. Sedgwick," he called. Sedgwick froze with his back to Sam. Sam didn't take another step, not wanting to startle him. "It's Sam Fox." He could almost hear the other man's sigh of relief as his shoulders dropped and he turned to look at Sam. "What in God's name do you think you're doing in a neighborhood like this?" Sam demanded.

"I'd like to know what business it is of yours." Sedgwick's voice was utterly frigid, which Sam supposed was no more than he deserved. They had parted awkwardly last week, and Sam winced whenever he thought of it.

"If you want to get yourself killed, that's your concern, but you could maybe do it in another part of town. My pub is nearby, and it won't do business any good if word gets about that people are getting murdered on my doorstep." In truth, the Bell wasn't so close, and Sam doubted whether any of the regulars would be bothered if half a dozen toffs were killed directly on the premises as nightly entertainment. But Sedgwick didn't need to know that.

"I'm not going to get myself killed." The moonlight shifted, throwing a play of light and shadow over Sedgwick's face. He looked tired. Bored. As if the prospect of getting killed wasn't so very upsetting.

A cold fear gripped Sam's gut. It wasn't a good sign when a person acted like staying alive was a chore. "I'm walking you home," he said.

"That's entirely unnecessary. I often walk this way."

"And do you often do it with a gold chain hanging out of your pocket in plain view of God and everyone?"

He heard the man sigh. "Fine. Suit yourself." Sedgwick resumed walking, leaving Sam to trail in his wake. But Sam was much taller and he soon had to adjust his stride so as not to outpace the smaller man.

"What were you doing in that neighborhood, anyway?" Sam asked, after they had walked in awkward silence a few minutes.

Sedgwick was silent for long enough that Sam thought he was going to get ignored the rest of the way to Mayfair. But then Hartley held up a parcel he had been carrying under his arm. "Getting my supper," he said.

"What is it?" Sam asked with professional curiosity.

"Pork pie," Sedgwick said, and Sam would have bet that he was rolling his eyes. "Why, did you want a bite?"

"Not really." Now that Sedgwick was holding the parcel

up, Sam could catch the aroma of slightly burnt pastry and a muddle of different kinds of meat. No kind of herb had even been waved over the dish. "Where'd you get it?"

"The pie man at Moorfields."

"You walked all the way to Moorfields for a slice of dodgy pie?" Sam's sensibilities were outraged.

Sedgwick sniffed. "If you must know, I happened to be in the neighborhood, calling on my brother, and I bought the pie because all my servants but one have quit and I don't fancy starving."

It was frustrating when someone told you only half a story. It happened at the Bell when people wanted to make themselves sound more interesting, or when they wanted Sam to ask questions that would give them an excuse to talk about themselves. He didn't much care for that tactic. But he didn't think that was what Sedgwick was doing by casually mentioning that his servants had quit. It was more as if he assumed Sam knew more than he did, and was airing a source of potential awkwardness to get it out of the way.

"Not starving is good," Sam said, which for some reason made Sedgwick laugh, a surprisingly low and throaty sound that was at odds with his usual mannered accents. Sam smiled down at him helplessly. When they squeezed closer together to pass beneath an archway that spanned between two buildings, Sedgwick didn't pull away, and Sam found himself looking forward to the times their sleeves would brush against one another's.

They wound their way through side streets and narrow alleys, and Sam couldn't have said whether it was his doing or Sedgwick's, but it gave him an odd feeling to think that they both knew the streets well enough to choose the route that cut across London in the path most nearly approaching a straight line. Maybe that was why Sam kept walking even after they had crossed into a perfectly safe part of town, the streets wide and clean and lit with gas lamps. Sedgwick didn't complain, didn't tell Sam to turn around and go home. When they got to the Davies Street crossing where Sedgwick ought to turn off to go to his front door on Brook Street, they paused, as if by common consent.

The street light reflected off a strand of Sedgwick's hair that fell onto his forehead beneath the brim of his hat. He must have noticed Sam's gaze, because he hastily smoothed his hair before slapping the hat back onto his head. It was such a self-conscious gesture, so unrefined and inelegant that Sam was almost touched. The man was young, somewhere between twenty and twenty-five. And while Sam, at twenty-eight, wasn't much older, he was certain he had done a lot more living than this fair-haired gentleman who didn't seem to know the value of his own life.

"I'm sorry about what I said last week," Sam said, wanting to do at least this one small thing right by the fellow.

Sedgwick's eyes widened, then he looked down at his boots. "It's quite all right."

"No, it isn't. I only meant that I didn't want you to *let* me do things to you. I hadn't meant to make you feel like what you were offering wasn't good enough."

"It isn't good enough, though, and it's fine for you to say as much." He performed another nervous adjustment of his hat brim. "This isn't a dinner party where you're obliged to sample every dish that's set before you."

Sam laughed from deep in his belly, the sound surprising himself and causing a gentleman in a many-caped great coat to look at him twice.

"Come this way," Sedgwick said, indicating the mews behind his house.

Sam didn't speak until they were in the safety of darkness. "What I'm trying to say is that I've been kicking myself all week for not having taken you up on your offer." He lowered his voice to almost a whisper. Sedgwick leaned in to hear, and Sam wondered if the man even knew he was doing it. "More than that. I think I would have liked whatever you had in mind."

CHAPTER SIX

Hartley's mouth went dry. "I see," he said slowly, frozen still. He could feel his watch ticking in his pocket, counting down the time he had left before Fox walked away. Much to his surprise, he found that he didn't want Fox to walk away. He had gotten so used to avoiding people that it took him a moment to realize that he was actually pleased to see Fox. It had been presumptuous and preposterous for Fox to insist on walking him home, but Hartley's first reaction upon seeing him had been unalloyed relief. Not only relief that it wasn't some former acquaintance come to make trouble for him, but relief that he was seeing Fox again. After that debacle last week—which Hartley was quite certain was his own fault more than Fox's—Hartley had wondered if Fox would ever turn up again. Perhaps he had come to his senses and decided that neither the painting nor Hartley were worth the risk.

"It's Sunday again," Hartley said, about twice as loud and twice as fast as any normal person would have. But Fox only nodded as if this were a perfectly reasonable observation.

"What I mean is that the house is empty." Alf was out on the lash, so they'd have the house to themselves for an hour at least. "You could come in and share some dodgy pie with me," he suggested, holding up his parcel, and then winced at his own attempt at comedy.

But when Fox smiled it was the filthy grin of someone who was about to get something he very much wanted. Hartley's chest tightened at the desire in Fox's gaze. Other men's desire had historically not worked out well for Hartley, and it was hard to look at Fox while remaining optimistic. But Hartley wanted Fox in return, wanted him enough that maybe it outweighed his trepidation. Fox was wearing buckskins tonight, and the fabric clung deliciously to his strong thighs. Even in the shadows Hartley could see that his jaw was dusted with stubble of the darkest black. Hartley wanted to run his fingers over the scratch of new beard and the softness of his lips.

"I'll pass on the pie," Fox said. His voice was a soft rumble and Hartley knew that however the next hour went, his dreams would be infiltrated by that voice saying things utterly unrelated to pie.

Hartley indicated the door with his chin and somehow they got inside without Hartley further making a fool of himself. His heart pounded madly in his chest. Whatever happened with Fox was likely to end with Hartley uncomfortable and Fox disappointed. But his prick had decided opinions and was not capable of learning from past mistakes, so he abandoned the pie in the kitchen and led the way to the library.

Once the door was shut and bolted behind them, Hartley

knew a moment of raw panic and darted across the room, only stopping when he reached the window.

Fox cleared his throat. "I'm going to speak baldly. How do you usually fuck if you don't like being touched?" There was no judgment in Fox's voice, just the recognition that most people found touching fairly goddamned fundamental when it came to fucking.

But Hartley hadn't quite figured out the answer. "Sometimes it almost works if only I do the touching." It was never enough, never quite right; ultimately he had resigned himself to celibacy, figuring it was better than encounters that were alternately frustrating and terrifying.

Besides, the sort of one-sided arrangement that almost worked for Hartley didn't appeal to every man. Most men weren't content being passive. Especially large, strong men like Fox, who likely were accustomed to certain things from a lover. Although, at the moment Fox—still at a safe distance, hands shoved in his pockets, brow creased with concern—didn't look like he was harboring fantasies of roughly bending Hartley over the sofa. No, Hartley was the only one with fantasies of being bent over things, and he couldn't even act on them.

Fox was silent long enough that Hartley thought he was coming up with an excuse to leave. But then he cleared his throat, and when he spoke his voice was a bit rough. "Right then. You do the touching, eh? Let's see what we can do."

"Really?" Hartley's voice was nearly a squeak, damn it. He coughed. "I mean, good. Very well."

"How do you want me? Never done it without touching someone, so you'll have to tell me what you like. Or need."

Hartley didn't need anything. Well, what he needed was not to be crowded, not to be pawed at, not to have his own desire turned into a weapon against him.

"Maybe if you could stand where I am? Against the window?" They still hadn't touched, and it was strange but wonderful to be negotiating an encounter without there having been any touching yet. Words, Hartley could do. Words were safe. Touching was when things went awry. "And, um, let me suck you?" Fox's eyes flared. Good. He moved to where Hartley had indicated, his back against the drawn curtains. Hartley stood before him, absent-mindedly smoothing the silk of his own waistcoat and fingering the row of brass buttons, one at a time, before he dared to touch Fox. First, he smoothed his hands down the coarse wool sleeves of Fox's coat, stopping before the exposed skin of wrists and hands. Fox's arms were huge, and maybe if Hartley were half right in his head he'd figure out a way to properly get a good look at them, but right now the layers of fabric between their bodies were reassuring.

Hartley stood there a minute, appreciating the sight of Fox against the wine-colored curtain, enjoying the fact that Fox had a bulge in his breeches but wasn't doing anything about it, instead waiting for Hartley to act. Hartley dropped to his knees and heard the air rush out of the other man's lungs. That was good. He liked knowing that Fox wanted this, that he wasn't just letting Hartley have his peculiar way with his body.

He ran his hands up the sides of the man's thighs, feeling the restrained strength beneath the rough buckskin. He took his time getting to the placket, both because he enjoyed exploring this man's body with his fingertips and also because he wanted to draw this out. It had been a while since he had been with anyone, and in all likelihood it would be a while before he chose to do it again. Might as well make it last. He skimmed his hands over Fox's hips and arse, only the most featherlight of touches. Fox's hands were already gripping the curtains, large fingers twisted in the velvet.

Leaning forward, Hartley pressed a kiss to the place where the buckskin strained at the placket of Fox's breeches, just a small closed-mouth kiss, utterly chaste except for the location. He heard the man make a sound that was somewhere between a sigh and a hiss, and under his lips the erection grew larger. Now he was running out of patience, so he worked open the buttons and shoved breeches and drawers down all at once. Fox's cock sprang free, dark and heavy and gratifyingly in proportion to the rest of him. Hartley flicked his tongue across the head, and at the first taste of that salty bitterness, his own prick hardened in his breeches. There was so much more to these encounters than touch; there was that familiar taste and musky scent, there was the little gasp the other man made at the slow progress of Hartley's tongue. When he glanced up at Fox, he saw that the other man was staring at him. He liked Fox's gaze on him, could almost feel the heat of it.

"It's fine," Fox said, sounding strangled. "I don't have to be anywhere."

Hartley snorted with laughter, then glared up at Fox because snorting had not been part of his plan. To prevent any further levity, he closed his lips around the head of Fox's cock and gave it a thorough suck, letting his tongue swirl languidly around the head. Fox made a sound at the back of his throat and his fingers twisted even more violently in the curtain. That velvet would be permanently crushed by the force of Fox's grip, and that thought alone made Hartley's prick twitch with interest. Fox's body was taut with restraining himself, all because that was what Hartley wanted. He didn't even know Hartley, didn't have any reason to care what Hartley wanted or didn't want. Who even was this man? Did he go door to door granting unusual sexual favors? Hartley might have smiled if his mouth wasn't busy doing other things.

After another suck, he pulled off and started kissing and licking his way down the shaft. He skimmed the sensitive underside with taunting flicks of his tongue, then traced the vein with tongue and lips. When he got to the root, he pressed his face into the wiry hair and breathed in the other man's scent. His own cock was thoroughly hard now, and he wanted to reach down and adjust his trousers. Instead he wrapped one hand around the base of Fox's erection and slowly started to slide it as far into his mouth as he could. God, he missed this, the taste of incipient climax, the feeling of fullness, of almost not being able to breathe, the sense of another man's pleasure hinging entirely on his whim.

"Christ, you're good," Fox groaned. "Hell."

Hartley gave a little hum to let Fox know his words

weren't unappreciated, and really he could feel free to keep talking like that and then some. Maybe Fox took the hint, because he kept up a stream of murmured praise. "Just like that. So good." And then his words became a more urgent. "God help me. Your mouth is—I need to—I don't know—" His hands were fisted in the curtains, his body taut with stillness.

If Hartley took himself in hand, he'd last three strokes, maybe four. He wouldn't do it, though. For now he needed to store up as much of this as possible, to memorize every detail of this encounter. Hoping he still remembered the trick, he swallowed the shaft as best he could. And, success; Fox let out a muffled oath. Hartley could do this for a good while but decided to take pity on the man. He took the two globes of the man's arse in his hands and tugged him forward, then released. He did it again, building into a rhythm that he set himself. Fox wasn't moving so much as letting Hartley move him. A few more strokes, a swirl of his tongue, a muttered warning from Fox, then the burst of climax. Hartley lingered a moment, then wiped his mouth with the back of his hand.

This was the awkward part. Well, there were a lot of awkward parts, but this was the worst of the lot. Now they would both be wanting to get away from one another, but it was dashed odd to slap your hat back on your head and take off into the night after having your cock sucked. Hartley quite felt bad for Fox for having to manage it.

Then Fox slid to the ground where Hartley still knelt. "Bugger," he said, and Hartley gathered it was meant to be a compliment. "Didn't think I'd manage to come for a while there. Making myself hold still . . ." He shook his head and made a sound of appreciation.

"You managed," Hartley said, primly adjusting his cravat. His voice was hoarse and he was glad of it.

"You're still . . ." Fox gestured at the visible erection in Hartley's trousers.

"Yes, well. I imagine I will be for a while."

Fox tucked himself back into his buckskins. "Anything I can do?"

"It's a hard prick, not a fatal condition," Hartley snapped. "It'll keep."

"Oh well, as long as you don't actually die, then, I guess it's nothing to worry about."

Hartley huffed out a laugh despite himself. "I'll deal with it later. Did you really think you weren't going to be able to come?" he asked with no small interest. Hartley wanted to hear more about that, knowing he'd think about it when he took himself in hand later that night, in the safety and solitude of his small bedchamber.

"Damned hard when you can't move."

"I never said you couldn't move."

"You didn't say I could. And I didn't think you'd like it if I did. Was I right?"

Hartley thought. "Yes," he admitted. He had felt safe with Fox, but he had felt other things too. Things he'd be remembering alone, with his hand wrapped around his frustrated erection. For now, it was time for Fox to go home and leave Hartley to his empty house and turgid prick. He was still kneeling, but sitting back on his heels. Fox had landed in a sitting position, with his knees tucked up in front of him. It felt oddly companionable. Hartley didn't like it. "Well, Mr. Fox, I thank you—"

"No. After that—" he gestured in the vicinity of his breeches "—you're going to turn around and call me Mr. Fox? Everyone other than the excise man calls me Sam."

Hartley felt his face heat. Looking away from Fox, he brushed some dust off the knees of his trousers.

"Unless you want me to call you Mr. Sedgwick," Fox said, letting his words linger on the air.

That sounded all wrong. "No, please call me Hartley. Sam," he added.

"Right then. When am I calling you Hartley?"

"Pardon?" Hartley tilted his head in confusion.

"When am I going to see you again? It isn't a come on, I just like to know things in advance. If you tell me to bugger off, that's what I'll do, no hard feelings. But you're helping me with Kate's picture. Maybe you'll think of something I can do to help that won't risk my neck."

That was the first time Hartley had heard the name of Sam's friend and it kicked up some dust around an old memory that still remained just out of reach. "Come back next week. My house is always empty Sunday after midday." It was pretty empty most hours of most days, to be fair. "We won't be interrupted," he added, in case Sam thought they were only going to spend the afternoon planning a burglary instead of pursuing better uses of their time.

They got to their feet and Hartley absently led the way

toward the front door. It was nearest, and it was the door he habitually used, so it was only natural.

He froze, his hand on the door pull. "Oh, I beg your pardon. I forgot myself. I'll bring you to the kitchen. Much safer that way." Hartley had no reputation to speak of, but Sam kept a tavern and might be recognized for that reason as well as his dark skin. Sam's reputation wasn't Hartley's to throw away, which could very well happen to any man seen coming and going from Hartley's house.

But when he looked at Sam, he saw confusion on his face, followed by a blank coldness. After the pleasure, closeness, and sheer bloody relief of the last hour, Sam's stony expression was a bracing shock. Hartley didn't understand, perhaps because he was so carried away by the novelty of having forgotten himself for a time. All he could be sure of was that this encounter, like so many others before it, had ended badly.

Sam was no stranger to men who looked to him for an anonymous fuck, something rough to go along with his size and his looks. They wanted to be shoved up against a wall and used, and then afterward they left without more than a few embarrassed words. That wasn't Sam's ideal way to get off, but it was fine. Or at least he was used to it, and sometimes he thought being accustomed to something was maybe the same thing as accepting it.

That's not what he had expected from Hartley. Hartley hadn't wanted Sam to use him, hadn't assumed that Sam wanted to hand out a brutal fucking. They had talked and then Sam had damned near lost his fucking mind trying not to shove his prick down Hartley's throat. At one point he thought he might pass out or start whimpering if he didn't come, and he thought Hartley liked that. God knew Sam had.

Once, at a time when Sam had less concern for law and order than he did presently, he had met a man in an alley behind the Cross Keys. When they went back to the man's lodgings, the fellow had wanted Sam to tie him up. Sam had obliged, mostly because it wasn't any skin off his back if a bloke wanted his hands bound while he was rogered, but he couldn't say the practice had done anything special for him. Now he thought he understood what it did for that other fellow, though. The inability to move, the physical helplessness—it had scratched an itch Sam hadn't known he had. Sam didn't think he'd go in for actually having his hands bound. But knowing that he wasn't supposed to move was even more of a restraint than any ropes could ever be.

He had lived his life entirely aware of his strength and power. Hell, he had never been allowed to forget. Not in the ring, not when people crossed the street in alarm upon seeing him, certainly not in his brief encounters with men. He hadn't ever thought his strength was something that he wanted to put away temporarily, to escape from. But now he craved another chance to do exactly that.

He had seen Hartley's face after their encounter. He had been as taken by surprise as Sam had by the force of whatever it was that sparked between them. "A lid for every pot," his mum had often said, usually when referring to some slightly odd cousin who had finally settled down. Sam had always dismissed this saying as one that could never apply to him: what business did a man like him have looking for matches? Sitting on the floor with Hartley, though, he had wondered if that was what his mother had meant.

It wasn't Sam's usual encounter, and he was annoyed that it had ended the usual way. As if he even wanted to go out Hartley Sedgwick's precious front door. It would serve the fellow right if Sam never darkened his doorway again. The only problem with that plan was that Sam already knew he wanted to see Hartley again. And that just made him more irritated with himself. Because who was Hartley to him, anyway? A fellow who didn't have the sense God gave a duck, walking through bad streets with gold chains hanging out, and all to get a slice of dodgy pie. "Pitiful," he said aloud, and didn't know whether he meant himself or Hartley.

"It's anybody's guess which of you is more cross," Nick said, dropping a tray of empty mugs on the bar.

"I'm not cross." Kate yawned. "You're cross," she said, perched on a stool. Sam worried she would fall asleep and topple off the thing.

"I'm not cross, just busy, mate," Sam told his brother. He hadn't meant to snap, but he was pretty sure that's how it had come out. Besides, he wasn't cross so much as thoughtful, and even if his thoughts happened to stray toward everything in the world that annoyed him, that didn't mean he was cross, he was quite certain.

"No, not a hint of crossness here. Everyone's right cheerful," Nick said, rolling his eyes.

"It's the moon," Kate said, yawning again. "Puts everyone on edge. I've had three births in two days and I need to sleep."

"That doesn't explain Sam," Nick said.

Kate looked at Sam with bleary eyes. "You're right," she said to Nick, as if Sam didn't have ears. "For days now he's looked like he needed a dose of Senna tea. Maybe some syrup of figs." Nick evidently found this hilarious, because the two of them laughed and bumped imaginary mugs together in a mimed salute.

"Oh hell, what's going on with Johnny Newton now?" Nick asked, looking over Sam's shoulder, toward the entry of the back room. Sam turned in time to see Newton toe to toe with a man he didn't recognize as one of the Bell's regulars. He caught a snippet of conversation that seemed to have something to do with Johnny's mother.

"You stay back," Sam said to his brother and Kate. "I'll deal with it." Breaking up fights was one of his duties at the Bell. He managed to get to the two men just in time to grab Johnny's wrist and prevent him from swinging at the stranger. But the stranger's reflexes weren't as fast. Sam felt the blow collide with his cheekbone.

"Oi!" He brought his hand instinctively to his cheek. His fingers came away red with blood. He had probably been hit in the same place dozens upon dozens of times, but not lately, and the sharp pain of broken skin was familiar and surprising at once. "The hell is the matter with you? Get out of my pub."

The stranger didn't step away. He was plainly furious and utterly soused, and looked ready to swing at Sam now. His pale skin was flushed with drink and rage.

"None of that. Away you go." Sam grabbed the man by his shoulders and steered him toward the door. But before they reached the door, a man Sam recognized as the constable entered.

"Now, what do we have here?" the man asked. His name was Merton, Sam thought, but Sam had tried his damnedest to avoid having any reason to deal with the police. "Don't tell me there's fighting in this pub." He spoke with the glee of a man about to make trouble.

"There was a friendly altercation, sir," Sam said kindly. He dabbed at the cut with his bar apron. There wasn't much blood, at least.

"Doesn't seem too friendly to me," said Marston. "Let's have a look at that back room."

Sam was confused about what the constable wanted with the back room, but murmured his assent as he led the way.

They used the back room to store casks of beer. It smelled of hops and the sawdust they kept on hand to dry up spills. In a slightly more elevated establishment, this room would be a snug or a private parlor for more genteel customers. In a slightly lower place, this would be the place for cock fights or, as in Sam's youth, boxing matches.

Boxing matches. He understood, then. Merton thought they were holding prizefights. He opened his mouth, but snapped it shut when he realized that a hasty denial would only confirm the constable's suspicions.

"I remember you," Merton said, holding up his lamp to examine Sam's blood-streaked face. "I saw you in Croydon. I thought it was you. Did that lad ever wake up?"

Sam had fought several matches in Croydon, but he knew the one Merton meant. "He woke up," was all Sam said. That had been Sam's last match. After that, he had started training Davey, who was made of stronger stuff, he had thought.

"What was it they called you?" Merton tapped his mouth with one finger as if he had trouble remembering the filthy nicknames people had given Sam. "You were a beast." His lip curled in slight distaste. "I won't have any of that on my watch," he said. He glanced around the back room. "I don't know what you're doing, but I'll bring you down."

Sam wanted to protest that there was no evidence of fighting in the back room. There was a broken glass and drops of his own blood in the taproom, and a dozen witnesses who would say that he had been breaking up a common tavern brawl. But he thought of what Constable Merton had seen upon entering the Bell: a crowd of people on their feet, looking in the direction of the back room. A prizefighter with blood on his face. The same prizefighter who had only escaped a manslaughter trial because the man he had knocked out had finally woken up, three days later.

When Merton left, Nick had already begun sweeping up the broken glass, and Kate had topped off everyone's drinks. Sam let out a sigh. They weren't doing anything wrong. The business was entirely aboveboard. But he felt dirty and small, he felt like he had when Hartley had maneuvered him away from the front door. He felt like all the nasty things he had ever been called.

Sam was saved by any further ruminations by the entry of Kate's dog, which had been banished to the outdoors during the busiest part of the evening and now came in with grievances to air and food to scrounge. Now he was perched in Nick's arms with his tongue hanging out and his ears up as if he had done something remarkably clever. When he and Nick had been boys, their mother had never let an animal into the house, let alone onto anyone's lap.

Maybe sensing his gloominess, the dog scrambled out of Nick's arms to dance around Sam's feet, as if Sam's mood would be improved by having untold foulness on his clean clothes. He had to wonder what neat, fussy Hartley would think about this dog. A man who kept his hands so clean and his hair so smooth would not be impressed with a dirty mongrel. He pictured the look of revulsion that would doubtless appear on the man's face, how he would shudder and turn his nose up.

Later he and Nick did the washing up while Kate dozed by the fire with the dog in her lap. "If you want to talk about it—and I'm not even saying there's an *it* to talk about, even though there definitely is, but it's fine if you want to pretend I haven't noticed—I'm here. And I'm not talking about Merton. He's an arsehole, but a bog standard one. I'm talking about whatever had you bothered earlier today. I'm here. For God's sake. If you killed a man, all I'd ask was where you wanted me to help you bury the body. You know that, don't you?"

"I know," Sam lied. He wiped a dish and stacked it on a shelf. Sam hadn't ever told Nick that he preferred men. He hadn't ever told Kate, either, but she had guessed; he hadn't corrected her when, a few years ago, she had tipsily whispered to him that she wished he'd find some nice bloke for himself.

But it was different with his brother. After not mentioning it for his entire life, he felt that he couldn't start now. And there was always the risk that Nick would react badly. Still, Nick had to have noticed that Sam was nearly thirty and had never so much as walked out with a girl.

Even if he could speak freely to Nick, he couldn't very well explain that he was feeling miserable because a near stranger had sucked him off and then told him not to use the front door. Not so many years ago, he had risked his life and his safety while crowds of people hurled insults at him. He might think it was silly for a former prizefighter to complain about being put in his place by a single unarmed gentleman. And Nick might ask what on earth Sam was doing with a rich man in the first place. Sam didn't have an answer to that, not even one he could voice to himself.

By the time they finished tidying up the kitchen, they could hear Kate snoring by the fire, and had to bite the insides of their cheeks to keep from laughing too loud and waking her. Tiptoeing as quietly as two large men could, they peered into the parlor. The dog was passed out on Kate's soft lap.

"I cannot believe she lets that dog sit on her lap," Sam said.

"She says it's earned all the fine things life has to offer," Nick whispered.

"Not lately, it hasn't. Sleeps, steals food, leaves fur on the floor of the Bell."

"I used to wash him under the pump when Kate wasn't looking," Nick admitted. "But she caught on and told me not to. Said he's been through enough."

Inspiration struck Sam. "Tomorrow I'll take the little fellow for a long walk." Tomorrow would be Sunday.

Nick looked at him suspiciously. "He's old and has three legs. He won't get far."

"I'll carry him then," Sam said, and refused to answer any more of Nick's questions. He told himself he'd bring the dog to Hartley to settle the score, but he knew that he just wanted an excuse to see the man. The fact that he couldn't even convince himself of his own lie was a bad sign indeed.

CHAPTER SEVEN

It didn't take long for Hartley to figure out what had gone wrong with Sam. He had time on his hands, endless empty hours to puzzle out what that blank expression on Sam's face had meant when Hartley had showed him to the kitchen door. Sam must have thought Hartley was putting him in his place, or that Hartley didn't want the world to see a black man in a worn coat leaving the front door of his house.

He was mortified, embarrassed out of all proportion to the significance of the event. But when one didn't have that much going on in one's life, things didn't stay in proportion. That hour with Sam Fox had been one hundred percent of Hartley's social calendar. Bollocksing it up was therefore a signal failure. He tried to tell himself that it didn't matter at all whether Sam was offended, but even though Hartley wasn't one of nature's most warmhearted creatures, he couldn't quite convince himself of that.

Compounding this failure was the fact that Sam had provided the only even minimally satisfying sexual encounter in

Hartley's recent life, even though Hartley's own climax didn't happen until late that night, alone in his room, thinking of hands twisted in velvet curtains, a body taut with the effort of not touching him. Sometimes he thought his mind might have gotten a bit warped. Most people liked being touched. And they liked going places and having friends and doing things that weren't sitting alone in a library and staring at the rectangles that marked where paintings used to hang.

The autumn sun had already set, and rain beat down on the windowpanes. The fire had burnt low, but the coal scuttle hadn't been refilled today and Hartley hadn't sunk so low that he was about to fill it himself. Instead, he let the chill of the room seep into his bones. If it was possible to be cheerful under these conditions, Hartley didn't know how.

Instead he thought of Friars' Gate and revenge. He could almost smell the mineral spirits, feel the blade in his hand, see the destroyed remains of those paintings. With every ruined canvas, he'd take away some of the power that Easterbrook had stolen from him.

He thought of how for years his only sexual release had been while barely enduring anonymous back alley cock sucking, and how eventually even that was out of his reach. He thought of these past months since his disgrace. Now that everyone knew what he was and what he had done, he couldn't tear his mind from those facts; it was as if other people's worst thoughts about him had wormed their way into his own thoughts about himself.

It had all been the Easterbrooks' doing, father and then son.

Sometimes he wondered what he'd have done if his god-father hadn't left him the house. He hadn't really had a chance to figure out what he wanted in a world where he had to make his own way, and he feared he was too broken to think in terms of the future.

It was now cold in the library, and Hartley realized he'd let the fire burn out entirely. He considered building it up again, but instead he sat in the cold and the dark.

The knock startled him. His first thought was that Alf had lost his latchkey. Then he remembered it was Sunday and Sam had said he would come. He glanced down at his clothes. Not his best, but adequate. The looking glass on the landing confirmed that his hair was acceptable but his cravat askew. Well, there was no time to retie it, not unless he wanted to risk Sam leaving. For reasons he chose not to fully examine, this was not a risk he wished to take.

He ran down the stairs and flung open the door. Sam stood in the shadowy passage, holding what looked to be a fox stole that had been dredged out of the Thames.

"What in Christendom is that?" Hartley asked by way of greeting.

"It's a dog."

"Are you quite certain? Have you checked?" It could be a large, furry rat. Or a ragbag. Anything was possible.

"Definitely a dog."

Hartley didn't ask why this alleged dog was being brought to his house, figuring that any answer he got would be beside the point. "Come in before you get drenched."

"Too late for that." Sam indicated his dripping hat.

"Sit here. Both of you. The fire's banked but it won't take long to build it up. If you like, take off your coat and your boots so they dry faster." He fussed with the fire, adding some coal and using the bellows until the hearth had taken the chill out of the room and filled it with a warm glow. Turning around, he saw Sam, still wearing his soaked coat and boots, holding the shivering dog.

Hartley cast his gaze searchingly around the room before settling on a large apron one of the girls must have left behind. "Here, give it to me."

"Give what to you?"

"The dog. It's shivering." When Sam didn't hand the dog over, Hartley sighed and scooped the dog up himself. "Poor creature. Only has three legs. It's no wonder you had to carry him."

"He's dirty," Sam cautioned.

"I should say so. Filthy. Not to mention a bit ripe." He wrapped the dog in the apron and cradled it in his arms. "Where did you find him?"

"Uh. He's my friend's dog."

Hartley tilted his head in confusion. "Then why is he in my kitchen, frozen stiff?"

"Because I'm an idiot? He's going to ruin your coat."

"I have others." The dog was trying his best to wedge himself into Hartley's armpit, presumably for warmth. Hartley gave it a vigorous rub with the apron and poked the fire to help it blaze back into life.

"I wouldn't have guessed you liked dogs." Sam's teeth were chattering.

"Take off that coat. Shirt too. Put them on the back of that chair to dry by the fire."

Hartley carefully didn't watch Sam peel off his coat, but out of the corner of his eye he could see the other man hesitate over his shirt. "The house is empty, so you can strip as much as you please." He blushed, not having meant the words as a come-on. Hartley averted his gaze as Sam pulled the shirt over his head. "My only servant has taken to sleeping in the loft over the carriage house. Presumably so he can freely debauch himself without my interference." He was blathering nervously, which was so lamentably unattractive. Extracting the dog from his armpit, he peered at the mongrel's face. "Good lord, what happened to you?" The little fellow had a bite out of one ear.

"He spent some years in the rat pit."

Hartley wrinkled his nose at the mention of rat baiting. He had never seen it, but he knew the general thrust was that a dog was put into a pit with a pack of vicious rats, while spectators bet on how many rats the dog could kill in a given time. "You poor sod," he told the dog. "I hope your days are filled with bacon and cuddles." The dog licked his nose, and Hartley wriggled away. "That's a step too far, my friend."

A crack of laughter came from Sam, and Hartley looked over despite his efforts not to see the man bare-chested. Sam's broad shoulders were shaking with laughter, firelight flickering off dark skin and outlining the heavy muscles of his arms and chest. Hartley had known that Sam was a large man, had felt that his body was strong and hard, but he hadn't quite been prepared for this visual proof of power. His mouth went dry and he hastily looked away. But he was weak and Sam really looked a treat so he stole another glance. This time Sam caught him looking and stopped laughing. Hartley's breath caught when he realized what was happening; they were both enjoying one another's company—not planning a burglary, not dancing around the topic of sex, but simply taking pleasure in their time together. The air between them felt charged with the intimacy of the moment and the shared recognition of what it meant.

"I'd like to know what's so amusing," Hartley said, even though Sam had long since stopped laughing.

"Just what a dolt I am," Sam answered, because that was God's own truth. "I brought him here to annoy you. I thought you wouldn't like a dirty dog in your house."

"To annoy me? We're talking about the front door, aren't we? I owe you an apology about that, and an explanation too."

Sam was taken aback, not only by the fact that Hartley had brought up the door incident, but that he looked so conscience stricken. "Yes," he managed.

Hartley frowned. "I know how it sounded, and I'm sorry for that. You must have thought me a high-handed bastard who had treated you like a servant—"

"Not quite," Sam said, remembering the servants who had come in and out of the kitchen door when he had been spying on the house. They had been clean and tidy, and Sam had felt very aware of his rough coat and shoes.

"As someone unfit to use the front door, then. And to get even with me, you decided to arrive with a filthy old mongrel who would most definitely not be granted access to the front door."

That was about the size of it. "Right."

Hartley turned his attention to the dog. "You poor dear, to have been used so poorly." He spoke in the sort of singsong voice a fond mother might use to talk to a baby. The dog was looking at him with wide eyes, likely confused because nobody had ever spoken to him that way in his entire miserable life. "Dragged out into the cold and the rain, just so this rude man could make a point. And at your age." And then, in a normal voice, "How old is he?"

"It didn't start raining until we were halfway here," he protested. "Kate got him about eight years ago, and he wasn't a puppy then."

"What's his name?"

"We call him Dog."

"You've called him Dog for eight years," Hartley said, in obvious disbelief.

"Well, the rat pit man called him Duke, but Kate said she has no use for any lords in her bed, so she wouldn't call him that." He realized too late that he shouldn't have repeated Kate's ribald joke. His face heated. "But he won't answer to anything at all. I think he's deaf. Watch." He patted his leg. "Come here, Dog." The dog didn't even turn away from Hartley. Sam whistled, which at least got the dog's attention. "Heel, Duke." Nothing.

"Oh, for heaven's sake." Hartley, still holding the dog under one arm, opened one of the doors off to the side of the kitchen, probably leading to a pantry or larder. He returned with a loaf of bread and a hunk of cheese. After setting the dog on the floor by the fire, he took a few steps away. "Here, Dog," he said, holding out a bit of cheese. "Good Dog." Eventually, the dog came and ate the cheese. "See," Hartley said smugly. "He answers."

"Of course he comes when you put food on the floor. He's deaf, not daft."

For the next hour, Sam sat by the fire while Hartley trained the dog. He put the bread farther and farther away, and sometimes called the dog even without a bribe. By the end of the hour, the dog was looking at Hartley with wide, pleading eyes every time he heard the man's voice.

"I grew up with dogs," Hartley explained after the dog had fallen asleep at his feet. "Usually sheepdogs that weren't fit for work, which my brothers took pity on. And they always had the run of the place."

"I didn't. Ever. My mum was house proud. No dogs, not even shoes, only a cat in the kitchen to keep away the mice." And looking at the amount of filth the dog had tracked onto the stone floors of the kitchen, he could see why.

Hartley must have caught the direction of Sam's gaze, because he asked, "Now who's fussy?"

"Ha. Point taken. You grew up in the country, then?"

"In the north. Not far from Keswick."

Sounded like the middle of nowhere. "Are your people farmers?"

"No. My father is—well, more or less an idler. He writes poetry and sponges off his friends. The poetry is supposed to be good, which I daresay counts for something. I haven't eaten," he said, rising fluidly to his feet. "The day rather got away from me. Let me see if I can scrape together something for both of us." He disappeared again into the larder. "Do you care for ham? I still have some bread," he called, but didn't wait for an answer. "That cheese was meant for my supper, so I hope you appreciated it, Dog." He came out laden with a couple of dishes, some pots of what looked like jam or mustard, and a jug that proved to contain ale.

As they ate, they talked about nothing in particular. The dog sniffed around the edges of the kitchen and made a general nuisance of himself, which Hartley seemed to enjoy. Sam's shirt dried, so he put it back on. He was warm, his belly was full, and his frame of mind much improved from when he had arrived. Hartley met his gaze and looked hastily looked away, but not before Sam saw the shadow of a smile on his lips. This could be the beginning of something, Sam realized. And while only a fool would believe that a kitchen table supper between a rich man, a black boxer, and a three-legged dog could be the beginning of something *good*, maybe Sam was more foolish than he thought.

"What happened to your face?" Hartley asked, gesturing to his own cheekbone.

"Fight." Sam saw a pale eyebrow shoot up. "Breaking up a fight," he added hastily. "At the pub." Something—either concern or distaste—flickered across Hartley's face.

Suddenly, the dog's ears pricked up and a moment later Sam heard footsteps outside. Without thinking about it, he got to his feet, positioning himself between Hartley and the door, clutching a fire iron in one hand.

The door swung open, revealing a gangly youth with a

shock of unkempt hair, accompanied by a girl in a somewhat disordered frock. Not a likely pair of housebreakers, but still Sam didn't move.

"Alf," Hartley said, coming to stand beside Sam. "This is Mr. Fox. He's come for supper. I take it this is your friend who is to be the new help?"

"Yes, sir. Sadie Russell." The girl managed an awkward curtsy and jabbed the lad in the side. "You could have told me he'd be in the kitchen, Alfred," she muttered.

"The housekeeper's room is down that corridor," Hartley said. "I'll leave you alone while you get settled."

Sam was suddenly conscious once again that Hartley was a man with servants. It had been easy to forget this essential fact when Hartley had been on the bare stone floor playing with a mongrel. But it was dangerous for Sam to have a damned thing to do with Hartley. "You can't trust them to look out for you," had been his father's constant refrain during Sam's childhood. *Them* sometimes meant white Englishmen and sometimes meant rich people, and Hartley was both.

They came from different worlds, and while tonight had been cozy and familiar, that would only make it more jarring the next time Hartley chose to look down his nose at him. Sam had to figure out a way to keep a safe distance from this man, otherwise he'd only wind up getting hurt.

Even though they were once again alone in the kitchen, their earlier intimacy was gone, and Sam finished his ale and bread in a hurry while Hartley kept up a stilted, one-sided conversation. When Sam got to his feet, announcing that he had to go help close the Bell, he headed straight for the kitchen door.

CHAPTER EIGHT

When Hartley returned from a long early morning walk in the park, he found the house in an unprecedented state. All the curtains were open and the floors and furniture polished to a satiny shine. He followed the aroma of roasting meat and buttery pastry down to the kitchens.

In the scullery he got his first good look at the new maid. She was a young woman in a faded brown frock, up to her elbows in dishwater. Upon seeing Hartley, she wiped her hands on her apron and executed an awkward curtsey. When she straightened, Hartley perceived what he assumed was the reason her parents had cast her out: a significantly rounded belly. He looked carefully at her face. She was about Alf's age, which was to say no more than eighteen.

"I beg your pardon," Hartley said, trying not to stare at her belly and calculate how much longer before the blessed event. "I wanted to thank you myself for the work you've done. The house hasn't looked so fine in years. Did you do it all yourself?" It had required a staff of five to keep the house reasonably presentable, and he recalled his godfather having had at least eight servants.

"No, sir," she said, not taking her eyes off the floor. "Alfred helped."

"Nah," Alf said, emerging from the coal cellar. "I only did what Sadie told me. She knows how things are meant to be done." He spoke with an audible note of pride.

"You're not from London, are you?" Hartley asked. He thought he heard a bit of a burr in her voice.

"No, sir. Was born near Exeter, sir." Yes, a distinct country burr. And also a hint of refinement that made Hartley's ears prick up. Her father had most likely been a gentleman. Hartley felt distinctly uncomfortable by the idea of a young gentlewoman, indeed one who was in a delicate condition, toiling in his kitchen.

"And how did you learn to cook?" he asked, because she was too young and too genteel to have risen from the ranks of kitchen maids.

"Sometimes we had a cook who would let me help," she said, "but when we had no cook I'd have the fixing of the meals to myself, so I learned."

Hartley pursed his lips. In the girl's words he heard an echo of his own childhood: unpredictability of household arrangements, servants coming and going, children pressed into service as unpaid help. But if her family had a cook, however sporadically, they had certainly been well-to-do. She oughtn't to be scrubbing floors and washing dishes. This was what Will would call reactionary twaddle, but Hartley couldn't quite rid himself of the notion that some people scrubbed floors and other people paid them to do so. Complicating matters was the fact that his own background placed him more comfortably in the former group than in the latter: his family hadn't had servants or even a functional roof until his older brother was old enough to take things in hand.

"Have you found your work and your quarters to your liking, Sadie?"

"Oh, yes, sir." Another curtsey.

"That's enough with the 'sir' and the curtseys." He was afraid she would pitch forward if she attempted it again. "I assume Alf has told you about my situation, so you know that I'm fortunate to have you." Her face reddened beneath her cap, which he took as confirmation. "If there's anything you need, please tell me. I want you to be comfortable here."

Later, when Alf cleared the supper dishes, he said, "I didn't know you had it in you."

"Had what in me?" Hartley asked.

"You were right sweet to her."

Had he been? He wasn't certain whether it was proper to be sweet to one's servant, or indeed whether he had ever been sweet to anyone in his life. "She's a very capable cook and housemaid, and I want to keep her."

"She'll be relieved to hear it."

Hartley sat back in his chair. "I don't like that her parents turned her out. Do you know anything about how she got—" He mimed a round belly, then felt foolish for not being able to speak the suitable words.

"Uh, the usual way, I reckon," Alf said.

Hartley pressed his lips together. "I mean, does she wish to marry the father?"

"She won't talk about it," Alf said, confirming Hartley's worst suspicions.

"Alf, she was raised to be a lady. She shouldn't be cooking my supper."

Alf gave a disappointed shake of his head. "What a sodding snob you are."

Hartley didn't deny it. "I realize that girls are put on the street for far less than—" again he mimed a large belly "—but that doesn't make it any less galling. The fact is that my father would never have kicked any of us out for anything. He was—is—a bit scattered, and he's deliberately ignorant about how the world works, but he'd never have turned us out into the cold."

"That's a low bar you have there."

"What I'm trying to say is that he always knew about me."

"There are newborn babies who know about you, mate."

Hartley glared. "Anyway, keep her safe and make sure she has whatever she needs."

"You know I will." Alf's voice was gruff.

Hartley was getting ready for bed when he heard the wailing. At first he thought it was an injured child, so he ran down the stairs toward the back of the house, from where the sound was coming. But when he opened the door, he saw

Dog. *Dog*, honestly. Who had a dog for eight years without bothering to give it a proper name?

"You again? Your mistress will be beside herself." If he knew the name of the pub where Sam worked, he might have sent word. But it was late, and it was raining again, and he couldn't stand to leave an elderly three-legged dog standing out in the cold. Sacrificing another apron, he dried the dog and put it in front of the banked fire to sleep. He'd figure out how to get in touch with Sam tomorrow.

Sam had spent nearly two hours in Hartley's kitchen the other day, most of that time with his shirt off, and they hadn't so much as touched one another. They had talked about dogs and ale; Hartley had spoken of his brothers and Sam had talked about some of the patrons at the tavern. Neither of them had mentioned the painting; neither of them had even made a move to get the other's trousers off. The entire visit had been as chaste as a tea party. In fact, Hartley had enjoyed it more than any tea party he had ever attended. He had been at his ease, eating what amounted to table scraps in his empty kitchen, sitting with a shirtless tavern keeper. He had felt at home for the first time in months, if not years.

He knew that to be a dangerous illusion. He couldn't spend a pleasant evening with a man he wanted to take to bed without everything getting muddy in his mind. No—his mind was already muddy. It was an oozing pit of quicksand. There was no way for Hartley to have what he wanted out of a man; his brain wouldn't let it happen. Every minute together would only remind him of what wasn't possible, of what his mind was too broken and muddled to allow.

The dog followed him upstairs, wagging that appalling stub of a tail. It looked like somebody had meant to dock the thing, then only done the job halfway.

"No. No, sir," he whispered so as not to wake Sadie. "You stay downstairs."

The dog tipped his head again. Hartley couldn't tell what kind of dog it was supposed to be. He had the pointed muzzle and long legs of a rat terrier, but its fur was long and shaggy. Its ears looked like they wanted to prick up but were too floppy to quite manage the trick. Well, one of his ears was floppy; the other had that chunk missing from it. "Fine," Hartley said, sighing. "Come upstairs."

At the first landing, the dog stopped walking, instead holding one of its paws in the air and mewling plaintively.

"This is emotional blackmail," Hartley said.

The dog whimpered. Hartley picked it up and placed him at the foot of the bed where he would doubtless ruin the coverlet.

No sooner had Hartley slid between his clean sheets, then the dog started howling.

As Sam swept the floor, one eye on the straggling patrons who were still nursing the remnants of their drinks, Kate came downstairs. Sam gathered that she had been paying a visit to Nick.

"Where's the dog?" she asked, scanning the room.

"In the courtyard. I gave him a ham bone."

Two minutes later she was back. "He's not out there. And

it's raining again." She had circles under her eyes, and she really ought to be asleep. "I'm going to go look for him."

"I'll go look if you'll keep an eye on the till and refuse to give anyone so much as another drop to drink."

He slapped his hat onto his head and went into the rain. "Dog!" he called, which sounded ridiculous enough to earn him a glance from a passerby. After a quarter of an hour, Sam still hadn't seen any trace of the animal. Constable Merton, however, was trailing a few paces behind, as if waiting for Sam to step out of line. In defeat, Sam headed back toward the Bell.

From the shadows came the gleam of moonlight glancing off a row of silver buttons. Even if Sam hadn't been preoccupied by buttons lately, the sight would have been arresting enough in this neighborhood, even more so at such a late hour and in such bad weather, and when the wearer of the expensively buttoned garment was being propelled through the streets by a scruffy dog on a string.

"Oi!" Sam called, when he saw Hartley twice walk past the alley that led to the Bell. The dog was jumping and barking, and generally looked like he was going to have some kind of fit if Hartley didn't turn where he was meant to.

Hartley turned his head and spotted him. "Thank God," he said, sagging with relief. "Did you know this dog can bay like one of the hounds of hell? When I left him outside my bedchamber door, I thought he'd wake the neighborhood. I put him at the foot of the bed—"

Sam realized that the little bastard had gone back to Hartley for some more bread and cheese. "You put that—"

he gestured at Dog, who was at least fifty percent filth at this point "—in your nice clean bed?"

"I wanted to sleep! I would have shared my bed with half a dozen piglets if it meant an end to the racket." A man gave Hartley an odd look, but he didn't notice, and Sam bit back a smile. "I didn't know which pub you worked at, or if you'd even be there, so I put the dog on a lead in the hope that he'd find his way home."

"It looks like it worked."

"Ha! No. This imbecilic mongrel has led me on an impromptu walking tour of what must be half of London. I've brought him to a dozen taverns in this neighborhood alone. It's been quite the adventure." He didn't sound too put out, though. Even in the moonlight, Sam could see that Hartley was smiling despite his wet hair and muddy clothes.

"I can take him from here," Sam offered. Hartley didn't quite flinch, but the smile momentarily dropped from his face. "I didn't—"

Hartley waved his hand imperiously, cutting Sam off. "Quite."

Sam wasn't in the habit of turning away people who needed warmth and rest, certainly not people he was growing rather troublingly fond of. But Hartley seemed to accept as his due that he would be cast out, alone, into the cold. Sam knew he'd have to turn that over in his mind, but for now he only gestured at the small gap between buildings that would bring them to the Bell. "Follow me," he said. "If you think I'm sending you home without a pint of something to warm your way, you can guess again.

To get to the Bell, you had to turn down a small street that ran somewhat perpendicular to Fleet Street, and from there you had to know where to look for the lane that led to the courtyard that fronted the Bell. Leading Hartley along this path, Sam wondered that they did any business at all. But the regulars knew the way, and that was good enough.

When he opened the door, he was greeted by the sound of Kate's laughter and the scent of hops, wood polish, and a bit of sawdust. These scents belonged to the Bell and it was disconcerting to have them mixed with Hartley's cologne, or hair soap, or whatever it was he used that smelled like spring woods. He hesitated on the threshold, but he couldn't keep Hartley standing in the cold and rain, so he stepped inside.

Hartley looked around the way anyone did when entering a new place. Not disapproving, not inspecting, just getting the lay of the land. Sam feared that he was being measured and coming up short. Then Kate looked up from the table she was wiping—he would have to remind her that nobody was paying her to do that sort of work anymore—her face stern as if she were about to turn out a late-arriving patron. When she saw that it was only Sam, her face relaxed.

When she caught sight of Hartley, she dropped the rag and ran to him.

"Oh my God," she said, staring. "Hart?"

Hartley stared at her in return, his pale eyes wide and his hand clapped over his mouth. Then they sort of fell into one another's arms. Sam started to warn Kate that Hartley didn't care for being touched, but Hartley was hugging her back while they both laughed and cried. It seemed Sam didn't need to perform an introduction.

Sam could make out only a few of the jumbled exclamations and half-interrupted questions they peppered one another with.

"That week—"

"My *dear*—"

"I looked for you!"

"His servants wouldn't give me your name."

"And you were using a false surname, I think."

"Was I?"

Sam turned away to finish wiping the tables and putting the chairs up, wanting to give them some privacy. But after a moment, Hartley called him.

"You didn't tell me your friend was Kate Bradley," Hartley said, his hands on his hips. "We, ah, traveled in the same circles."

"What he means is his godfather wanted to shag me," Kate chimed in. "He'd invite me round, offer me sweets and ribbons. Gave me a sodding fortune for that painting. Proper old pervert. But Hart and I made friends."

"We had such fun," Hartley said. "I had almost forgotten. Until one day you didn't come back. I thought you'd been killed."

"Nah, I went with my father to watch one of Sam's fights up north. That was about when I took up with Nick—Sam's brother—and I didn't think he'd like the idea of me stringing old men along for presents."

Hartley nodded comprehendingly, but he crossed his

arms across his chest in a way that made Sam wonder again exactly why Hartley wanted this revenge, or whatever it was, against his godfather. Easterbrook had taken advantage of Kate, and Sam's fists clenched at the idea that he might have done the same to Hartley.

Kate yawned. "I'm run off my feet. Come by tomorrow, Hart, will you? I want to know how you came to be friends with my dog. And with Sam," she added with a sidelong glance in Sam's direction. "The till is empty and the mugs are clean," she told Sam. "I'll lock the door on my way out. I banked the fire here, but Nick came down to say that he has yours roaring, so you ought to take Hart upstairs and get him warm. Night!" she called before heading for the door, the dog trotting behind her.

Sam watched as Hartley walked around the circumference of the taproom, peering at the sketches on the wall and warming his hands over a brazier that still held some heat. He paused at the print of Sam's father in the ring that somebody had clipped from one of the boxing rags, and then again at the sign behind the bar that proclaimed that the Bell, Samuel Fox, proprietor, was licensed to sell beer and spirits. He peered into the darkened back room, then ran his fingers along the smooth wood of the bar.

"Not your sort of place," Sam ventured.

Hartley looked over at him. "What do you know about my sort of place?" His voice was sharp. "You just heard Kate say that she and I are old friends. You and I shared a meal in my kitchen and much more in my library." There was enough light coming from the single lamp for Sam to see Hartley's cheeks flush slightly. "Any claim to gentility I might have had was taken away when—" He shook his head and turned half away. "You didn't tell me you had been a boxer. But Kate said something about one of your fights."

"For a bit. That's my da." He gestured at the prints on the wall.

Hartley squinted at the prints. They were decades old, faded, the type almost unreadable. "I remember my father and his friends talking about Hiram Fox. He was undefeated for a while, wasn't he?"

Sam nodded. "He was the best." Hartley looked like he was about to ask another question, but Sam didn't want to talk about his own time in the ring. "You want a drink?" he asked.

Hartley shook his head. "No, and you don't have to bring me upstairs. I'm only a bit wet."

Like hell he was a bit wet. There was a puddle at his feet. "It's late," Sam said.

"So it is." Hartley took a step closer.

"Not sure how I feel about you going home alone."

A corner of Hartley's mouth twitched. "I got here alone."

"Right, but you had the dog to protect you." He was proud that he managed to say that without even the hint of a smile. "Now the pubs will all be closed and the streets will be emptying out. It's not safe."

Hartley made a halting movement, as if he were trying to step forward but found his feet rooted to the spot.

"You heard Kate say I have a warm fire upstairs." He kept his voice low and soothing, and was reminded of how

Hartley had coaxed the dog to him on his kitchen floor. "Doesn't that sound good?"

"It sounds so good." There was a note of wistfulness in his voice.

"Same rules as last time, Hartley. Nothing you don't want."

"Rules," Hartley repeated. "You didn't mind my . . . rules last time."

"I can't get enough of your rules," Sam said hoarsely.

A flicker of mischief lit Harley's face. "Lead the way, then."

Chapter Nine

Even the stairwell was clean, not so much as a cobweb in the corner or a speck of dust on the banister, at least none Hartley could see by the light of Sam's lantern. The building smelled of lemon and beeswax, with an undercurrent of ale and maybe somebody's Sunday roast.

"I'm at the top," Sam said, his voice low. They climbed another set of stairs that opened onto a small landing with two doors. Sam pushed open one of them and Hartley was met with a wall of heat.

"That's a proper fire," Hartley said.

"Nick knew I'd be wet after chasing after the dog so he might have gone a bit overboard." Sam had his hands in his pockets and looked a bit embarrassed at his brother's solicitude. It figured that Sam had a houseful of people who cared to keep him warm.

Hartley had lied earlier about not being cold. His coat—now ruined, to be sure—had been designed for style, not warmth, and now had neither virtue. He peeled it off and laid it across a spindle-backed chair. In only his shirtsleeves, he felt bare, so he crossed his arms against his chest.

"When you said the painting you were after was of a woman named Kate, I thought it might be her," he said. But he hadn't dared hope that he might once again see the person who had been a true friend to him despite knowing him for who he was. "Kate was lovely to me," he added. "She was a bit older and much wiser."

"She's probably going to marry my brother, but she doesn't like the idea of Nick being ashamed to have a wife whose naked picture is hanging on somebody's wall."

Hartley could well imagine. "Would he be? Ashamed, that is."

Sam shook his head. "He's thinks your godfather was a bastard—"

"He's right."

"—but he doesn't hold it against Kate. Besides, she was young, her father was unreliable, and five guineas meant a lot."

Hartley had been toying with the top button of his waist-coat, debating whether to undo it, but now he let his hands drop to his sides. "You think it matters that she was young and in need of the money? You don't think it's a sign of bad character?"

Sam was silent for a long moment while he put a kettle on the fire. "Even if she had been thirty and rich, I wouldn't think it meant she had a bad character. There's nothing wrong with sitting for that kind of painting, if it's what you want to do. But the fact that she was poor and young means the old man took advantage of her. She had a choice, but it wasn't much of a choice. Not really."

Hartley reflexively smoothed the fabric of his waistcoat, counting the row of buttons. It was relatively dry. Perhaps he didn't need to take it off. The cuffs of his shirt, however, were cold and stiff with wetness, so he rolled them up only far enough to keep the damp fabric from touching his skin. His boots had kept his feet dry, at least.

While Hartley was deliberating over how little clothing he could get away with removing, Sam placed two cups of tea on the table. It looked like there were two small rooms: the sparsely furnished parlor they stood in now and what must be a bedroom through that open door beyond. Hartley sat in a chair facing away from the bedroom door and wrapped his hands around the warm teacup.

Sam straddled the other chair, facing him. "You like dogs," he said, not making it a question.

Hartley was slightly startled that Sam had gotten him upstairs and wanted to spend their time drinking tea and discussing the merits of dogs as a species. But he decided to play along. "What's not to like?"

"Dirty, loud, make you go across town on a rainy night?"

"He didn't make me," Hartley said, ready to jump to the dog's defense. "I just thought he'd be missed. Sam, he was pining. Howling. I had to bring him back."

"You could have left him in the alley. Would have served him right, showing up at your door begging for more cheese."

"I would never," Hartley protested. "He'd freeze or get hurt by bigger dogs. I'm not a monster."

"I noticed."

Hartley shook his head and made a rude noise.

"I think you're secretly softhearted," Sam said, with the air of someone who had discovered a secret.

"Then you're bad at thinking."

Sam snorted with laughter. "Drink your tea and warm up."

Hartley wrapped his hands around the cup, letting the heat seep into his body, then took a sip.

"You didn't mind when Kate touched you," Sam said. "Is that because she's a woman?"

"Perhaps." If Hartley knew why he felt the way he did, he might be able to think his way through it. "It's . . . I don't know how to put it."

"You don't have to explain. I shouldn't be nosy."

Hartley waved away his concern. "It's partly that she doesn't want anything from me."

"And men do want something from you."

"Some men do." Hartley knew what question would come next and didn't try to forestall it.

"What did you think I wanted from you? That first night in your library, I mean."

"I didn't know you at all then." His face heated as he said the words, because he knew he was implying that they understood one another now, that what lay between them was more than pleasure and convenience.

"And now? Now you'd let—no, that's not it. Now you'd want my hands on you?"

"Want might be a bridge too far. I tried, you know." God, he had tried. He had spent years trying to pretend that he could manage something approaching normal if he pushed through his fear. "It just doesn't work."

"I'm not asking you to try," Sam said. "I only want you to know that it's fine by me. Whatever you want is enough."

Maybe because Hartley was born contrary, Sam's acceptance made him want to try again, even though he knew how it would go. But there was a table between them, and Sam would let go of him if he asked. He was safe everywhere but his mind. He slid his hand across the rough surface of the table. When Sam didn't take it, he said, "Come on, touch it. I'm not going to lose my nerve yet." Sam brought his hand near, palm up, so their fingertips met. That wasn't bad, but it was hardly a touch at all so it didn't count. "Come on now, don't be shy," Hartley taunted.

"My hand is right here. Have your way with it."

Hartley rolled his eyes but he couldn't help but smile. Feeling like a fool, he rested his hand on top of Sam's. He could feel the callouses on the other man's palms and didn't know if they were from boxing or maybe carrying casks of ale. After a moment Sam curled his fingers so he was stroking the underside of Hartley's wrist. It was an innocuous touch; it shouldn't have done anything to Hartley, but his heart beat faster, and not from fear. Sam kept up that steady stroking as if he didn't have anything else to do in the world, as if he didn't want anything from Hartley other than to touch his wrist, and Hartley started to believe that maybe it was true.

"You look a mess, you know," Sam said, his voice sounding a bit rough.

"Well, thank you. I was just getting carried away thinking you a perfect gentleman."

"It's a compliment. You look like you've been up to no good, even though we both know you spent the night doing good deeds to bad dogs."

"What does it look like I've been doing?" He dropped his voice and put enough interest in the words to make them a clear invitation.

"Ah, Hartley. You were still hard when I left last week, weren't you?"

Hartley swallowed. "You know I was."

"What did you do about it?"

The force of the memory sent a spasm of lust through Hartley's body. "I brought myself off."

"No, you can do better." His voice was a rumble, a soft entreaty. "Where were you?"

"My bedchamber. In bed." When Sam kept looking at him expectantly, he added, "In my nightshirt."

"How did you do it?"

"Uh, the usual way?"

Sam clicked his tongue disapprovingly. "A hand on your prick, all right, that's a given. Where's your other hand? Bollocks? Arse? Nipple?"

Hartley hoped it was too dark for his blush to be visible. "Nipple," he managed.

"And what did you think of?"

"Sucking your cock, obviously."

"Anything else?"

"You fucking me." Silence, during which all Hartley could

think of was that he was now gripping Sam's hand hard enough for his fingers to hurt, but he didn't slacken his hold and Sam didn't pull away.

"Huh. Wasn't expecting that," Sam finally said. "Thought you wouldn't go in for that."

"It's only pretend," Hartley snipped, as if he needed to explain how masturbation worked.

"How hard are you right now?"

Hartley drew in a sharp breath. "Very."

"So am I. You can take it out, you know. The table's there. I wouldn't even have to see." The noise that came from Hartley's mouth might have been a whimper, but he preferred not to think of it. "Or you could leave it be, either way suits me."

"I could show you what I did that night," Hartley said.

"So you could," Sam said equably. "If that's what you wanted."

Hartley imagined it: Sam's warm brown eyes on him, hungry and intent, but not demanding anything. The familiarity of his own hand, but with someone else nearby. "Or I could do it with your cock in my mouth."

A strangled oath, and the hand beneath his own flinched. "Jesus."

"Unless you—"

"Yes. Do it." His voice was a rasp. "I mean, if you please."

"It'll probably be a mediocre cock-sucking at best. I'll be too distracted."

"Don't sell yourself short. If it's half as good as the last time it'll still be the best I've ever had."

He was probably just saying that to be kind, but Hartley

still preened a bit. "Well, then." With that, he pushed his chair away from the table and slid to his knees.

The sight of Hartley kneeling between his spread knees made Sam's mouth go dry. But he wasn't ready. "No. Wait. Get up for a minute so my cock doesn't get ahead of my brain." Hartley let out a near-silent laugh, but he stood and then perched on the edge of the table, looking down expectantly at Sam. "Where do you want my hands?" Sam asked. "Or where do you not want them?"

Hartley opened his mouth, then snapped it shut, as if he were giving this serious thought. Good. Sam wanted to get this right. "You can touch me, but don't move me around."

"Right. You're in charge." Sam had never been with anyone with this amount of haggling beforehand, but it turned out he liked it. He liked knowing that they were both doing what pleased the other. He also liked knowing that he was keeping Hartley safe, and that Hartley trusted him with his safety. "You tell me right away if something's not right, you hear?"

Hartley nodded. "I, ah, liked it when you talked."

"I can talk," Sam said, maybe too quickly. "I can definitely do that." His face heated at the memory of some of the things he had said the last time.

Hartley slid off the table and in one fluid movement landed on his knees in front of Sam. The look he shot up at Sam was equal parts teasing and wanting, with a shadow of unease. Sam guessed that shadow was always there with him during this sort of encounter. But if Sam could help the shadow not turn into an obstacle, then that's what he'd do. He held on to the sides of his chair. But, no, Hartley had said touching was acceptable, and Sam had better find out if that was true before they got much farther. With one finger, he brushed aside a lock of hair that had gone askew in the rain. Hartley's hair had dried slightly wavy, in pale tendrils that lay across his forehead. He pushed it back, letting his fingertip linger on Hartley's scalp.

"That all right?"

Hartley nodded and swallowed. "It's good." He unfastened Sam's trousers and took him in hand.

"Are you hard now?" Sam asked. "Show me." He paused. "If you want."

Hartley bent his head to lick away the moisture that had gathered at the tip of Sam's cock. Last time Sam had thought Hartley really liked doing this, liked the feel and taste of him in his mouth. Now, watching Hartley fumble with his own trousers, feeling Hartley's sigh of relief against his sensitized skin, Sam knew it. Sam stroked his hand through Hartley's hair, letting the strands slip between his fingers as Hartley took him into his mouth.

"Your mouth feels so good. I hope you're giving your prick what it needs." He felt as well as heard Hartley moan, the vibrations traveling up his prick and through his body.

Last time, Sam's pleasure had been tangled together with holding himself back, with staying still and keeping his hands to himself. He might have thought that touching Hartley would undo some of that magic, but it had the opposite effect.

He was only letting himself touch the other man so slightly, so gently, firmly within the rules Hartley had set, that he was still very conscious of all the things he wasn't doing.

After a bit, Hartley's rhythm faltered, and Sam guessed it meant he was nearing his climax, and that thought alone pushed Sam close to the brink. He grabbed the base of his erection and started stroking in time to Hartley's sucking. "I'm close," he warned, and he came in his hand as Hartley threw his head back with his own release.

Sam didn't know how much time passed afterward with Hartley's forehead resting on Sam's knee, Sam sifting strands of pale hair through his fingers. When they fumbled for handkerchiefs and cleaned themselves up, that ought to have brought an end to the moment they were sharing, but Hartley still didn't stand.

"You can stay," Sam offered. "It's late."

"I can't. I mean, thank you. But I wouldn't be able to sleep. And I really need to sleep."

Sam held his hand out to help Hartley stand up. Hartley didn't take it, but he also didn't step away, and Sam told himself that was fine. "I'd like to walk you home. I know you can take care of yourself . . ."

Hartley let out a long, soft sigh. "I really can't, though," he said with such an air of defeat that Sam wanted to fold him into his arms.

They walked the distance mainly in silence. The rain had abated into a heavy mist that muffled noise and deepened shadows, creating the illusion that they were alone in the middle of the city.

"I'll call on you next Sunday," Sam said when they got to the kitchen door. "Same time."

Hartley nodded.

Sam glanced around. The lane was empty and dark, and they were in a place that would be sheltered from anyone who happened to be looking out a window. "Can I kiss you?"

In the moonlight he could see Hartley frown. "I think it's best that we don't."

Well, that would have put Sam in his place if he had been forming illusions about the nature of their relationship.

"Stop that," Hartley said, as if he knew what Sam was thinking. "What I meant is, I can cope with small touches that are relevant to orgasms. Kissing isn't."

Sam raised both eyebrows. "I don't know, Hartley. Your lips felt pretty relevant on my cock just now."

Hartley laughed, a surprisingly husky rumble. "That's not what I meant and you know it."

Smiling at one another in the lonely, midnight shadows of an empty alleyway, not kissing or touching or even speaking, was somehow more intimate than anything Sam had shared with a lover. It felt precious and dangerous, baffling and strange, and judging by the look of acute confusion that replaced the smile on Hartley's face, Sam was not the only one to feel that way.

Chapter Ten

Sam hadn't expected Hartley to turn up at the Bell again. Maybe he still thought Hartley above a place like the Bell. Maybe he thought Hartley considered himself above a friendship with someone like Kate.

But there the two of them were, cozied up at table in the warmest corner, sharing a pork pie Nick had made that morning. Hartley was wearing one of those waistcoats with a good dozen buttons. Since meeting him, Sam had been obsessively counting the waistcoat buttons of every man he met, and now knew to a certainty that Hartley had twice as many as anyone else. Did he have his waistcoats specially made? Then he realized he was being daft, because of course a man like Hartley had everything made special for him.

If he was honest, he wasn't quite comfortable having Hartley in the Bell. First, because he was afraid that by some stray look or word, one of them would inadvertently give away the truth of their relationship. Second, because it was odd to see anyone as rich as Hartley in the Bell. But mainly because it was a strange collision of his worlds to see Hartley here, his silver-blond head bent toward Kate's dark curls.

The Bell was Sam's own. After Davey died and the very idea of boxing had been enough to turn Sam's stomach, he had used his saved-up prize money to buy the place. It had been run to seed and in need of a good deal of work, and the building's owner had been glad enough to give it to him on a repairing lease. He and Nick rolled up their sleeves and made the place into something decent, something good. Something necessary.

Some black families, like Sam's mother's people, had been in England for centuries. But a generation ago, Britain had promised black Americans freedom if they fought against the colonists. Sam's father had been one of them. But nobody had quite figured out what to do with an influx of former soldiers, many of whom didn't have a trade and were barred either by law or prejudice from learning one. There were schools, now, and even some apprenticeships, but they wouldn't do any good if people were cold and hungry, or if they didn't know about these opportunities in the first place.

That was where the Bell came in. It was a place for people to meet, to find work, to talk to other people like them. And if it came right down to it, it was a place where they knew they could get a hot meal. It was so much easier to make your way when other people had your back, and there was nobody you could count on as much as other people who had been through the same troubles as you.

Sam knew he couldn't explain that to Hartley. What would a man like Hartley know about making his own way?

"Are you going to stand there gawping or join us for a pint?" Kate called, ruining Sam's half-formed plan of pretending not to have noticed them.

"I thought I ought to actually work, as this is a place of business," he said, hearing the stodginess in his own voice. He deliberately looked at Kate, not trusting his expression if he saw Hartley.

"Sam. If anyone needs another drink they'll call for you. I mean, you've wiped down that bar seven times and it's not going to get any cleaner."

"There was a drop of water," he protested. "It would have left a mark."

With an exhausted sigh, Kate got to her feet. "Sorry, Hart, but Sam needs help polishing things that are already clean."

"Sit down, you," Sam said, exasperated. "Fine, I'll join you." He grabbed a chair from a nearby table and hesitated before deciding where to put it. On Kate's side? On Hartley's side?

"Oh bollocks," Kate muttered, hooking the chair with her ankle and dragging it to the short end of the table between her and Hartley.

Sitting, he turned to Hartley and tried to get out a reasonably normal-sounding "Good day" like he would to any customer, but his voice sounded strange. He probably ought to have cleared his throat. He probably ought to go hide behind the bar.

Hartley was watching him with baffled amusement. "Good day," he answered. Only then did Sam notice that Hartley had the dog sleeping across his lap.

"Daisy likes Hartley," Kate said.

"Who the hell is Daisy?" Sam asked.

"I named the dog," Hartley said. "You can't go on calling him Dog. It's rude."

Sam looked at Kate, expecting her to protest. "Daisy's a good name," she said.

"You'll get fleas," Sam cautioned.

"Don't listen to the bad man," Hartley told the sleeping dog. He was wearing his usual fine clothes, but in subdued browns rather than the blues and greens he seemed to favor. Sam wondered if he had chosen these garments to stand out less at the Bell. If so, he had done a terrible job. He looked bright as a new penny in a coal bucket. Sam was going to have to spend years trying to forget that Hartley had ever been here, wiping and polishing away traces of a foreign substance.

"This pie is incredible," Hartley said. "I asked Kate what was in it but she won't tell."

"Mainly because I don't know," Kate said.

Sam looked at the nearly empty dish. "It's my mum's pork pie. Well, it was my mum's recipe, but Nick makes it now. I think he uses porter from the tap and chops the pork shoulder himself."

"And he makes the pastry with equal parts butter and lard," said a voice over his shoulder. He turned in his seat to see Nick, still wearing a floury apron. Kate sprang to her feet and kissed his cheek.

"Nick, this is Hartley Sedgwick, an old friend of mine," Kate said. "Hart, Sam's brother, Nick."

Hartley inclined his head and said "Mr. Fox" in a way

Sam had only ever heard on stage. Maybe that was how gentlefolk talked to one another all the time. But if Nick thought it strange, he didn't show it, probably because all his attention was on Kate.

"I'm done for the day and now I'm going to take a nap," Nick said, his eyes on Kate. Sam supposed he was trying to discreetly invite Kate to his bed.

Kate gave him a frank leer that showed she hadn't missed his meaning. Then she bent across the table to kiss Hartley's forehead. "Come back, you hear?"

He didn't answer, but Sam saw him give her a tight smile. Then Kate disappeared up the stairs after Nick, leaving Sam alone with Hartley.

"You can go back to work, if you need to," Hartley said, and Sam was tempted to take the excuse. After all, the Bell would soon be filling up with the midday crowd. Hartley looked ready to dart for the door. Then they caught one another's eye and both froze for an instant before Sam smiled and Hartley made a sound suspiciously close to a giggle.

"I have a few minutes," Sam said. In the center of the table was a pair of gloves that could only belong to Hartley. He picked up one of them and held it against his own palm. He couldn't have gotten half his hand into it without tearing the seams. They were the sort of gloves gentlemen wore, thin and soft and clean, and would be shredded after a few minutes' honest work. Sam touched a pair of delicate buttons that fastened the underside of the glove; they would rest against the soft part of Hartley's wrist. He glanced across the table to where Hartley's hands gripped a tankard, then

upward to the other man's face. His eyes, pale and disconcerting, were wide.

At first Sam thought Hartley might be afraid, might
consider his gloves too close a proxy for his hand. But then
he saw that Hartley's lips were parted with something like a
sigh. Not fear, then, but desire. And Sam couldn't help but
feel an answering rush of want. Here, at the Bell, of all places,
in plain view of everyone.

Sam ought to put the glove down, pour some beers, get
back to his damned job. Instead he turned it over on the
table, gave it one final caress, and when he handed it back to
Hartley, let his fingers graze over the other man's palm.

His breath hitched, and from the other man's stillness, he
thought Hartley wasn't breathing either.

Hartley watched Sam deftly pour drinks, collect coins,
and make passing conversation with patrons. This was
a public house of the halfway respectable sort. He had
guessed as much when he saw the place the other night,
but then it had been empty and almost dark. Now most
of the tables were occupied by patrons who had the air of
tradesmen and clerks. In front of about half the people
were dishes of food, either the pie that he had just shared
with Kate, or something simpler, like bread and cheese.
Maybe a third of the patrons were black. Hartley hadn't
ever seen so many black people at once; he hadn't ever
really thought about it, but he supposed it stood to reason
they'd feel at home in one another's company in the same

way Hartley might theoretically feel at home in the company of men like him.

Sam didn't talk much while he worked, but he acknowledged every person who walked through the door, and he seemed to know everyone's orders before they even spoke. Customers slid coins onto the bar before Sam asked, and Hartley watched in some surprise as Sam sometimes put those coins not into the till, but into the hands of other customers. Hartley already knew that Sam was preposterously good and kind, but at the Bell he fairly radiated warmth. People drifted toward him as surely as they drifted toward the hearth and the braziers. Hartley, too, had been drawn to him as helplessly as a man on a cold street might yearn for the warmth of a place like the Bell.

Sam Fox was good and kind and warm, and it filled Hartley with perverse satisfaction to know that he was able to satisfy the man's darker desires. There had been something Sam wanted—fingers twisted in curtains, the strain of muscles not allowed to move—that only Hartley had given him. And Hartley found that he wanted to give him that. It had been so long since Hartley had given anyone anything, since he had even thought of doing so.

Sam returned to the table with two pints of ale and slid into the seat Kate had occupied rather than diagonally from Hartley, as he had earlier that afternoon. He didn't say anything, apparently waiting for Hartley to talk. Hartley didn't know how Sam had guessed he had something to say.

"Why did you give money to that woman in the green cloak?" Hartley asked, wanting to avoid the real topic at hand and also curious about what had been going on with the three shillings six Sam had given away.

"She needed it." Sam, whose expression was usually so open, suddenly seemed very interested in examining a scratch on the table. Hartley was rather too gratified by the prospect of Sam having a secret.

"Do you do that often?"

"How is this your concern?" Sam asked, bristling. "The Bell does decent business, and I give some of the takings to people who need it more than I do."

"Shouldn't they go to proper charities?" Hartley set no store by charities and had heard Alf complain at length about rich ladies who tried to rescue happy whores from the streets and send them to church so they could learn to feel ashamed. But he wanted to provoke Sam into saying more. He was probably being a git, but he had never heard Sam speak so passionately on a topic. "You can't possibly give money to everyone who needs it."

"God, you sound like Kate. First of all, it's not charity. Most people don't like the idea of charity, and most charities set up for black people just want to ship us off to Africa."

"Really?"

"When I was a kid there were meetings right here at the Bell where people talked about it. Emigrating might be fine for some people, but it's a rubbish plan for somebody whose family is in England. And it's a bit insulting when the best idea anybody can come up with is to literally tell us we don't belong here." He was leaning forward in his seat, not raising his voice, but speaking with a low urgency. "When I give someone a shilling, or when Nick gives them a hot meal, it reminds them that they do belong here, and that there are people who have their backs. And that even if they don't have anywhere to go, they can come here."

It was the longest speech Hartley had ever heard Sam make. "Damn it, you're decent." All the more reason to let him know why he ought to stay away from Hartley. "Do you know why you need to use the kitchen door at my house?" he finally asked, staring into his ale.

"Listen, Hartley, you may not have guessed, but I'm not in the habit of calling at gentleman's houses." Sam's voice was low enough not to be overheard by anyone at neighboring tables, but Hartley could hear him well enough to detect the current of frustration underlying his words. "But if I were, I know I'm supposed to go to the back. I don't need to have this explained to me."

"Stop. It's nothing to do with what you're thinking." He wrapped his hands tightly around the smooth pewter of the mug. Watching Sam work and hearing him talk, Hartley realized what Sam stood to lose if his name were mixed up with Hartley's. While Hartley had alluded to his disgrace, he hadn't ever spelled it out for Sam. But now he needed to. Sam had a business and a family; getting mixed up with Hartley could ruin that. "You know that most of my servants left," he said, keeping his eyes on Sam even though he wanted to look away to spare himself the sight of Sam's unease or disappointment.

"You mentioned as much."

"Well, they had a good reason for not wanting to work for me."

"You don't have to talk about this," Sam said, and Hartley thought he could hear the pity in his voice. That would not do.

"No, I need to." He hadn't wanted to, but he couldn't let things go on with Sam without telling him the truth. If he were a decent person, he wouldn't go on with Sam at all. "I told you about my godfather." He braced himself for a reaction, but Sam only nodded. "There was gossip. Nothing concrete enough to put me in the pillory, but certainly bad enough to draw attention to any friend of mine. Any male friend, I mean." He was almost whispering at this point, half out of discretion and half because his voice didn't seem to want to come out. His body was braced, as if ready for a physical blow. He knew Sam well enough to know the man wasn't going to throw him into the street, shouting epithets behind him. The worst outcome would be for Sam to politely say they were never going to see one another again, which would hardly be the worst thing either of them had endured, so why did Hartley dread this as he might dread sharp knives or loaded guns. Sam *ought* to be concerned, he told himself; moreover, he ought to be angry that Hartley hadn't told him sooner. But still, he clenched his hands, fingernails digging into the bare skin of his palms.

"Who started the gossip?" Sam asked.

"Martin Easterbrook, my godfather's son." Hartley frowned. "I can't think of who else. He resents me for having an inheritance that ought to have been his. And he's right about that."

"Can't say I have much sympathy for people who don't get left money."

"Oh God no. I don't have any sympathy for Martin,

either. He's an ass." Hartley swept aside long ago memories of climbing trees and swimming in the lake with Martin and Will. "He didn't take kindly to my seducing his father and doing him out of a London property, which I suppose is natural enough."

"You didn't seduce him," Sam said quietly.

The only way Hartley had achieved anything resembling complacency with his current state was by deciding it was his own fault for making bad choices. If he stopped feeling guilty and ashamed, he couldn't imagine what other unpleasant feelings would rush in to take their place. So he waved his hand to dismiss Sam's words. "This is worse than I would have expected from Martin. I always thought him selfish and self-serving, not suicidally vindictive. And telling people I—" he lowered his voice "—prostituted myself makes his late father look almost as bad as me, not to mention how foolish it makes Martin look." But Hartley had given up puzzling out Martin's motives at about the same time he decided that revenge would be an excellent way to cleanse his palate of all that bitterness. He realized Sam hadn't said anything for a while, and glanced up from his ale.

Sam's face was fixed into something almost severe. "How old did you say you were?"

Hartley didn't need to ask what Sam meant. "Sixteen."

"Right. Just seems like it's hell to be paying for something that happened when you were a kid. This fucker took advantage of you."

Hartley shook his head, ready to object that he hadn't been a child, but when he thought of how stupidly trusting and naive he had been, he knew he hadn't been an adult either. "I know that he took advantage of me," he snapped. "That doesn't make me feel better. I already feel like a fool. But the fact is that I'd do it again if it was what I needed to help—" He stopped short. He didn't want to talk about his brothers. He didn't want to sound like he was blaming his brothers or even his father for the predicament he was in. "I was compensated very well and I can't complain," he said instead, and watched Sam almost flinch at the sharpness in his voice. He took a long drink of ale and continued more calmly. "I came here today to let you know that I'm planning on going to Friars' Gate next week." He had delayed this trip long enough, and now he realized it was because he didn't want his association with Sam to end. But it had to end.

Sam frowned and swirled the ale in his mug. "I still don't like the idea of your breaking into houses. But if you insist, then I'm going with you. I'm afraid that otherwise you'll get yourself arrested or killed and nobody will—" He stopped abruptly.

"You're afraid nobody would know I was in trouble. Quite right. I don't get about much these days." He glanced wistfully around the Bell, at the groups of people who seemed to know one another, to belong to one another. "No. We've already been through this. It's too risky for you."

"Not your call, mate. I can worry about whoever I please and take whatever steps I like to keep them safe." Sam's voice was a near growl, far from his usual mellow tones. "I am not standing by while you get hurt."

Bewildered by the raw feeling behind Sam's words, Hartley

decided on a different tack. "Traveling with me won't do your name any favors."

"I'll meet you there, then," Sam said.

Hartley threw his hands up. It would be easier to go along with Sam than to spend another moment in the presence of this fierce protectiveness. "Very well, then. Shall we say Thursday next at the Red Boar in East Grinstead?"

Neither of them mentioned this coming Sunday, which was for the best, Hartley told himself. Those Sundays had been rash for both of them, and it was best to stop before he got in over his head.

Chapter Eleven

"It's a bad idea. No, it's several bad ideas wrapped together into a terrible idea." Nick leaned in the doorway to Sam's room, his arms folded across his chest as he watched Sam stuff clean linen and a razor into a satchel.

Sam couldn't argue there. It was a bad idea for reasons Nick didn't even know. As the reason for his absence, Sam explained that he was visiting a brewery in Sussex to sample their light ale and decide whether he wanted it for the Bell. He had no talent for fabrication, and this excuse was just this side of preposterous. Kate had responded with narrowed eyes, but if she suspected he was up to anything, she didn't say so. Since they had first talked about the painting a month ago, neither of them had brought up the topic, so he doubted whether she'd think his trip had any connection with her portrait.

"The brewery that supplies us now is perfectly good," Nick said for perhaps the tenth time. "There's no need to go jackassing around England. It's not safe. The farther you get from London, the less likely you are to see anyone darker than a pail of old milk."

"I know that, Nick. I fought all over the country, and I know what it's like." Leaving London meant people staring at Sam as if he were on exhibition, and that was the least of it. "Anyway, it's not that far. Three hours by the stage, I think."

Nick folded his arms across his chest and for a moment he looked so much like their father that Sam had to look away. "Do you even have someplace to stay?"

"I'll stay at the inn."

"And they'll give you a room? I doubt it."

"They'll give me somewhere to sleep."

"Out by the bogs, maybe."

Wincing, Sam hoisted his satchel onto his shoulder. The day before, he had pulled something when lifting a cask of porter. He had injured that shoulder in the ring and from time to time it acted up as a reminder of bad times.

"Christ," Nick muttered. "You're more stubborn than Kate. At least take the liniment." Nick rummaged around in Sam's chest of drawers until he produced the jar of comfrey salve that he got from the apothecary the last time he strained that muscle.

Six hours later as the stagecoach pulled into the Red Boar in East Grinstead, Sam was biting his lip to keep from swearing with pain. The last stretch of road had been a misery, pitted with holes and strewn with stones. On the top of the coach, Sam had felt every bump, and by the time he climbed off, he was afraid he had injured himself in some new and interesting way.

The innkeeper did the usual bit of staring but took Sam's money and promised him a bed in a shared room. Sam ordered a pint and scanned the taproom. When he found Hartley sitting at the bar, reading a newspaper in such a way as to occupy two seats, Sam knew a surge of relief at the sight of a familiar face. A voice within him whispered that what he felt was more than relief, and Hartley's face was more than familiar, but he was paying no attention to that voice. He was here to keep Hartley safe, and that was all.

Hartley looked up when Sam approached. "Oh, I beg your pardon," he said, moving the paper aside and twisting on his stool to make room. "Do sit." His voice was sniffy and formal, and Sam guessed that they were going to pretend to be strangers.

"Thank you, kindly," Sam said with equal courtesy. He didn't know where to go from there. He wasn't used to being on this side of the bar, he wasn't interested in playacting, and he wasn't in the habit of striking up conversations with strangers anyway. But he had an inkling that all he had to do was wait, and Hartley would carry on with whatever scheme he was cooking up. Sam was almost eager to see what happened next.

What happened was that Hartley turned the page of his newspaper, took a sip of his beer, and proceeded to ignore Sam for the next quarter of an hour. Then, moving to turn the page, he knocked over Sam's still-full pint. It landed in Sam's lap, dripping down his legs, into his boots. Sam sprang to his feet, trying to mitigate the damage.

"Oh, I beg your pardon. A thousand pardons. I'm so

terribly clumsy. Innkeeper, please get this man a towel. Oh, the state of your clothing, whatever shall we do?" Bemused, Sam watched him go on in that manner until the innkeeper's wife appeared and Hartley had begged her to launder the unfortunate man's clothes. Coins changed hands, then the innkeeper arrived and more coins were produced, until Sam and his satchel were being escorted up the stairs to a room.

"I don't know what the devil you're about," Sam said when the door had shut on them.

"Yes, well, now we have an excuse to be together in private, and we've effected an introduction. This enterprise requires privacy and discretion." His pale eyes were bright and Sam realized he had been enjoying this farce.

"How long were you waiting for me?"

"Hours. Your coach was appallingly late." He glared at Sam as if it had been Sam's doing. "You have no idea how rude people think Mr. Sullivan from Tunbridge Wells. I sat at the bar for three hours, drinking a single pint, and taking up two seats."

"I didn't realize were using false names. I signed the book as Sam Fox."

"Naturally. Now, get out of those trousers."

Sam raised his eyebrows. "I'm not sure lounging around in my drawers is going to be discreet."

"Don't be absurd. You'll wear my dressing gown, Mrs. Wilson will launder and press your clothes, and I'll order supper while we wait."

Sam wondered how much Hartley had paid to buy everyone's willing cooperation. The innkeeper's wife appeared with an ewer and basin and left with Sam's clothes. While Sam washed, Hartley lay back on the bed and filled Sam in on what he had learned so far. Sam could feel Hartley's eyes on him, intent and appreciative. Sure enough, when he glanced over at the bed, he saw Hartley regarding him from beneath heavy lids. Sam felt his skin heat under the other man's gaze.

"The house hasn't been let," Hartley said. "I walked through the property and there wasn't even any sign of a caretaker. It's ideal for a first burglary, I'd say."

He sounded so cheerful about the prospect that Sam laughed. And then he winced, because every sinew in his body felt knotted with pain.

"What's the matter?" Hartley asked.

"I hurt my shoulder," Sam said. "It's an old injury, but the journey made it worse."

"Anything I can do?"

Sam turned to look at him. As far as he knew, there wasn't any way to help a sore muscle that didn't involve touching; surely Hartley knew that, and wouldn't have offered if it were off the table. "Bet I could think of something."

Hartley flushed but he didn't look away. They were interrupted by a knock at the door and the arrival of supper. It was a shoulder of mutton, some stewed cabbage, and a loaf of bread. None of it was out of the ordinary in itself, but it was a rare treat to have a meal on dishes he wouldn't have to wash himself, and in the company of a man whose gaze kept darting down to the triangle of bare skin at the neck of the dressing gown. Sam did his share of looking too. Hartley was at his most buttoned up (fourteen tiny waistcoat buttons, a personal record), but Sam knew by now that the starch and the buttons were armor that Hartley needed. To call Hartley handsome was to miss the point; he would have been delicately pretty if not for the set of his chin or shrewdness of his pale eyes. If Sam had to conjure up the ideal looks for a bed partner, he wouldn't have come up with Hartley in a million years—too fine, too fragile, too sharply dangerous. But with Hartley sitting before him, he couldn't imagine wanting anyone else.

Hartley had badly miscalculated. His little drama in the taproom had come off without a hitch, but now that he had Sam in his bedchamber, he wanted to crawl all over him and make terrible choices.

The innkeeper's wife brought Sam's clothes so promptly that they were still hot from the iron. "My compliments on supper, Mrs. Wilson," Hartley said, pressing another coin into her hand. "And many thanks for having attended to this good gentleman after my clumsiness. I'll ring when we've finished this superb meal." All smiles and excessive gallantry, he showed her from the room and shut the door.

"You do that well," Sam said.

"What? Order servants around?"

"No, the thing where you confuse everyone but pay them enough that they don't worry too much about what's going on."

Hartley snorted and handed Sam his clothes. "We can meet tomorrow in the taproom at about nine and go for a walk, now that we're acquainted. It's about a mile to Friars' Gate."

"Nine o'clock," Sam repeated, moving toward the door. Indeed, it was high time for Sam to leave, because with every passing minute the chances increased of Hartley attempting to climb his body like some kind of wild cat. The problem was that Hartley was blocking the closed door, and his feet weren't doing a damned thing to move him away.

"Nine o'clock," Hartley said again, because he was a brilliant conversationalist. This time he got his feet to move away from the door but instead of stepping to the side like a sane human being, he moved closer, so he found himself face-to-face with Sam. Well, more like face-to-shoulder, thanks to the height difference.

"Hartley," Sam said. "I'm still wearing your dressing gown."

"Oh. Right." To be utterly accurate, it wasn't Hartley's dressing gown. His own would have been too small for Sam, and while lilac suited Hartley, it was perhaps not Sam's favorite color. He bought this one when he thought of his beer-spilling scheme. It was made of a soft wine-colored wool that looked just as good on Sam as Hartley had thought it would. He would have offered it as a present, but feared Sam was too proud to accept costly presents, especially from a lover. "Are you going to get dressed?"

"That depends," Sam said. He wasn't smiling, thank God, because Hartley didn't think he could live with Sam laughing at whatever rapid mental decline he was suffering. But he did look kind, as if he knew Hartley's head wasn't on straight and didn't mind.

"What does it depend on?"

"On whether you want me to leave."

"Right." Of course. Sam was waiting for Hartley's invitation. He was reliably considerate in that regard, as well as all other regards, which was why Hartley really ought to steer clear of him.

"I don't think you want me to leave."

"Was my blocking the door a subtle hint?"

"Something like that." Sam rubbed a hand along his jaw. "We don't have to do anything, you know. Whatever you choose is fine."

Sam had made that clear from the beginning, that whatever Hartley wanted would suit Sam. Hartley was unspeakably grateful, but at the same time wished he didn't have anything to be grateful for. He wished these decisions were straightforward for him.

"I'm going to sit by the fire and put some salve on my shoulder before I get dressed," Sam said. He was making it easy, Hartley knew. He watched Sam take a jar out of the canvas satchel he had arrived with, and he knew that he could offer to help. Easier still, he didn't have to offer. He could just take the jar, which, after filling his lungs with a shaky breath, was what he did.

Sam held his gaze for a moment, then took the hint and climbed onto the bed.

"Probably most people you go to bed with aren't this much trouble," Hartley said.

"Maybe I like trouble," Sam said, lying on his stomach,

his voice muffled by the pillow. "I like when you take what you want. What you need. That's not what men usually expect from me." And then, after a moment of quiet, "I didn't know it could be like this."

Hartley went utterly still as he contemplated how thoroughly ruinous this was going to be for both of them. This, he supposed, was the moment he could turn back. He could step away, send Sam to his own bed, keep his heart protected and Sam's life intact. Instead he uncorked the jar of salve and slid the dressing gown off Sam's shoulders. "Neither did I," he whispered.

The salve smelled lightly of herbs, but nothing flowery or overtly medicinal. He scooped out a bit and rubbed it gingerly onto the dark, smooth skin of Sam's shoulder blade. He hadn't ever been this close to so much bare muscle and it took his breath away. Clothed, Sam was impressive. Unclothed, he was beautiful.

"It's the right shoulder," Sam said. "Put your weight into it."

Hartley complied, first rubbing circles with the liniment and then using both hands to work the stuff into Sam's flesh. When Sam wriggled his arms out of the sleeves of the dressing gown and folded them under his head, Hartley began touching and rubbing down the length of his back. The only sound in the room was the crackling of the fire and the pounding of Hartley's own heart.

"Do you still box?" Hartley asked, wondering how Sam had acquired this degree of musculature.

"No. I was glad to give it up." His shoulder tensed beneath Hartley's touch. "I broke men's noses and knocked out their teeth. It's hard to tell yourself that you're a decent person when the floor is wet with blood you've spilled."

"You're more than a decent person." Hartley realized he had stopped rubbing Sam's shoulder, his strokes having devolved into mere pets. He resumed pressing slow, firm circles.

"Have you ever been to a boxing match?"

"No," Hartley admitted. Large groups of rough, rowdy men were not his idea of a good time.

"The crowd is usually more than a bit drunk by the time the boxing starts. And one of the things they do, I suppose it's a tradition, or a way of getting the men to put up a good fight, is to harass the boxers. They really let their tongues loose. It was bad watching it happen to my da, but I always thought he was invincible. When it was me, I knew I wasn't."

Hartley's stomach turned at the thought of what revolting epithets a crowd of half-drunk men might shout at a black man. "I'm glad you don't do that anymore."

"Easy now," Sam said. "You don't need to strangle me."

Hartley loosened his hands from where they were perhaps a bit too firmly massaging Sam's shoulder muscles. He scooped up more salve and rubbed it into the top of Sam's back until he felt the muscles relax.

"I stopped boxing when I nearly killed a man," Sam said, in a voice so quiet and low Hartley could almost pretend not to have heard it. Sam hadn't ever confided in him before. All the confessions and embarrassments had been on Hartley's side. Hartley suspected that he was being offered this truth as compensation for the secrets he had shared and those he had hinted at. But he was being offered it all the same, and he didn't want to brush it aside.

"I'm glad you didn't," Hartley said, rolling his eyes at his own obviousness.

"I think the crowd would have torn me apart if I had killed that fellow."

Hartley sucked in a breath. He had read about another black boxer who had been injured when an angry crowd, annoyed by his victory against a white fighter, stormed the ring.

"If I had been smart," Sam went on, "I would have gotten out of boxing altogether after that. Instead, I trained a friend. David. Davey. He was younger than me, strong, angry as hell. He was killed with a single punch."

Sam's entire upper body was taut with tension, the sinews in his neck standing out. Hartley futilely smoothed his fingers along Sam's shoulders. "That wasn't your fault."

"Somebody paid Davey to throw the fight, and he did. I knew matches were fixed all the time. Backers had offered me money to pull punches or take hits. Knowing that, I shouldn't have let Davey anywhere near the game."

"So why did you? Why did you train him?" Hartley asked.

"He was shaping up to be a proper young ruffian, and I thought he'd be better off in the ring than at the end of a rope."

Hartley knelt on the bed to get a better angle. "It sounds to me like you did the best you could with the tools you had. If you had been a butcher or a baker you might have taken

him on as your apprentice, but you were a boxer, so you
trained him to fight. You're a good man, Sam." Hartley heard
the earnestness in his voice, and decided they were quite
done with the soul-baring portion of the evening. He gave
a dramatic sigh. "It's really very tiring to be surrounded by
saints. You ought to meet my brothers. Sickeningly decent,
every last one of them. Makes me feel such a villain."

Sam let out a breath of laughter and relaxed slightly
under Hartley's touch. When Hartley shifted his weight
onto his hands, Sam groaned. "God, that feels good, Hart."

Hearing his nickname on Sam's lips sent curls of warmth
spiraling through Hartley's belly. Feeling reckless, he swung
a knee over Sam's back, straddling him. Now he had a proper
grip on Sam's shoulders, fanning his fingers and watching
how his hands were dwarfed by Sam's body. He shouldn't
feel so safe, alone in a room with a man this large, a man
who wanted him. But Sam Fox really was a good man, and
Hartley knew he had never been safer. In the kitchen that
night Alf had stumbled in with Sadie, Sam had instantly
positioned his body between Hartley and what he assumed
was an intruder. Any strength Sam had, he'd use for Hartley, not against him.

He slid his hands lower still, skimming his fingers along
the length of Sam's spine, dragging down the dressing gown
as he went, but stopping at the small of his back.

"Whatever you like, Hartley," Sam said softly. Hartley
tugged the dressing gown down further, and then threw it
aside entirely. The strange thing was, he wanted his hands
all over Sam. He wanted to feel every inch of him. Getting

another dab of the salve, he smoothed his way back up Sam's broad back and down his arms.

"You're touching some irrelevant parts there Hartley," Sam said, calling back to Hartley's pronouncement that he wanted to confine their contact only to places that were relevant to orgasms.

Hartley pressed his lips together to keep from smiling, even though Sam couldn't see him. "I suppose you think you're terribly droll."

"Yeah, that's right, I do."

He wrapped both his hands on one of Sam's biceps and couldn't make his fingers touch. Incredible. "Is that your way of asking me to touch more relevant areas?"

"If that's your way of asking me whether you can fuck me, the answer is yes."

Hartley stilled his hands. That hadn't been what he was asking, but the idea made his head spin. "That's not my—I mean, I would if that was what you fancied. I'd oblige. But it's not my favorite way to get off. At least, I don't think it would be. I haven't. Never really wanted to, either." His cheeks were hot and his heart pounding.

"I can take it or leave it. What is your favorite, then? Or, what would be your favorite, if you . . ."

"If I could? God, I liked getting fucked." The past tense was bitter in his mouth, but it felt good to say it aloud, to admit what he had lost. "Not that I've done it much. I just think I would, if I could."

"Ever do it to yourself? With fingers or with something else?"

"Something else?" he echoed. "If you think I'm sticking a vegetable marrow up my rear, you can guess again. As for fingers, of course I have, but it's a bit of a hassle."

Sam's shoulders were shaking with laughter and Hartley hadn't been trying to be amusing, so he pinched Sam's arse. That made Sam gasp and then squirm in a very decorative manner. Hartley rubbed the place where he had pinched, and since that felt good he kept doing it. By the time Sam shifted on the bed to spread his legs slightly further apart, Hartley was already hard.

He dipped his fingers in the salve and traced them down the crease of Sam's backside, his eyes on Sam's face to see if this was what he wanted. He had said Hartley could fuck him, but maybe he'd be interested in this instead. Sam's eyes flickered shut, his lips parted on a sigh. He brought his fingers lower still, circling the pucker of Sam's entrance. When Sam stilled for a moment, Hartley could almost feel the touch on his own body.

"You're teasing me," Sam mumbled.

"That's right I am," Hartley agreed, and proceeded to do it again. Sam parted his legs further, giving Hartley unfettered access and providing an unsubtle clue. He slid in the tip of a finger. God, it had been a long time since he had touched a man this way. Because just as Sam's lovers had expected certain things of him, so had Hartley's few lovers, and touching like this wasn't it. Adding more salve, he probed deeper. Sam's hands were twisted in the bedsheets, and Hartley remembered those same strong hands gripping the velvet curtains in his library. But this time he wasn't holding himself back; he was letting himself go, letting himself have what he wanted. Hartley added another finger and twisted, causing Sam to swear into the pillow and tilt his hips up, rocking back into Hartley's touch.

"Yes," Hartley said, "just like that." He reached underneath Sam's body and took hold of his cock, which was already hard and wet. Hartley still had all his clothes on, but he pressed his aching length into the back of Sam's thigh for some relief.

"I'm close," Sam groaned when Hartley started thrusting his fingers in with purpose and stroking his cock in rhythm. He realized he was rocking into Sam's leg with the same rhythm, as if this were something they were doing together.

Sam groaned when he came, strong arms spread out on the bed, eyes shut in pleasure. The image would be seared into Hartley's mind forever. His heart still pounding and his prick absolutely furious with him, he got off the bed and wiped his hand off. Then he brought a cloth for Sam and cleaned him too.

"Is your shoulder all right?" he asked.

"Every part of me is all right. Come here." Sam patted the bed beside him. "If you like."

Hartley wished he were the kind of person who could leap unreservedly into his lover's arms. Instead, he gingerly climbed onto the bed and arranged himself about eighteen inches away from Sam.

"I wouldn't mind if you touched me," Hartley said. Sam gave a sleepy smile and stroked Hartley's hair. "I meant my cock."

"You touch your cock while I make a fuss over you."

Hartley unfastened his trousers and pulled himself out, then sighed in relief as he finally touched himself. It wasn't going to take much. Sam smoothed a hand down his arm, then up his side, covering him with lazy, tender caresses that somehow weren't too much, didn't ask for things that he couldn't give.

His climax washed over him easily. Everything with Sam was, if not precisely easy, at least not impossible, at least not a constant reminder of things he couldn't have. Being with Sam gave him the hope that he could perhaps live contentedly alongside the demons he would never vanquish.

Chapter Twelve

Away from London, in the crisp autumn sunshine and far from everyone he knew, Sam could almost pretend that he hadn't lost his entire mind. He could pretend that it was reasonable and sane to have given over a solid portion of his heart to thinking and worrying and caring about Hartley. He was used to caring about people, to offering whatever aid or protection he could. He tried to tell himself that was all he was doing with Hartley, but he knew he was lying to himself.

If he had truly wanted to protect Hartley, he wouldn't let him attempt a burglary, that was for certain. He wouldn't let the man do what they had done last night in Hartley's bed. He wanted to keep Hartley safe, but Hartley was a man who couldn't be kept safe. His very existence was dangerous; he had been exposed for what he was, for what he and Sam both were. Not only could he not be protected, but being around him meant Sam was courting danger too.

Sam had spent the past ten years watching nearly everyone around him marry and settle down. First the lads he had grown up alongside, now Nick and Kate, who were plainly in love, whether or not they saw their way to getting married anytime soon. He had been raised by parents, who, however awkward he had found it in his youth, had been thoroughly in love with one another. He remembered his mother worrying the hem of her apron while waiting for his father to come home after a fight. He remembered them staying up late, laughing and whispering, when they thought Sam and Nick were long asleep. His mother had died holding his father's hand; his father died not too long after, his late wife's name on his lips.

He hadn't held out any hope of that happening to him. Since he was fourteen, he had known that he wasn't one for the girls, and while he knew it must be possible for two men to pair up the way men and women did, he didn't know any who had done so. He could count on one hand the number of black men he had ever even seen in the places frequented by men who preferred men. Besides, the odds of finding a fellow he was really fond of were long when you only met for expeditious pleasure in dirty alleyways and the seedy edges of parks.

He smiled to think that he had met Hartley in an alley of sorts, then had to stamp on the idea that what existed between them could ever amount to anything.

"The gate is on the other side of the village, but if we take this lane we can approach the house from the stables," Hartley said. They had met that morning as arranged after spending the night apart, Hartley in his fine bedchamber and Sam in a room he shared with three other men, one of whom snored like a bellows. Hartley had brought a small hamper of sandwiches, insisting that the innkeeper's wife wouldn't let him leave on a long country walk without provisions.

Lit by morning sun rather than flickering lamplight, Hartley looked young and a bit frail. He looked exactly like someone a country innkeeper's wife might fret over. He wasn't skinny, not exactly, but there wasn't much of him. His nose turned up pertly and was sprinkled with a smattering of freckles that had been invisible in weaker light. His eyes, which had seemed pale and shrewd in London, now reflected the dusty greens and browns of the autumn countryside.

"If you know this place so well, why did you take the trouble to draw out a map?" Sam asked after they had taken a few turns at Hartley's direction. He remembered that map, all straight lines and precise penmanship, tidy and orderly to a fault while still being decorative. Much like Hartley.

"Until I put it on paper, I wasn't sure I did remember it properly. There was always a chance my memories weren't reliable."

Sam looked over and saw the familiar set of Hartley's jaw. "I think your memories are pretty reliable, Hartley."

Hartley's shoulders rose and fell with a deep breath. "I'm afraid so."

When the house came into view, Hartley went still.

"We don't have to do this," Sam said.

"You spend a lot of time reminding me that we don't have to do things." They were beneath an oak tree that had lost half its leaves, casting Hartley in a dappled light, shadow and sun playing across his face.

"I think you need the reminder," Sam countered.

Hartley glanced away. "He didn't make me do anything I didn't agree to, if that's what you're thinking."

Sam made a scoffing sound. "Do you think you owe him a fair hearing or something?"

"No, I just—"

"How does a kid agree to anything like that, Hart? Especially when the man was making you promises."

Hartley crossed his arms and scuffed the toe of his boot in the dirt and leaves before him. "I don't know what you're imagining, but I chose to sell my body—"

"Stop," Sam growled. "I hate that expression. If you fucked for money, that isn't selling your body any more than a bricklayer sells his body by building a wall for money."

"I fucked for money, then." His chin was up, as if daring Sam to take issue with that bald statement.

"So? I let men blacken my eyes for money." Sam leaned against the broad trunk of the tree. "My father used to tell Nick and me the story of what he did when he was in the colonies."

Hartley shot him a startled glance. "I hadn't realized."

"He was a blacksmith's assistant in Virginia. Decent work, he'd always say. Safe work. Sometimes he'd get an extra chicken to put in the pot if he had done someone a favor. Usually people were civil to him. But after the war started, he ran off to join the British army. He knew that if he even survived the war and made it to England, the only work he'd get would be dangerous. He was lucky to get work at all. He worked on the wharves, sometimes fighting for wagers until Kate's father took him on to train. But he said every punch he took, every drop of blood he shed, every time he broke a bone—all of that was his choice, because he was free."

Hartley remained silent for a long moment. "I think if your father knew you were comparing his tribulations as an enslaved person to my bedding a man for the promise of advantage to my brothers, he'd be a bit put out."

"It's not the same, and I'm not saying it is," Sam said, exasperated. "But my point is that sometimes what seems like a choice really isn't."

"Maybe so. But what good does that do me now?"

"I think that because you blame yourself for what happened, you think you deserve to feel the way you do about being touched." Hartley drew in a sharp breath, and Sam knew he was on dangerous ground. "And that you deserve the shunning you've been getting. You don't deserve either of those things, Hart."

"You don't know what you're talking about."

"Maybe not. I'm not trying to tell you how to feel. Whatever you feel, I like you just the same. You know that, don't you?"

Hartley looked away, but not before Sam saw his eyes grow bright. "Oh, damn you. I don't like you at all, just so you know. I think you're terrible." But he stuck his hand out, reaching blindly for Sam's. Sam grabbed it and squeezed, his larger hand almost completely enveloping Hartley's.

In the end, they hardly had to break in at all. The French doors leading to the garden were latched, but creaked open when Sam gave them a shove with his shoulder.

The drawing room smelled of dust and damp and all the fine furniture was gone, but it was unmistakable. Hartley clenched his fists and realized he was gripping Sam's coat sleeve like a frightened child. Absurd. It was only a house, a collection of bricks and wood and plaster. He had come here only a few times with Sir Humphrey, when the baronet had hosted house parties of the disreputable sort.

After having lived in London society for a few years, the only thing that Hartley now found surprising about Sir Humphrey's parties was that the man had dared bring Hartley. The other gentlemen had brought women—courtesans, opera dancers, sometimes girls who had been more or less picked up off the street. Looking back, maybe the other men had thought Hartley was a guest. Or perhaps some of those men were planning to visit one another's beds as surely as Sir Humphrey was going to visit Hartley's; perhaps the women were nothing more than a screen. Hartley had since encountered some of those men and they had never alluded to Sir Humphrey or his parties; every last one of those men had cut Hartley dead after the letters became common knowledge. Now he wondered if they had secrets like Hartley's own, and had cut him rather than be found guilty by association.

"It's empty," Sam said, unnecessarily.

"I suppose Martin sold off the furnishings." He would have had to sell off everything not nailed down in order to pay off the legacy duties, Hartley supposed. "That'll make it easier to search. We ought to check every room, one by one," he whispered. Something about an empty house made him want to keep his voice low.

Sam nodded his agreement and they passed through the ground floor rooms in near silence. Hartley didn't know exactly what he was looking for. The paintings could be on a wall, stacked on the floor, or even removed from the frames and rolled up. Had Sir Humphrey sent them here to adorn the walls during a party? Or had he some other motive in removing them from the London house? Was there a possibility that Martin had sold them after all, but somehow Hartley hadn't found out?

With every door they opened, Hartley held his breath, not sure what he'd see on the other side. But so far there were only empty rooms.

"Hell of a lot of rooms," Sam said, his voice low.

"This is nothing," Hartley said. "It's maybe a third of the size of the family's principal seat in Cumberland."

Sam muttered something about the guillotine that Hartley didn't quite catch. "Is this how you grew up? In a place like this?"

Hartley had to stifle a laugh. "No. God no. I grew up in a sort of semi-genteel poverty. There were always too many mice and not enough beds to go around. Plenty of books but never any ready money at all. How I use to envy proper ladies and gentlemen." He had imagined that anyone who lived in a decent house and had clean clothes would never have to worry about getting enough to eat. With a child's belief in magic lamps and good fairies, he had thought that if only they were gentlemen, he and his brothers could be safe. So he had set about to make sure his brothers got to be gentlemen. All his worst choices, all the troubles that had been visited on him and his brothers, stemmed from that fundamental error. He supposed Ben was happy enough despite not having a penny to bless himself with. As for Will, he was infinitely worse off than he would have been if Hartley had never intervened, never begged Easterbrook to use his influence for Will's advancement in the navy.

As they climbed the stairs to search the upper floors, a noise came from above.

"Probably rats," Hartley whispered. Sam didn't answer.

Hartley directed Sam to the room that had been his own. It was partly the instinct to walk a path he had followed many times before, but also a feeling of dreadful certainty in the pit of his stomach. The door was shut, of course, and when they opened it, the draft dislodged a cloud of dust that made them both cough into their sleeves. Before it cleared, Hartley had a fleeting sense of relief that he hadn't come here alone. Sam's solid presence beside him was a reassuring reminder that it was not seven years ago.

This room was empty too. Gone was the old-fashioned clothes press, white with gilt leaves painted on the edges. Gone was the spindle-legged writing table where he had penned cheerful letters home, assuring his brothers that he was having a jolly time with the toffs. Even the bed was gone. It ought to have been comforting to see that the room held nothing to remind him of his past, but instead it was disorienting. His memories became unmoored from reality and took on the cast of a troubled dream.

"You all right?" That was Sam, always checking on him.

"Not really, no." He could have lied, could have said that

he was perfectly well, that being in this house meant he was one step closer to getting what he wanted and that he was glad of it. But his heart was racing, his hands sweating inside his gloves, and he didn't have the wherewithal to put up a front.

"I hear footsteps," Sam hissed. "Someone's here."

Hartley heard the sound too. Footsteps upstairs, almost directly over his head. "You have time to leave, if you're quick," he whispered. "Leave the way we came. I'll meet you back at the inn." He could talk his way out of trouble with a caretaker or groundskeeper, he was certain of it. Failing that, he had brought enough money to make up a handsome bribe.

"Hartley, *no*. This house is empty. There are no paintings. We both need to get out of here." Sam's voice was an urgent whisper. "It could be a madman with a pistol. A gang of smugglers. You don't know who's been using this place. Come with me. Now."

"Go. Please. I'll be fine." Surely he didn't need to explain why Sam wouldn't be safe. "Please," he repeated.

"I'm not leaving you here, damn it."

The footsteps were on this floor now, approaching them. Heavy footsteps. Boots, most likely. "It's too late." Hartley searched the room. "Get over there," he said, gesturing to the curtains that covered a large window.

"Sod this all." Sam sounded furious, but he got behind the curtains.

Hartley's hands had stopped sweating and his heart had slowed down. He was much more at ease than he had been when they entered the room, far more at ease than he might have imagined he could be when about to be discovered mid-felony. He patted the knife that he had brought with him to destroy the paintings. He'd wait for the footsteps to pass, and then he'd go room by room until he found the canvases.

The footsteps fell silent. Hartley was about to step out of the room and peer into the corridor when he saw the shadow in the doorway.

Chapter Thirteen

There was a gap between the curtains, just a hair's breadth, but through it Sam could see Hartley. The man in the doorway remained frustratingly just out of view. For a moment the small cramped space turned into a corner of a boxing ring; the pounding of his heart and the rush of blood in his head became the cries and jeers of the crowd. Sam realized it was because he was ready to knock that stranger's teeth out—his own bloodlust on Hartley's behalf had put him back in the ring.

Sam remembered his da telling him to imagine that his opponent was someone who had done him wrong. But even when the other boxer repeated one of the uglier phrases shouted by the crowd, Sam didn't want to strike him. Because if he started hitting everyone who looked down on him because of his race or his class, he'd wind up going on some kind of spree. And he knew men who had done exactly that. There were plenty of people all too ready to raise a hand for the wrong reasons, and Sam didn't want to be one of them.

Despite all this, despite his loathing for violence and his relief to have done with that part of his life, if the man in the doorway took a single step closer to Hartley, Sam knew he would do whatever it took to keep Hartley safe, consequences be damned.

That didn't mean he wasn't furious at Hartley for not having left when Sam told him to. Now Sam was risking his safety, maybe even his life, to keep an eye on Hartley. No man was worth this kind of danger. If Sam were arrested for housebreaking, his family would never get over it. And if Hartley's name was as much a byword for scandal as he claimed, then Sam could imagine what kind of construction would be put on today's events. His family would never live it down. All the work he had put into the Bell would have been for naught. It wasn't healthy to care enough about someone to want to take that kind of risk.

But as Sam watched, his heart was pounding so loudly it seemed a wonder that Hartley and the other man couldn't hear it, Hartley's expression shifted from tense watchfulness to bewildered relief.

"Will?" he asked. "What in God's name are you doing here?"

"Really?" The other man sounded exasperated, rather than upset. "Pretty sure that's my line, Hart." Sam wasn't sure who this Will was, but it seemed that he and Hartley knew one another well.

"I'm here to destroy some paintings," Hartley said with a shrug.

"Paintings," the other man repeated, sounding confused.

Sam gathered that Will didn't know what kind of paintings Hartley was searching for. "I won't ask why. I'll assume you break into places whenever the spirit moves you. And maybe you do, for all I know. But you can see for yourself that this house doesn't have anything in it. I've been over it with a fine-tooth comb."

"Why *are* you here, Will?" Hartley asked.

There was a silence that lasted a few beats too long. "I'm looking for Martin."

Hartley's sharp intake of air was loud in the empty room. "I should have guessed. I thought you had gotten past that. After what he did to me, I thought—well, never mind."

"Jesus. Why will you not listen to reason about this?" Will's frustration made it clear this was a topic they had discussed many times. "He's not responsible for what his father did."

"He exposed me, Will. That was his own doing."

"That doesn't make any sense! His father's reputation was the last thing he had. Why would he throw that away? He has nobody, Hart. He's alone. He doesn't have anyone who cares about him, and he never has."

"Except you," Hartley interjected, his mouth curling into a sneer.

"I'm looking for him because I'm afraid he's done something stupid."

"I hope he has." Hartley's voice dripped with venom.

"We can't see eye to eye there," Will said. "I can't find him. And he's all alone. Hartley, he has nobody, and you have so many people if you only looked around."

Hartley gave a bitter laugh. "I haven't had a single caller at my house in months." Sam felt Hartley's words like a slap. He had suspected that he didn't count as anything in Hartley's life, not as a visitor, not as a friend, certainly not as anything more; he was a bit of rough trade, and now he was hearing it for himself. This was the man Sam had been willing to risk his neck for.

"You have Ben and Percy and Lance, which you might know if you ever bothered to answer their letters. Ben is worried sick. And I suspect you also have whoever the fellow is in the window."

Sam had to give Hartley credit; he didn't even glance in the direction of the window. He was a born deceiver, and it made Sam smile inwardly despite his sense of betrayal. Hartley raised his eyebrows. "Back at the opium, are you?" And there it was, more of that casual cruelty in Hartley's voice. Sam hardly knew how to reconcile that coldness with the kind words and gentle touches they had shared last night.

Sam could hear Will suck in a breath. "I see that we're done here. I'm leaving. Call on me in London, Hart. I miss you."

Hartley didn't respond to that. Sam waited until the footsteps had died away before shoving the curtains aside, feeling like a fool. But Hartley was now sitting on the floor, his knees drawn up and his head cradled in his arms, and Sam couldn't stop himself from crouching beside him, wrapping his arm around Hartley's shoulders, offering whatever comfort he could.

"**I**'m getting you out of this house," Sam growled, pulling Hartley to his feet. "And then we're talking." He made it sound like a threat, but Hartley was too worn out to complain; besides, he liked the feel of Sam's arm around his shoulders as they left the bedroom.

The sun was high in the sky when they stepped outside. Somehow it was only noon. Hartley winced at the light; he felt as though he had spent hours in the dusty shadows of Friars' Gate, but it couldn't have been more than ninety minutes.

"That was your brother?" Sam asked when they reached the edge of the woods where they had left the hamper from the inn.

"One of them. I have a lot of brothers."

"He must be one you're not particularly close with, I suppose, seeing as how you've never mentioned him and he's mates with your godfather's son?"

"We're close." Hartley sat on the ground, not caring about the state of his trousers. "Or, we were." When had things gone so drastically wrong? It had been two weeks since he had seen Will, and they lived in the same city.

Sam sat beside him, leaning his back against a tree. He didn't angle himself toward Hartley or place his hand palm up beside him. He didn't do any of the things that silently let Hartley know that touching was an option, should Hartley be so inclined. Hartley hadn't realized how much he depended on this silent conversation of unspoken questions until it was absent. Sam's body was oddly rigid against Hartley's, and he didn't know why. He supposed he had bungled something, stepped on Sam's toes, said something unfeeling. Somewhere along the way, Hartley had lost the knack for friendship, if he had ever had it to begin with. He thought of the pile of letters on his desk, thought of how he had just treated Will with deliberate callousness.

He took a long drink from the jug of brown ale that the innkeeper's wife had tucked into the picnic basket. "I'll visit my godfather's solicitor," Hartley said. "He must know something."

"About what?"

"The paintings," Hartley answered, holding out the jug to Sam. "Isn't that what we were talking about?"

Sam shook his head and waved away the offer of ale. "Forget about the paintings. You don't know where they are and you're not going to get them back."

So, it was *you* now instead of *we*. Hartley put the stopper back in the bottle. "I thought you wanted Kate's painting." Hartley's voice sounded small and peevish.

"I did, but not anymore. Kate would have my hide if she knew what we just did."

"That's fine," Hartley said. "I can manage it on my own."

Sam made a sound of frustration. "Are you going to spend the rest of your life alone in your grand house, scheming to get those paintings back? You're what, two and twenty?"

"Three and twenty."

"Do you have any reason to think you won't live for another half century? Are you going to spend all that time alone in your house?"

"I want to go away," Hartley said, the idea occurring simultaneously to the words leaving his mouth. "I've never been to Paris. Or really anywhere at all." During the past two days away from London he felt as if a weight had been removed from his chest. He wasn't certain exactly what he wanted to run away from, only that the prospect of doing so was soothing. "Would you come with me? Someplace warm, perhaps." A terrible idea, an utter fantasy. But he could imagine weeks and months of lazy picnics with Sam, nothing to do but amuse themselves and explore one another. He wanted that daydream of a future more than he had wanted anything in a long while. "Italy," he said, remembering how he had once meant to run off to a place with blue seas and cheap wine.

"I can't afford to bugger off to Europe," Sam said slowly.

"I'd pay your way, naturally," Hartley said quickly.

Sam regarded him with an expression that Hartley couldn't quite decipher. "I have the Bell."

"You could hire someone to cover while you're gone." Hartley looked eagerly up into Sam's face, and was perplexed not to see answering enthusiasm. "I'd pay for that too." He didn't have unlimited funds, but surely money went farther on the Continent than it did in England, which was why people were always running off there. He would have to figure out how that worked.

"It's not that simple."

Hartley couldn't see why not, but he nodded anyway. "No, no, of course not. I thought you might like a break."

"A break?" Sam repeated the words as if they were an insult. "I earn my keep. I do my job. I have a place in the world, even though there are plenty of people who don't want me to have that much. And that place is the Bell. That's where my life is. There's Nick and Kate, my aunts and cousins and everybody else. It's where I do some good." He said those last words with a ferocity Hartley had never heard from him. "And you want me to walk away from it, as if none of that matters to me. It sure as hell doesn't matter to you."

"Of course it—"

"And all that when not an hour ago you told your brother nobody had visited you in months. Either you like lying or you don't count me as a person."

Hartley froze. "Of course I count you as a person. When I said visitors, I meant—" Too late, he realized he had no way to end the sentence that didn't put Sam into a different category of person than himself. "I meant ladies and gentlemen, all right?" Hartley was a gentleman, however loose his upbringing, however disgraced his current status. Sam wasn't. "I meant people from my old life." The people who gave him the cut direct when they passed in the street.

"You meant your equals, which I'm not. True enough." Sam's usually warm, open features were closed and hard. He was angry. And Hartley had earned that anger. Really, he ought to be accustomed to being the object of contempt or disdain, but there were some things a person couldn't get used to. And some sad, pitiful part of him had been so glad that Sam liked him despite knowing what a mess he was.

Hartley sighed, resigned. He pulled his gloves out of his pocket and began tugging them onto his hands. "I don't know what to say to that," he said, smoothing the soft leather over his fingers, carefully fastening the buttons. He didn't know what Sam wanted to hear, but he had a sinking feeling that whatever it was, he couldn't say it.

"Listen, Hartley, I don't want to spend time with people who don't count me as their equal."

"I do! You are!" Hartley protested. He clenched his gloved hands in his lap.

"When you told Will that nobody had visited you, it sounded like you meant it."

"Honestly, Will isn't even my social equal, so I don't know what you're going on about." Hartley felt Sam's body go rigid beside him.

"Jesus, Hartley." Sam was on his feet now. "Let's go back to the inn."

Every spot on Hartley's body where they had been touching now felt like it had been plucked bare. He rubbed his side. "I didn't mean—"

"I'd stop," Sam snapped. "You're not going to make it better."

Hartley half wanted to admit that while he had spent his entire adulthood as a gentleman, despite being all too conscious that he hadn't come by that designation properly, he now doubted what that status was even worth. It certainly wasn't doing him any good. The only people he spoke to these days were Alf, Will, Kate, and Sam. All were decidedly not gentry.

But Sam had already started toward the inn, the picnic basket hefted in one strong arm. They walked back in silence.

Chapter Fourteen

Hartley had been prepared to retreat to the house on Brook Street and lick his wounds. He had no reason to leave; he had surprisingly excellent meals brought to him regularly and he subscribed to a lending library, so perhaps he'd simply spend the remainder of his three score and ten as a hermit. At the back of his mind he suspected that most recluses either enjoyed solitude or found it spiritually fulfilling, whereas Hartley, having grown up in a busy household and seldom even having a bedchamber to himself until he moved into this house, found solitude somewhat disturbing. Silence let his mind swarm with unwanted thoughts; solitude filled the room with the difficulties of his own flesh.

He tried to tell himself that it was for the best that Sam keep away, that this estrangement would save Sam from exposure and ruin. But this knowledge was not as sustaining as he had hoped, and he had to admit that he would rather have Sam's company than his safety. When Sunday came and went without Sam's knock on the door, Hartley was dismayed rather than satisfied.

He maintained his habit of long walks, timing them to even more improbable hours of the early morning and late afternoon, wishing to avoid any attention at all. Every pair of eyes saw through his fine clothing and recognized him for the shallow, hurtful person he truly was, so it was best that nobody see him at all. He returned from one of these walks to find Sadie sobbing in the kitchen and Alf apologizing for the fact that there would be no dinner.

"It's my fault," Alf said.

"That's right it is," Sadie said in between sobs.

Hartley was about to make himself scarce, when the light caught Alf's face and he remembered he was dealing with two very young people. They were both about eighteen, and while Hartley wasn't so much older, he was at least out of that fraught period of adolescence. Both, effectively, were children, and he was the only responsible adult they had.

"Let's not worry about dinner," he said. "But what's the matter?"

"There were some blokes at the market," Alf said. "One of them needed to be punched in the jaw and so that's what I did."

"But now where am I supposed to do the marketing?" Sadie asked. "I certainly can't go back there. I'll have to walk all the way to Fleet Market and that's no small matter with my feet all swollen like this." She held out one booted leg.

"Couldn't go back anyway, not with those bastards talking about you that way," Alf said, hands in his pockets. "Wouldn't be safe. I'll do the marketing for you, Sadie."

"No, you won't, because now they'll be looking out for you." Sadie's fists were clenched, and she appeared to have moved from sorrow to anger. "Or, worse still, they'll follow you back and find me here. I told you to keep your mouth shut and your head down and you ruined it for me."

"I'm sorry, Sadie, I really am," Alf said meekly. "I didn't think about them coming here. I just couldn't stand to hear them saying those things about you."

"What you can or can't stand isn't the point," she spat.

"I think we'd all do better with some hot food. Alf, will you go to the Bell to get one of Mr. Fox's pies?" He looked at Sadie, who was still too thin except for her belly. "No, make that two."

"The Bell?" Alf asked.

"It's in one of those lanes behind Fetter Lane where it meets Fleet Street." He hoped the vague directions would mean Alf took long enough on his errand that Sadie might be in a more forgiving frame of mind upon his return.

When Alf left, Hartley sat on a stool beside Sadie's at the large worktable. "I'm so sorry that happened," he said. A sob wracked her slight frame and he watched helplessly before venturing to pat her tentatively on the back.

"I already think everyone is watching me. Because they probably are, and I'm not even sure I can blame them. They know what I did at the docks, and I'm a bit conspicuous now." She gestured at her belly.

"Bollocks on anyone who can't mind their own business."

But that was easy to say, and not the entire truth. "I feel like that too," he admitted. "I feel like people are watching me, thinking about what they know about me." She looked up at him with red eyes, waiting for his next words. He swallowed. It was grossly improper to be having this conversation with a servant, but she didn't have anyone else and neither, really, did he. "When they see me, all they see is a whore and a sodomite. And after a while it's all I think I am. It's as if everyone else's thoughts are so loud I lose track of who I really am. But we're more than that, you hear?" She didn't look at him. "I mean it, Sadie. We're more than that."

"I'd like to hide in this kitchen forever."

"So would I, if I'm honest. You can stay here as long as you need, but you deserve more." It was an easy platitude, and he was almost ashamed of himself for saying it.

She let out a small unladylike sound of indignation. "I don't know what *more* would look like for me."

Neither did Hartley. He didn't know what an actual life could look like for either of them. But he knew he wanted Sadie to have that. "Is Alf giving you trouble? I thought you were mates, but if I have it wrong, say the word."

She reddened and twisted her hands in her apron. "We're friends. And he doesn't give me any trouble, not what you're talking about. He's a gentleman."

"Good," Hartley said, although he was certain Alf would loudly protest being called a gentleman. "Glad to hear it. Now, why don't you splash some water on your face and have a drink with me while we wait for our supper?"

"You did *what?*" Kate put the tankard onto the bar with enough force that beer sloshed over the rim. It was early afternoon, and the Bell was only starting to fill up, but she pitched her voice into a low hiss that wouldn't be overheard.

"We talked about it," Sam protested, regretting that he had decided to come clean to Kate about the real reason behind his travels. "You said you wanted to know what happened to that painting."

"I want any number of things! Two hundred pounds. The Hodges baby to get itself born so its mum will stop calling me around every day." She sat heavily in a chair at an empty table. "I thought you were just going to ask some questions. Not break into houses!"

"The doors were practically unlocked," he said feebly.

"Sam." She shook her head.

"You said you wanted to know!" he repeated.

"I did! But even more, I want you safe. I'd rather stroll down the street stark naked than have you go to prison."

"And I'd rather burn down half of Mayfair than know you and Nick are spending one second worrying about that painting. It isn't right, Kate." He poured a beer for a customer and then sat beside Kate. "Look, I'm not going to do any more prowling about for that painting, so you don't need to worry your head about it." That moment of raw panic behind the curtains at Friars' Gate had been enough to remind him of his priorities. If he were arrested, he wouldn't be of any use to anyone. It would be as if nothing had changed after that day Davey died. "I know it wasn't the wisest decision—"

"Ha!"

"But I wouldn't have done it if it really were dangerous," he said, knowing it was a lie. He would have walked into fire if it meant keeping Hartley safe, and that was a terrifying realization. "The house was empty," he said, mainly to convince himself he hadn't done anything truly mad. "Besides, I wasn't alone." He had meant that to be reassuring, but Kate's dark eyes lit up with the brightness of a spark about to hit a powder keg.

"Really, now? Who were you with?"

Sam knew there was no escaping Kate's interrogation. "Your friend Hartley."

Kate pressed her lips together and regarded him with narrowed eyes. "I have a mind to go tell Hartley what I think of him going along with this scheme of yours." She pushed away from the table, rising unsteadily to her feet. Kate looked even more tired than usual these days and he wanted to suggest that she go to bed for a bit of a kip before the Hodges baby really did make an appearance. But nobody told Kate what to do unless they wanted their eyes clawed out.

"It wasn't like that," Sam said quickly, thinking to spare Kate the trip across town and Hartley the tongue-lashing. "He had his own reasons for wanting to get back at that family."

"Oh?" Her brow furrowed. "*Oh.* I see." Kate's dark eyes assessed him. "And you went along to help Hartley avenge his own honor rather than to be an idiot on my behalf?"

Sam didn't know how to answer. Kate had laid a trap for him and he didn't know how to get out. "Well," he started. Kate's eyes narrowed further, but she sat back down.

"You never told me how you met Hartley. I made certain assumptions about how you might have run across one another." She paused, letting that sink in. She had apparently assumed that Sam and Hartley had met in precisely the sort of place Sam had suggested Hartley visit to pick up men that first night. Sam opened his mouth to protest but held his tongue. She may have been wrong about the precise circumstances of their meeting, but she wasn't wrong about the substance of their friendship. He waited, and even though he'd give it twenty to one odds against her being disturbed, he felt a creeping sense of dread until she reached over and squeezed his arm.

"That's not how we met, not exactly, but you have the lay of the land," he said. That was the first time he had ever spoken openly about who he went to bed with. It was almost dizzyingly strange. He went on to tell her how he had gone to the address she gave him and found Hartley living there; he left out the more explicit details, just like anybody would, but he also didn't pretend nothing explicit had happened.

At the end, Kate pursed her lips. "You and Hartley. He and I used to get along like a house on fire and I'm glad to see that he's made out well. And here I've been worried about your being lonely."

"It's not like that," Sam said quickly. "It's . . . We had an arrangement."

"You have a lot of arrangements that involve your sticking your neck out for another man? A rich man, even?"

She was right there. "Just an arrangement," he repeated.

"He being decent to you? I'll murder him if he isn't. Wait. Are you being decent to him? I'll murder you both if you hurt one another." She looked so torn about not knowing who to murder that Sam couldn't stop himself from smiling.

"Does Nick know?" Sam's cheeks were hot. "About . . . me?"

Kate frowned. "Nick isn't a noticing sort of person, bless the man. He might have seen that you don't have an eye for the ladies, but that's it."

Sam nodded. That sounded like Nick. And he still didn't know whether he was relieved Nick probably didn't suspect, or whether he wished Nick knew and hadn't let it change anything between them.

"It's as good as over," Sam said a bit later, after he had cleared some empty mugs and wiped down the bar. "With Hartley."

"You don't seem pleased."

He thought about denying it. But he had lied enough today, and if he knew Kate, she was already well aware of it. "I'm not. I'm fond of him. And he doesn't have anyone to look after him." He remembered what Hartley's brother had said about Hartley not answering letters or talking to his family, and wondered if the reason that Hartley didn't have anyone to look after him was that he didn't let anyone. Or maybe he didn't think he deserved looking after.

"He's a man, not a stray animal," Kate said, petting the dog on her lap. "You can't just keep him because he doesn't have anyone else."

"That's not what I'm doing," Sam said.

"Then what are you doing?"

"I don't rightly know, Kate," he admitted. And that was the truth.

CHAPTER FIFTEEN

It was with a sense of great satisfaction that Sam finally dislodged the bird's nest from the chimney. It was old and brittle, the birds long since having hatched and flown away. "There, now," he announced to the taproom at large. "That ought to take care of the smoke."

"That's just a chimney swift's nest," said an elderly patron, bent over the sooty remnants of twigs and mud. "A wee little thing like that won't have caused all that smoke. What you've got is a bad chimney cap."

"Or a faulty flue," chimed in another patron.

Sam suppressed a groan. They had already paid good coin for a chimney sweep to put in a new chimney cap and to repair the flue, but still the chimney smoked.

"It's a down draft," said the first patron in ominous tones.

"Not good," agreed the second. "Not good at all."

The reason he had been able to get the Bell on such favorable terms was that he had a repairing lease, meaning that he alone was responsible for repairs. The building's owner had, as far as Sam knew, no obligation beyond taking Sam's money. Whatever additional expenses they incurred fixing this blasted chimney were Sam's responsibility alone. If they failed to keep the place in good repair, the landlord would have every right to kick them out.

He had worked hard to make this place a cut above the seedy alehouse it had once been. Now it was a place where black tradesmen and laborers could talk to one another over a pint or a bite of food and know they wouldn't get caught up in a brawl. Sam didn't want to see that all down the drain just because of a temperamental chimney. He'd just have to find a way to hire another, hopefully better, sweep.

When he caught Kate wiping a table, he didn't even have the heart to remind her that she didn't work at the Bell anymore and ought to be sitting down, or possibly be at home getting some rest. Instead he hefted a stack of dishes to bring to the sink when he felt a gust of cold air from the street.

"You," Kate said in a voice that meant she was scanning the room for likely weapons.

"You, yourself," answered a too-refined voice. "Honestly, darling, sit down. You look exhausted. When was the last time you slept?"

Sam held his breath. The patrons at the table nearest Kate edged their chairs away. There was a moment of dangerous silence. But instead of murdering Hartley on the spot, Kate sort of collapsed onto his shoulder in a fit of laughter and tears. "I *know*," she said. "I'm half asleep on my feet."

"There, there," Hartley said, patting her back. Sam was out of view of the table where Hartley and Kate sat, hidden in the shadows near the doorway. But he could see them clearly. Hartley had on one of his many-buttoned waistcoats and a coat the color of wet cobblestones. His hair was as tidy as ever, his face neatly shaved, but around his eyes were tiny lines that Sam thought hadn't been there before.

Sam watched, transfixed, as two of the prickliest people he had ever met dissolved into a puddle of affection. Hartley had Kate nearly in his lap, and she was sobbing into his collar. Any difficulties Hartley had with being touched didn't seem to apply to Kate. In fact, Hartley's starchy reserve seemed to disappear around women. Hartley had been downright charming to the innkeeper's wife. He wondered how much of Hartley's chilly demeanor was simply the fact that he was afraid of men.

Maybe fear wasn't the word. Maybe it was more physical than that—the instinctive flinch at a fast approaching fist. Maybe all men posed that same potential danger for Hartley. And wasn't that a rubbish bit of luck for a man who preferred men. Sam was glad that old Easterbrook was dead, otherwise he might be tempted to do something about that for him.

Nick appeared then at Sam's shoulder to relieve him of the stack of plates he was still carrying. "That Kate's friend who was here the other day? Some toff she used to know?"

"That's him." Sam hoped he had managed to keep his voice disinterested.

The dog rushed in through the door Nick had left open and ran over to leap around Kate's and Hartley's feet. Hartley promptly picked him up and started to talk to him in a daft voice.

"Not the sort of man you worry about your girl being around," Nick said.

"You don't need to worry about Kate around anyone."

"I know that," Nick said. "I just meant that I don't think that fellow is going to give her any trouble."

"How can you tell?" Sam snapped. "I didn't think you knew many men like that."

Nick looked at him, wide-eyed. "Well, he's not making a secret of it, is he?"

Sam turned his attention back to Hartley and Kate. It wasn't that Hartley was exactly feminine, but there was something about the way he held himself, something about the tone of his voice, too, that wasn't quite masculine either. Sam didn't think it was anything Hartley was deliberately doing, so much as something inborn in him, just part of who he was. And his looks didn't help; he wasn't handsome so much as beautiful. Maybe that was why the gossip had ruined him: it was just so easy to believe that Hartley was that kind of man.

Sam had always been able to keep his bedroom preferences separate from the rest of his life. He had good work and a family who loved him. That was the sum and substance of his life. Nobody who saw him had to know that he liked men, which meant Sam hadn't had to think about it much either. But he knew what it was like to be judged on appearances and found wanting. These days, he rarely heard the slurs that had been openly shouted at him in the ring. Cowed by Sam's size and his history, people tended to hold their tongues. Only men like Constable Merton, with the full force of the law behind him, weren't afraid.

Did Hartley walk down the street imagining the slurs that people were just barely managing not to say aloud? Did he suspect that everyone he met secretly disdained and distrusted him? Sam knew what that was like, knew it better than Hartley ever could. When Hartley had said that he wanted to travel, maybe what he really meant was that he wanted to get away from those hateful whispers, wanted to go someplace where people looked at him and only saw a finely dressed white man. Sam didn't have that as an option, and wouldn't have taken it even if he had; he didn't want to be anybody other than hardworking black Englishman that he was, but he knew that when many white Englishmen looked on him they saw someone inferior, someone who didn't belong.

It had hurt to hear Hartley speak words that seemed to carry the echo of that kind of ugly sentiment. Failing to count Sam as a guest in his house, suggesting that Sam could walk away from the Bell—even if Hartley hadn't meant to demean Sam, the fact that he didn't understand how Sam would interpret his words was itself a problem. But seeing the man bent over a table, deep in conversation with Kate, Sam didn't want to believe Hartley was just another Constable Merton.

What he wanted didn't matter, though. He couldn't put his dignity, his safety, or his work on the line for anyone, least of all someone who didn't respect him and who he was. He ought to cut his losses before he got in any deeper.

"Where's Sam?" Hartley asked, trying and failing to sound uninterested.

Kate gave a slight roll of her eyes. "He was here before you came, so I suppose he's avoiding you. You know why better than I do."

Hartley took a sip of ale before speaking with more sangfroid than he felt. "I can't imagine what you're talking about."

She regarded him carefully, as if deciding whether to say something. "He told me about the two of you," she said quietly. "Well, no, actually I told him and he didn't deny it. So you don't need to come up with any tales. Hurt him and I'll cut off your bollocks and feed them to Daisy."

"Duly noted."

"And if I ever, ever hear about you putting him in danger again, I'll slit your throat and dance in your blood."

"Christ, Kate. Anything else? Any other gruesome fates you need to threaten me with today? You don't need to worry about my putting Sam in any more danger, because it's over."

Kate raised a skeptical eyebrow. "That's what he said."

"As well he should. I was rude and stupid and thoughtless. You know, the usual."

"If you put your foot in it, which I can well believe, you'd better fix it. Sam is fond of you."

"Perhaps he *was*—"

"What is the *matter* with you?"

Really, Hartley hardly knew how to begin answering that, so instead he drained his tankard.

"If you bollocksed it up, fix it you daft sod," Kate said, slapping the table between them.

They talked until Sam appeared, hefting a cask of ale on one shoulder. That explained the muscles, Hartley supposed.

Even now, through the linen of Sam's shirt, he could see the man's arms and shoulders ripple as he set the cask down. He remembered the feel of those strong muscles under his hands, and he remembered everything else that had happened that night too—the sense that Sam would use his strength for Hartley, the warmth and security he had felt in Sam's company. And then he remembered the look of stunned hurt on Sam's face the next day. True, Hartley hadn't meant to hurt him, but it was also true that if his head hadn't been up his arse he would have thought before he spoke.

"Good of you to show your face," Kate called cheerfully across the taproom.

"New ale. Half a dozen more in the back." He addressed his words to Kate alone before turning to Hartley, as if only then noticing his presence. "Good day, Mr. Sedgwick."

Hartley hoped Sam never played cards because he was a terrible liar. "Good day, Mr. Fox," he said with exaggerated politesse.

When he turned back to Kate, she shook her head disgustedly at him. "Like a pair of old hens," she said. She got up, and for a moment Hartley thought she was going to leave him there. But she returned with two fresh pints of ale. "May as well tell me whatever it is. You'll feel better after."

"Fat chance," Hartley said. But three pints later his inhibitions had worn down. He wasn't going to talk about Sam, because if he told Kate about the swirling mess of stunned gratitude and baffled affection that comprised his feelings toward Sam, she'd think him a sapskull, and rightly so. There was another matter that Kate could advise him on, however.

"Can I ask you something, ah, delicate?" They had removed to a table away against the wall where they wouldn't be overheard. The dog had leapt into his lap and promptly fallen asleep, and its snores seemed to double the effect of the ale.

"If I don't want to answer, I won't," she responded pragmatically.

"My cook is increasing and I don't know what to do."

Kate's lips pressed tightly together. "I take it you didn't get her that way?"

"No! Of course not," Hartley protested, aghast. "I don't know the circumstances, but her parents turned her out, presumably due to her condition. After that, she worked the streets."

"Do you typically get your household staff directly off the streets?" Kate asked, her head tilted quizzically.

Hartley was about to insist that of course he didn't when he remembered Alf. "That's not the point. But you're a midwife and I thought you could attend her. I'll see to your fee when the time comes."

"Of course. That's your delicate question?" She looked rather let down.

Hartley's cheeks heated. "I thought you might also talk to her about whatever transpired in between leaving her father's house and arriving in mine. In case anything . . . happened." He filled his lungs with air. "To her, I mean. Or if the, ah, manner in which she got with child was . . . not of her own choosing."

Kate nodded. "I'll see what I can do."

"Thank you." Hartley knew a surge of relief that was

surely disproportionate to having secured a midwife for his cook.

Kate slid a hand across the table and laid it atop Hartley's, and he felt his cheeks heat even more at the recognition that this was not only about his cook. "If this girl has had an unfortunate experience, she might do better to talk to you than to me, Hart."

Hartley had not realized Kate was out of her mind. "I rather think that would drive her into the river, if she thought she might wind up like me."

Kate frowned but didn't say anything falsely reassuring. She didn't try to tell him that nothing was that bad, or that he had a lot to be grateful for. She squeezed his hand. "Is it that rough?"

Was it? A year ago Hartley might have said he was absolutely fine despite everything that had happened with Easterbrook. His days had been filled with engagements and conversations—all hollow and empty, but at least they passed the time. If he couldn't fuck, that was a small thing, really. But now his life had shrunk to the precise dimensions of the house on Brook Street, had dwindled to the size and shape of his own body. What he had lost loomed larger than what he still had. And he was furious. He wanted to raise his godfather from the grave just to have the privilege of sending him back there.

"It's all right, you know." Kate squeezed his hand.

"It really isn't," he said.

"Not what happened to you. That'll never be all right. But *you* will be."

"I'm fine," Hartley insisted. "Except for . . ." He wasn't going to say *fucking* in Sam's pub, and besides, it wasn't just fucking anyway. It was all the things that went along with it. "It's shit to want something and also feel sick at the thought of it."

"It's utter shit," she agreed, squeezing his hand.

"I mean, I know everyone has things they want and can't have. I'm not that spoilt. And what I want isn't important. I have wealth and health. My brothers and father seem to tolerate me. I shouldn't be feeling sorry for myself. But I still want . . ." He shrugged, not wanting to complete the thought.

"A cock in your arse," she murmured sympathetically.

He didn't know if it was the contrast between the coarseness of her words and the sympathy underlying them, but he burst out laughing. He laughed until his shoulders were shaking and the dog had woken up to lick the tears that streamed down his cheeks. When he looked at the bar, he saw that Sam was watching him, his mouth curved in the beginnings of a smile, as if he were happy to see Hartley laugh. As if Hartley's happiness mattered to him.

Sam kept himself busy wiping down the bar and collecting empty tankards while the last patrons left the warmth of the Bell for the cold autumn night. Hartley, though, was still at the same table he had occupied with Kate, even though she had long since left, taking the dog with her. He had put his gloves back on and held his hat in his hand as if he were ready to be sent on his way. Sam debated whether to lock the door.

He usually waited until the last patron had left, and some-times even longer after that, in case anyone needed him. But Hartley was still here, and he was a patron.

He wasn't fooling himself. Hartley wasn't here for the ale. He was waiting for Sam. Sam threw the bolt and turned to face him.

"I won't keep you," Hartley said, rising to his feet. "I only wanted to apologize. I never meant to hurt you, but I did. I ought to have realized before I spoke."

"What are you sorry for?" Sam needed to hear it.

"I'm sorry I suggested you walk away from the Bell. I'm sorry I suggested you didn't count as a visitor at my house, because truly Sam, I've enjoyed your visits more than I've enjoyed anything in the past twelvemonth, and not just be-cause . . ." He gestured between their bodies, a faint blush creeping onto his cheeks. "I understand if you don't want to see me again. After I destroy the paintings, I'll send word." He stepped toward the door. "But I didn't want to end things badly."

"I accept your apology," Sam said.

"Really?" Hartley stopped and turned to Sam, his expres-sion startled.

"Would you rather I didn't?"

"No, of course not. I—Thank you."

"Sit back down, will you?"

Hartley sat, and Sam filled them each a tankard of his best porter. Sam pulled out a chair, and Hartley began the process of unbuttoning and removing his gloves. Sam put out a hand to stop him.

"Let me help," Sam said, and Hartley held out his hands. Sam didn't dare look at Hartley's face, just kept his attention on the soft leather stretched tight and thin over Hartley's palms. They were perfectly clean, even the fingertips. He held one of Hartley's hands palm up in each of his, running his thumb from palm to wrist, tracing over the buttons and then the soft skin above the glove. Only when he heard Hartley sigh did he look up.

"It's not just fucking, is it?" Hartley asked.

"No," Sam said, and began unbuttoning the gloves.

"I was afraid of that."

"You would be." He flicked open the final button.

Hartley cracked a laugh and then looked very sternly across the table at him. "It's a bad idea."

"It was a bad idea a month ago. We've gotten beyond the idea stages now." He began tugging the gloves off Hartley's hands, one finger at a time, sliding the soft leather over each digit in turn.

"You're saying now it's just bad."

"No, it's good." Sam pulled the gloves off Hartley's hands and held them in his own, rubbing the hollow of Hartley's palms with his own thumbs. "There are damned few good things, but this is one of them, I think."

Hartley pressed his lips together and looked like he was about to argue. Sam didn't want to hear it, so he brought one of Hartley's hands to his mouth for a kiss.

CHAPTER SIXTEEN

In contrast to the bustle of the Bell and even the warmth of his own kitchen, Hartley's library had the stale quiet of a sickroom. More than once, he found himself wandering down the back stairs under the shamefully flimsy pretense of requiring Alf or requesting a dish from Sadie. Only that morning he had insisted on taking a heavy dish out of the oven to spare Sadie the trouble. This was highly ungenteel but he didn't quite know whether he cared. When Will showed up two weeks after their encounter at Friars' Gate, Hartley was too bored and lonely to even feign chilliness.

"Look," Will said, his hands shoved in the pockets of a coarse fustian coat that ought to go directly to the rag man, "either we patch it up now or we're going to be awkward together for the rest of our lives. You're my brother and my best friend. I don't see that a dead man needs to ruin that, in addition to everything else he ruined." Something in his tone suggested that Will's list of things Sir Humphrey Easterbrook ruined went beyond Hartley's personal life, but he didn't want to ask, lest they start quarrelling about Martin again.

"Quite," Hartley said. Really, he didn't deserve a brother as understanding as Will. Hartley knew he was prickly and difficult; he couldn't meet Will's generosity even close to halfway.

"So come with me tonight to see the new play in Covent Garden. I'm meant to write a review for the *Observer*."

It was supposed to be perfectly terrible, and Hartley, who liked picking apart bad plays almost as much as he enjoyed watching good plays, would have gone in a heartbeat if he didn't have misgivings about being on display in front of hundreds of people.

"Come on," Will said encouragingly. "It's going to be ghastly." He said this in the manner of one promising a special treat, and Hartley couldn't help but smile.

"Very well then," Hartley said. "If it turns out to be any good I'll be very cross."

"Afterward," Will continued, "the cast is having a bit of a do."

"No," Hartley said too quickly.

"It's nothing grand."

Hartley refrained from pointing out that Will was hardly likely to be associated with any grandeur whatsoever, and also that his boots looked like they had been dragged behind a cart for some distance before he put them on. He needed to get out of the house before he started offering to help Sadie peel vegetables simply to avoid his own company. If he could associate with anyone without fear of being ostracized, it was actors. It might be pleasant to simply be among other people who didn't whisper about his proclivities and scandals. Hell, most people thought actors were all sodomites and actresses all whores, so he'd be among fellow travelers, as it were.

"Fine," he said, and rang for Alf.

"The black coat and the violet waistcoat," Alf declared when Hartley said he was going to the theater.

"I was thinking of the dark blue coat with the gray waist-coat."

Alf's lip curled. "If you're only going to leave the house once a week, might as well look your best when you do."

"The gray waistcoat suits me."

"Makes me want to die from boredom. What's the point of having purple waistcoats if you don't wear them?"

Will watched this exchange like a spectator at a tennis match. Indeed, he had never seen any of Hartley's servants say more than two words to him, usually along the lines of "yes, sir," or "presently, sir." But things were different now and Hartley found that he didn't mind Alf mouthing off. Maybe it was because he had nobody else to talk to. Maybe it was because Alf knew the worst and tolerated him anyway. Or maybe it was because Will's presence reminded Hartley that he hadn't always been a fine gentleman. Will's appalling coat wasn't so different from what Hartley had worn a few years ago.

Hartley hadn't known that coats such as Will's were anything other than perfectly serviceable until his godfather had taught him so. Closing his eyes, he had the sense that when he opened them, the library would be as it was eight years ago: lewd paintings on the walls, expensive baubles still unsold, the room filled with wealthy sybarites. It was in this room, and at the house parties at Friars' Gate, that Hartley had learned what gentlemen were, what they wore, the unspoken codes of behavior that they followed. He had soaked up that knowledge with the callow certainty that being a gentleman would protect him from the vagaries of fortune. At his father's house, everything had been maddeningly unsettled—days without food, years without school, no plans at all for the children's future. Without trades or professions, the Sedgwick children would have had a lifetime of missed meals and empty hearths.

Easterbrook had been perfectly aware of the young Sedgwicks' predicament and his own ability to give them aid. But instead of freely offering help, he had taken advantage of Hartley's desperation. At the time, Hartley had thought only of the promise of future security for his brothers; he considered himself the author of his own fate. Now he looked back and saw his own actions as the tactics of a desperate child with nowhere else to turn.

He tried to remember what it was like to care so much about anyone else, and all he could think of was his growing pile of unanswered letters. When he opened his eyes, he saw Will staring at him with concern. Good God, if *Will* was worried about him, he must really be badly off.

He cleared his throat and tried to summon up a pedagogical manner. "In the best households," he told Alf, "a servant doesn't argue with his employer about waistcoats."

"Is that so?" Alf was speaking with what was doubtless intended to be a comic mockery of Hartley's own accent.

"Indeed it is," Hartley said, drawing on a dwindling reserve of patience.

"If I ever give a sod what they do in fine households, I'll be sure to remember that."

A strangled sound came from Will's direction and Hartley did not dare turn his head lest he see his brother laughing and find it contagious. "Fine," he conceded. "The violet waistcoat, then."

The play was every bit as bad as Hartley had hoped, and he enjoyed Will's scathing commentary more than the actual production. Afterward, they went to somebody's lodgings, where gin and cheap wine flowed freely and a few actors still wore their stage makeup. Hartley couldn't help but feel that he ought to be enjoying it more, and that it was his own fault for finding himself at the edges of the rooms, failing to take conversational bait, and in general being a bad guest.

"You're Will's brother?" said a man in a sloppily tied cravat and an inexpertly shaved jaw. "You look nothing alike."

"He's one of the legitimate ones," Will said, appearing at Hartley's elbow. "This is Edgar Graham, the actor."

Will wandered off, claiming to need another drink, but plainly leaving Hartley and Mr. Graham alone. "The play was very entertaining," Hartley lied.

Graham snorted. "The crowd did seem to like it, at least."

"The problem was in the third act," Hartley said before he could think better of it. He had downed two glasses of gritty, bitter wine in quick succession in order to combat his unease, and now his mouth was running a full minute ahead of his mind.

"Oh?" Graham said, raising his eyebrows. "Tell me more."

"Well, if the baron is meant to be a villain, he ought to act like a villain. Instead he pulls his punches. I kept waiting for the baron to abduct that poor daft Clara creature. Who, by the by, I would have abducted by myself if I hadn't been twelve rows back."

"Up close she's even worse," Graham lamented. "She simpers."

"Precisely!" Hartley said. Some kind-hearted soul had filled his glass once again so he drained it, and now he was in fine form. "She simpers, she wrings her hands, and her brother has the ancestral jewels that our villain requires for his fell purposes. Why on earth not abduct her?"

Graham raised an eyebrow. "Do you know the playwright?"

"No," Hartley said. "Is he here?"

"If you knew him, you'd understand that he's revoltingly decent."

"Oh, to hell with decent people. They're exhausting. Make one feel so evil, when really one simply has one's own concerns."

"I could not agree more." He leaned close to Hartley, and since Hartley was against the wall he couldn't step away. They were only a hair's breadth closer than normal talking distance, just enough to make it clear that this was an approach. It occurred to Hartley that in the right circles, his reputation would make picking up bedmates vastly less confusing and fraught with peril for everyone involved. Graham was even fairly good-looking, in a scraggy sort of way. If Hartley were an entirely different person, they could disappear to another room and pass a pleasant hour.

But the proximity made Hartley feel sick. Even the look of interest in the other man's face made Hartley feel pinned to the wall, exposed. Unsafe. "I need to leave," Hartley managed, and was out the door before he heard Will calling after him.

"Damnation," Will muttered, catching up to him. "Did Edgar do something?"

"No. I'm a bloody mess, that's all." Hartley leaned against the damp stone of a building. His head swam from an excess of wine and his heart raced but he no longer felt actively terrified. He had the relief of waking from a nightmare but the certainty that he'd have the same dream the next night.

"You are not," Will said with more loyalty than sense.

They walked a few paces in silence. "I met someone."

"Ah. The fellow behind the curtain, I reckon."

"I can almost stand to let him touch me and look at me."

"That's good, Hart. That's really good."

"It's nothing of the sort. It's a piss-poor thing to offer a good man."

"I reckon he's a better judge of that than you are."

They continued walking, and when Hartley found his feet straying from the pavement, Will steered him in the direction he required. "His name is Sam and he keeps a public house." He had to work hard to annunciate his words. "The Bell."

"The Bell," Will repeated. "Sam Fox? I know him. He's your man behind the curtain?" He let out a low whistle. Hartley elbowed him clumsily in the ribs and then lost his footing. Will laughed and tugged him upright, and they made their wobbly way home.

Hartley walked right past the clerk's desk and into the solicitor's office, somehow managing not to cringe at his own unmannerliness.

"Mr. Sedgwick," the clerk protested, calling after him. "Mr. Philpott is engaged."

Philpott was not engaged. He was at his desk with no company but a stack of papers.

"Thank you so much for seeing me," Hartley said with all the effusive gratitude of a client who had been granted a proper appointment, rather than someone who was no better than a trespasser. "No doubt your schedule is frightfully busy. I'm so glad you could find the time to talk to me."

"Mr. Sedgwick," Philpott said, plainly flustered. "I told you to consult another attorney. I'm not prepared to represent you in any legal matters."

"Of course not," Hartley said cheerfully as he settled into a chair, crossing one leg over the other. With a negligent air, he glanced around the room. There were four cabinets of the sort lawyers used to store papers, none large enough to hold paintings unless removed from their frames and rolled up. "But it's not a legal matter at all. It's quite illegal, in fact. And I do think you'll want this door closed while we discuss it," he advised.

"I don't know what you're talking about."

"Should we leave the door open, then?" Hartley kept his eyes wide and his expression innocent. Philpott called for his clerk to shut the door, and Hartley knew he had the whip hand in this conversation.

"What's this about, Sedgwick? Whatever filthy business you've gotten up to is no concern of mine."

"Oh, dear me, no. It's not my filthy business at all. Only, it's occurred to me that you must know where the paintings are."

"I don't know what you could possibly mean." But his eyes darted to a small lacquered cabinet by the door. Hartley pretended not to notice.

Hartley made a disapproving sound. "Come, now. Of course you do. I'd really have expected a better caliber of lies from the man who served as Sir Humphrey's solicitor. Either you have the paintings or Martin does. If Martin is on the Continent, then I find it hard to believe he's traveling with a trunk filled with paintings. I'm certain he didn't leave them at the Priory because it's been let to tenants." The tenants were Ben and his captain, and there was no possibility that the captain's hellion children hadn't run amok over every nook and cranny in the house. "And I also know they aren't at Friars' Gate because that place has been stripped to the floorboards. That leaves you."

"Why would Sir Martin leave these paintings in my care?"

"Because they're his principal asset." It had taken days for Hartley to realize it, but the paintings were worth a tidy sum. They were the best kind of blackmail fodder: respectable people painted in the nude. "If you don't have them—" he let his voice indicate how dubious a likelihood that was "—then we ought to ask Martin what became of them."

"Sir Martin is traveling," Philpott sniffed.

"Surely you have some mode of communicating with him. Where are you directing correspondence? A poste restante?"

A flicker of unease passed across the lawyer's face. "Sir Martin left no address." Philpott's face was scarlet. The redder the solicitor's face, the more certain Hartley became that the man knew exactly what had happened to those paintings. "This is highly inappropriate."

"It was highly inappropriate for your late client to use me as he did," Hartley said evenly. "And it was highly inappropriate for you to condone his behavior during his lifetime."

"I never did any such thing," the older man sputtered.

"Please, Mr. Philpott. You knew perfectly well what kind of man my godfather was, and you still took his money. You had visited his library and you had seen his paintings."

"Sir Humphrey didn't leave half his estate to those whores."

"Yes, well, he did leave half his estate to *this* whore, and there's nothing you or anyone can do about it. It's mine." Philpott's face was now purple with either anger or embarrassment; Hartley did not much care which. It had felt good to condemn Easterbrook; speaking the words aloud to someone who had known the man felt almost like retribution. "I'm giving you one more chance to tell me where the paintings are."

"And then what?" the solicitor scoffed. Philpott's implication that Hartley was, once again, helpless in the hands of a man with more power and influence made him want blood.

"Do you really want to find out? I have no reputation left to lose and I have a certain amount of money burning a hole in my pocket. I could bring an action against you for slander. Or, I could get Easterbrook's will sent to Chancery. That ought to keep us both busy for the next few decades." He was delighted to see Philpott's face drain of color. He had come here to inspect the lawyer's office for any likely hiding places, but wielding a little bit of power had been unexpectedly satisfying.

He stood up and put his hat on his head. "Good day, Mr. Philpott." By the time he reached the street, he was more sanguine than he had been in weeks.

The door to Hartley's house was opened by a tall girl in an enormous, starchy cap. Sam clutched the paper parcel under his arm. It was Sunday evening, and Sam had expected Hartley to be alone.

"How can I help you, sir?" the girl asked, as if Sam were the lord mayor coming to pay a visit.

"I have a delivery for Mr. Hartley Sedgwick," Sam said, startled to realize that this capped and aproned servant was the same disordered girl he had seen in Hartley's kitchen that night he had arrived with Daisy.

"I'll see that he gets it," she answered, holding out a floury hand.

"Ah, no, this has to go into his own hands."

"You should have come to the front door, then, sir," she said with the air of someone who knew exactly which doors people ought to be using and wasn't afraid to say so. "But perhaps Mr. Sedgwick does things differently," she conceded.

"You sit by the fire and warm your feet while I let him know he has a caller. What did you say your name was?"

"Sam," he said. When she continued to watch him, plainly waiting for the rest, he said, "Sam Fox."

"Well, there's hot cider in the pot if you care for some, Mr. Fox," she said before disappearing up the stairs. As she turned he saw that she wasn't merely plump, but increasing. Nearly done increasing, by the looks of her.

Sam ladled out some cider for himself, then sat in the chair he had occupied that afternoon he had watched Hartley play with the dog. Every time Sam had been in this room, it had been quiet and empty, with only the smell of old cooking. Now it was hot and bright, with three pots bubbling on the fire and the aroma of baking bread permeating the air. The cider was sweet and spicy and filled him with warmth.

There were footsteps on the stairs. "He says will you please join him in the library and, if you please, stay for dinner. It's roast squab and carrots, nothing grand." The girl said this not with the air of a cook apologizing for a humble supper, but with the intimation that Sam might run if he thought he was being invited for a three-course meal. And she was right.

"I reckon I'll stay. Thank you, ma'am . . ." She had called him Mr. Fox, and he didn't know what to call her.

She opened her eyes wide and stared at him. "I don't. I mean." She was stammering as if she had been asked to do a tricky sum rather than her surname. "Sadie Russell. Miss."

"Thank you, Miss Russell," he said.

He found Hartley sprawled on the sofa, reading a newspaper. His head was pillowed against one arm of the sofa and his bare feet were propped up at the other end, crossed at the ankles.

"I thought it was the servants' half day," Sam said.

Hartley folded the newspaper and got to his feet. "It is, but if I want her to eat a hot meal I have to pretend to want one. Otherwise she eats bread crusts. It's shocking."

"She?"

"The new cook. Sadie. Well, she's more of a cook-housekeeper, really." Hartley seemed looser and happier than Sam had ever seen him. "And, well, not to put too fine a point on it, I have every reason to trust her discretion." His cheeks flushed. "Not that your coming here means that we'll have need of discretion. Perhaps you really did come to make a de-livery." He glanced at the parcel Sam still held under his arm.

"Ah. Well. I thought you might need cheering up, so I brought you something. But you seem in fine fettle, so per-haps I won't—"

"Don't you dare," Hartley said, stepping toward Sam and reaching for the parcel. Sam held it over his head, well out of Hartley's reach. "I love presents."

"No, no," Sam said with a sad shake of his head. "I'll save it for a rainy day." Hartley was inches away now, one slen-der arm still raised toward the parcel and the other resting on Sam's shoulder. Sam felt a rush of heat at the unexpected contact. He rested a steadying hand on Hartley's hip, ready to pull it away. But Hartley didn't flinch.

"All right, I'll give it to you. But if you don't want it or if you're cross with me for thinking it was something you might fancy, I'll take it away."

"Now I'm curious as well as greedy."

Sam huffed out a laugh and handed over the parcel. He watched nervously as Hartley undid the string, hardly daring to breathe. Hartley was carefully picking at the string and the paper as if he needed to save them for later use, as if he weren't going to toss them into the fire or put them in the dustbin or whatever rich men did with rubbish. Finally, Hartley had peeled back all the layers of paper and stared at the object in his hand.

"I—" Hartley cleared his throat. "When you said you brought something to cheer me up, I thought maybe some boiled sweets. Not an enormous glass prick."

"It's not enormous," Sam said before realizing this was not the best ground on which to protest.

"It's very pretty," Hartley said dubiously, holding it out so it caught glimmers of firelight.

"Kate picked it out," Sam said, because apparently his brain had just stopped working at the sight of Hartley holding that thing. "I mean, I told her what I needed and she got it." Sam might be foolish fond of Hartley Sedgwick, but he wasn't fool enough to show his face in the sort of place that sold things like that. It was one thing for a woman to make that kind of purchase, but it was entirely more conspicuous for a man to do so. A girl like Kate could pull her cloak up to cover her head and come and go almost invisibly. Moreover, he knew he could trust her.

"She buy a lot of glass penises for you?" Hartley asked blandly.

Sam nearly choked. "I never saw one of those things until yesterday. But I've been thinking about how you said you liked being fucked, and how it's a pity you can't be. I thought it might be of use."

Hartley raised his thin, pale eyebrows. "When you thought about precisely how this might be of use, did you let yourself imagine it in detail?"

If Hartley hadn't been sliding his hand up and down the glass prick, Sam might have given a different answer. "You'd better fucking believe I did," he said. "Jesus." His own flesh and blood prick leapt to attention at the thought.

Hartley's hand slid up the fake prick, his thumb skimming over the head, his eyes fixed on Sam. "Would you want to watch me?"

Oh, would he. His mouth went dry at the thought of it. "You offering?"

CHAPTER SEVENTEEN

He *was* offering. Hartley could hardly believe it, but there it was. "I can't promise that I can go through with it, but at the moment the idea feels inspired."

When Sadie had announced that Sam was downstairs, Hartley's stomach flipped in some unholy combination of anxiety and relief that Sam still wanted to see him, even after Hartley had alienated him at Friars' Gate. Sam showing up was good; Sam showing up bearing gifts was better. The fact that the gift was a literal cock was *delightful*. No, more than that—it was kind and thoughtful and dear, because he was trying to give Hartley something he couldn't otherwise get. Sam was a lovely man who did lovely things, and he likely deserved someone who wasn't a colossal mess.

Well, if he wanted to be with a colossal mess, Hartley was going to make it worth both their whiles. He brought the glass prick up to his mouth and gave it a long, slow lick, watching Sam's eyes flare at the sight. God, he loved watching this man get worked up. It was so subtle, just a slight quickening of breath, a bite of his lower lip. With other men, men who wouldn't recoil in fear, maybe he let himself go, using his big hands and his strong body to take what he wanted. That was possible, Hartley conceded. But he knew that Sam liked this, liked the challenge of restraining himself. Well, Hartley liked watching Sam hold himself back. He liked it very much indeed. So much, he took the glass prick into his mouth and sucked the head.

"Oh fuck," Sam whispered.

Hartley took Sam's hand, meaning to lead him to the chair or the sofa or anywhere he could proceed to do lewd things with glass cocks. But Sam's fingers closed around his own so lightly, so gently, that Hartley was momentarily unable to draw in a breath. It felt so good to have someone else's hand around his own like this. Sam brought Hartley's hand up to his mouth. He was moving slowly, carefully, his eyes on Hartley for any sign of upset. Hartley gave a little nod to show that whatever was happening, he liked it. Then Sam bent his head to kiss Hartley's knuckles. The feel of lips on skin should not have felt like anything terribly special. Certainly it oughtn't to have sent desire spreading across his body like butter melting on hot bread. And there was more than desire; there was a wash of acceptance, of affection, of a whole host of things that Hartley hadn't known he wanted.

"Come over by the fire," Hartley said, getting his hand free. "Can't do this with clothes on."

He hadn't ever been completely naked with Sam. He hadn't ever been naked with anyone since—then. But this was totally different. This was Sam, and Sam was safe. Sam wouldn't do anything Hartley didn't want. Hartley went to the door and turned the key in the lock. When he turned around he saw that Sam had taken his coat off and was sitting by the fire, his hands resting on the arms of the chair. He watched Hartley unbutton his waistcoat as if he were witnessing a miracle.

"Blast," Hartley said. "I don't have any oil." It had been a while and he wasn't shoving any cocks up his arse without oil. As much as he trusted Sadie and Alf, he wasn't going to ask for cooking oil to be sent to his library.

"I have—" Sam took his coat off the floor where he had dropped it and retrieved a small jar from the inside pocket. Hartley recognized it as the salve he had used at the inn. "It worked when you used it on me, so I thought . . ." His dark skin flushed to a deeper color.

"Thank you," Hartley said, taking the jar. He made fast work of his cravat, tugged off his trousers, pulled the shirt over his head, and then he was bare. Sam's eyes were wide, his fingers pressed hard into the brocade of the armchair, and he looked at Hartley as if he were trying to memorize the sight. Hartley stood beside the matching chair, a few feet away. He had given this some little thought while stripping. If Sam wanted to watch, Hartley was going to put on a show. But he wasn't going to make himself ridiculous. Not that there was a way to bugger oneself with dignity—dignity was quite a moot point now that he was standing naked on his hearthrug. But he wasn't bending over the sofa and going at himself. If he was going to do this, he was going to do it beautifully, which probably meant he was compounding perversions with vanity, but so be it.

He sat, slinging one leg over the arm of his chair and tucking his other foot up beside him. He was totally on display, and when he saw Sam shift in his seat, he knew he had achieved precisely the reaction he sought. His own prick started to harden at the idea of what he might look like, what it must feel like for Sam to be able to look but not touch. He took the glass prick and teased it down his length, and heard Sam mutter an oath. Good. He needed to know that Sam liked what he saw. He spread his legs a bit further and brought the cock to the sensitive skin beneath his bollocks. It was cold, and very hard, and altogether nothing like a real cock, which was good because Hartley would have shied at a real cock. This was different, and Sam didn't want anything that Hartley hadn't freely offered.

When he scooped out some salve, spreading some on the cold glass and some on his skin, Sam loosened his neck-cloth. Hartley pushed inside himself with the tip of one finger and flinched a little at the sensation. It had been a very long time since he had touched himself this way, and even longer since anyone else had. He managed another finger, but this angle was terrible, so he lined the glass cock up with his entrance.

"Hartley," Sam breathed. He was fully hard, Hartley could tell, but he still hadn't moved his hands from the arms of the chair. "You're beautiful." He said it as if he were watching Hartley do something wonderful. As if there was nothing profane about this. Maybe there wasn't.

When he got the tip of the cock inside him, he had a moment of panic, but he made his body relax and accept the intrusion, and it slid in. "Oh God." He had been exaggerating when he called it enormous; in truth it was no larger than the average prick, but it felt quite sufficiently gigantic at the moment. It always felt like too much, he recalled, and that was part of what he liked about this act, the sense of being stretched and filled, the bite of pain that came along with the pleasure. This was what he had wanted. He twisted the cock to search out the spot that would make him feel like he was about to reach his crisis, and when he found it he moaned. Sam let out a choked sound and gripped the arms of his chair so tightly the muscles bulged beneath the thin cloth of his shirt. That was when Hartley stopped putting on a show and started . . . something else.

"Are you imagining that it's you inside me?" he asked, his voice thready and low.

Sam cleared his throat. "No. This is you. You're doing this. And I'm watching the most gorgeously filthy thing I've seen in my life." He ran a finger beneath his collar. "Because you're letting me."

Oh God, why did he have to be so good? It would be easier if he didn't always know what to say. Then Hartley might have some defenses left. As it was, his heart was as bare as his body, and it was too late to go back.

"I'm imagining it's you," he whispered, because at that moment it was true. He was imagining what it would be like to have Sam inside him, to share this pleasure equally. He imagined what it would be like to be able to have that. Not only the touching, but all of it—knowing how to care about a person, and how to let a person care about oneself. He tried to stroke himself, but his hands were shaking and he couldn't get it right. "Would you—" He swallowed, not able to form the words. "Help me, Sam."

Sam was on his feet at once, only pausing when he reached Hartley's chair. "You mean it?" Hartley was naked, open, doing unspeakable things to himself with a glass prick and still Sam didn't touch him without asking.

"Please," he said, his mouth dry. He reached for Sam's trousers, but Sam batted his hand away and got to his knees. Hartley nodded, because he didn't have any more words, and Sam bent his head. The feel of Sam's mouth on him, the feel of—oh God—that thing he was twisting inside Hartley's body, it was so much, and it was so good, that Hartley let his pleasure crest. He held Sam's head, calling out his name while spilling into his mouth.

"I'm sorry, I didn't mean to—" Hartley was babbling.

"Shh." Sam wiped his mouth against the back of his hand, then carefully removed the glass prick and put it aside.

"Let me touch you?" Hartley asked.

"Anything you want." There was something in Sam's face that made Hartley's stomach do a flip. "Always."

Hartley dropped to the floor beside him, tore open his trousers, and had his hands wrapped around him, hard and warm and all Sam. Sam hissed and swore and lay back to let Hartley have his way. Hartley licked and touched and in general gave him every bit of attention that a man could bestow on another man with a willing mouth and a pair of slick hands, because that was the least he could do.

"We have to eat downstairs," Hartley said after they had gotten cleaned up. "In the housekeeper's room. Otherwise Sadie and Alf have to go to a lot of trouble."

Sam imagined that servants generally went to a good deal of trouble, because that was the point of servants, but didn't question why Hartley seemed averse to this. Indeed, Sam would have eaten in a ditch, or on the roof, or just about anywhere Hartley required, and was baffled that Hartley didn't seem to know this.

So they went downstairs to the housekeeper's room and ate roast partridges and drank warm cider. It was perhaps the strangest company Sam had broken bread amongst: a disgraced gentleman, his cockney manservant, an exceedingly pregnant and unmarried cook, and himself, a black pugilist turned barman. Conversation oughtn't to have come easily but somehow it did.

When Sam put on his coat and reached for his hat, the servants made themselves scarce, which more or less confirmed that they knew what Sam and Hartley had been about upstairs.

"Come to the Bell tomorrow," Sam whispered, not sure why he was being quiet, except that they were standing so near to one another that a normal speaking voice would be too loud. They were still in the kitchen, near the back door that Sam would soon leave through, but neither of them were making any move to actually open the door.

"I'm not sure I can ever show my face there again, after

that errand Kate ran for you." But he was smiling, if a little shyly.

"Nah, in Kate's mind that's the sort of thing every gentleman ought to have at his bedside."

Hartley snorted and looked up at Sam. Sam wondered why until now he hadn't fully appreciated their height difference. Maybe it was because they seldom stood this close. If they stood any closer, Hartley's head might tuck neatly beneath Sam's chin. Sam found that he wanted very much to find out whether it would.

"Hartley?" Sam asked when they had been standing there for several minutes saying nothing of importance.

"Yes, Sam?"

"Thanks for tonight."

Hartley's pale eyes sparkled in the dim light. "I ought to thank you. For my present." He stood on his toes and kissed Sam's cheek. "I'll thank you for not making jokes about relevant body parts," he murmured.

Sam was hardly capable of speech, let alone humor. The soft brush of Hartley's lips against the stubble of his cheek was somehow more intimate, more precious, than anything they had shared before.

CHAPTER EIGHTEEN

It had been months since there was a proper fight at the Bell, but Sam supposed all good things came to an end. Right when he thought the place was on the edge of becoming decently respectable, Alf had gotten into it with some drunk. Sam had stepped between the two bloody oafs to break them up, but not before a chair was broken and a good deal of ale spilt. Some idiot threw open the door and shouted into the street that a rare good fight was on at the Bell, and the constable appeared moments later. Sam spent the next hour repeatedly explaining that it had been a regular taproom brawl, not a prizefight. Merton had demanded to see the Bell's license and insisted on inspecting the tankards to make sure they were the regulation volume. Sam's heart raced and his palms grew damp despite knowing that everything was in order.

"The second time in a month," the constable said, a smirk of satisfaction on his meaty red face. Ever since that dustup with Johnny Newton, Constable Merton had been prowling about the Bell every day, waiting for someone to put a foot out of line. This put a damper on the mood of easy comfort Sam had tried to cultivate at the Bell. "But I know there's prizefighting and gambling on the premises, and I mean to shut you down."

The man was a fool as well as a bastard. To anyone who knew the first thing about prizefighting, it would have been immediately clear that there was no boxing at the Bell. There were no bookmakers prowling about the edges of the crowd. The air smelled of meat pie, hops, and smoke from the bad chimney, not the blood and sweat of men fighting for their lives. And, frankly, if Sam had taken to organizing fights, he was pretty sure he'd have a bigger crowd than what he could fit inside the Bell.

"I saw one of your customers—" the constable put a nasty inflection on that last word that made Sam suspect he was referring to one of the black patrons "—collecting penny bets."

Sam suppressed a groan. That was Mrs. McCaffrey, not a bookmaker. She also collected bets on things like whether Nick would make pork pie or kidney pie. It was all innocent. And they weren't penny bets so much as farthing bets. "I don't allow bookmakers at the Bell," he said.

Most of the customers weren't bothered by either the fight or the constable's questions. Two men had picked up their mugs and moved to a table far away from the brawlers. While Sam dealt with the constable, Nick poured fresh pints for the people whose drinks had gone flying during the mayhem. All told, it hadn't been as bad as it could have been, but it reminded him of how little he liked having anything to do with the police.

The constable left with vague threats of returning the next day. Sam suspected nothing would happen; the man had only wanted to throw his weight around and frighten Sam. And he'd succeeded—Sam knew he'd worry about it for days. He closed the door behind the last of the patrons, reached for his broom, and started sweeping up the splinters of wood from the broken chair. He was interrupted by a knock on the door.

It was Alf. He had wiped the blood off his face, but he'd wake up tomorrow with a proper black eye. "You. Go home," Sam said sternly. "You've done enough for one night."

"I came to apologize." Alf scuffed his toe along the stone floor.

Sam grunted an acknowledgment and handed the broom to Alf so he could sweep up. While the lad swept, Sam grabbed two clean tankards, poured a couple of pints, and handed one to Alf.

"You get into a lot of fights?" Sam asked.

"Long story," the lad said, averting his eyes from Sam.

"How long?"

"The bastard was talking about Sadie."

"Ah." Sam figured as much.

"Don't suppose you have any pie left?"

Sam laughed despite himself. Trust a boy that age to never have thoughts of food far from his mind. "No, we ran out hours ago."

"Rats. Sadie and his nibs like the pork pie your brother

does. And I thought to bring them some to distract them from the, ah . . ." He gestured to the bruise on his face.

Sam pressed the cool pewter against his aching head. "My brother's been manning the kitchen on his own since my mum died. He can't keep up."

Alf nodded, as if considering the problem. "So you're looking to hire help."

Sam snorted. "That's well down the list of things I need to get done around here."

Alf took a long drink of his ale and studied Sam over the rim of the cup. "I'd do it, you know. Help out around here, I mean."

Sam shot the lad a sharp glance. "I thought you were happy in your position." Working in a pub would be a step down in the world for a gentleman's manservant: longer hours and harder work for what he guessed was about half the pay.

"I don't want to be a bloody valet."

"But you do want to be a barman?" Sam asked skeptically.

"It would suit me better than ironing cravats and polishing boots. And I bet he'd agree."

"He? You mean Mr. Sedgwick?" It felt strange to refer to Hartley in this way. It made Sam feel as if he ought to have been doing so all along, and all the whispered "Hartleys" had been somehow fraudulent. The man had servants, a fine house, a pile of money. Sam was the owner of a barely respectable pub.

"There's no way he'll keep on a servant who gets into scrapes. You should have seen the way he looked at me the last time I came home with a black eye. He and Sadie both. You'd have thought I was something that crawled out of the bogs."

Sam guessed that Alf was exaggerating, and that any reaction from Hartley or Sadie owed more to the circumstances surrounding Alf's fights than it did with the fact that he had been brawling. But he also knew that pointing this out wouldn't convince Alf of anything he didn't want to believe. Sam had a hard time believing it himself—he could imagine Hartley wrinkling his nose disdainfully at the idea of bloodshed or unruliness.

"Did you put anything cold on that eye?" Sam asked, and when the lad shook his head, he went to the back room to see if there was a slab of meat in the larder he could use.

He and Alf weren't terribly different. They were both products of the East London streets, with the difference that Sam had the advantage of a somewhat profitable talent and Alf had the advantage of his skin. Sam was freshly appalled that he was going to bed with this boy's employer. Hartley claimed not to have been raised a gentleman, but his brother had been a naval officer and his godfather had been a lord. He was enough of a gentleman to be miles away from Sam and Alf's experience. All of that was so easy to lose sight of when they were together. But there was no future for them, and it was best for Sam to get that through his skull before he got in any deeper.

"**Y**ou got robbed," Sadie said when she looked at the haddock Hartley had procured and heard what he spent.

"I wasn't going to haggle with the fishmonger. I have a bit of extra cash at hand and I daresay the fishmonger doesn't." Hartley had determined to take over the household marketing for the time being. Alf had once again gotten into fisticuffs with some boy who maligned Sadie's fair name, and the quantity of tears and recrimination that Hartley had endured in the aftermath had been quite enough to last a lifetime. He was entirely willing to overpay for haddock if it meant domestic peace.

Sadie shook her head and went back to stirring the pot. "That'll drive prices up for everybody else. It's extravagant."

"If you want to see extravagance, feast your eyes on this." He dashed upstairs, returning with a cherrywood box. Nestled inside was a silver christening cup he had purchased during an afternoon of going from jeweler to silversmith, searching for the most lavishly useless baby present he could turn up.

"What in hell is a baby going to do with that?" Alf asked, peering over Sadie's shoulder. He had a ghastly bruise on his eye that Hartley was trying to pretend he hadn't noticed.

"Nothing, I should hope," Hartley said. "I gather that the point of these things is that they can be easily sold down the line, either by the child when she's grown or by the parents if they hit a rough patch." Hartley wasn't entirely certain, not having been raised in a household where babies—or anybody else—had precious baubles. But it seemed a prudent practice to give a child something to hock later on, and meanwhile the cup was pretty, so Hartley approved.

"Bless me." Sadie stared at the cup as if it were a holy relic.

"My sister and I had a pair of those silver sauceboats that are meant to feed babies. Of course nobody used them," she said. "They sat on a shelf in the best parlor. I ought to have taken mine away when I ran off, I suppose."

"You didn't run off," Alf pointed out. "And you didn't have a chance to take anything with you."

"This is too fine for—" She gestured at her belly. "It's not right for me to have it. I can't accept." She pushed the silver cup across the table and her eyes filled with tears.

"It's not for you. It's for the baby," Hartley said. "No, that's not true. It's for you too. You said yourself that you had something like this. Surely it's proper for your own child to have such a thing."

"This baby will be the bastard of a disgraced lady and a married man. It's hardly the same."

"Indeed it's not." Over the past weeks Sadie had supplied Hartley with the essential details: she had been seduced by a handsome young soldier who promptly abandoned her, she refused to marry whatever ghastly suitor her parents had supplied to remedy the situation, and her parents had turned her out. "You were dealt a bad hand, Sadie. But what would you need to make the most of it? I'm certain you don't want to be my cook for the rest of your life."

"It's not a dream come true, but the work I do for you isn't any different from what I did for my parents, the main difference being that you pay me and don't call me names. And you don't think worse of me for this." She gestured again to her belly, but this time let her hand linger there. "Also, now I have my own kitchen with a proper range and it's glorious. Well, I suppose it's your kitchen," she said, looking at Hartley.

"No," Hartley said. "It's yours. And so is that christening cup." He felt insistent that she take that cup, that she and her child have what would have been theirs if the world were fair and right. He wasn't such a ninny that he believed in fairness, and at this point he didn't even know if he believed in ladies and gentlemen. This muddle-headed thinking was what came of associating with the likes of Will, he supposed. All he knew was that he cared for Sadie and wanted to make things right for her.

Sadie looked down. "I couldn't go back to Devon and I wouldn't want to. Now, try this and tells me if it needs salt." She blew on a spoonful of some kind of gravy or sauce and held it out for Hartley to taste. "It's béchamel sauce for the haddock."

"It's delicious," he assured her. It was velvety and rich. "Fit for a king. Everything you make is superb." He had tepidly appreciated the finest delicacies prepared by skilled French chefs in the grandest houses, but he found that he actively craved the simple dishes Sadie made. It had taken him days to realize this was hunger, and to wonder how long he had lived without it.

They'd share the haddock with Alf, eating together in Sadie's little parlor, three people who ought never to have found themselves around the same table. He looked forward to these suppers more than he had any elegant dinner. Admitting this to himself felt like releasing something he had held clenched in his fist for so long that he had forgotten it was there, and he didn't know if he was casting off a burden or losing a prize. Thus far, he was a disgraced gentleman. But if he carried on like this, dining with his servants and purchasing his own haddock, he'd be something else entirely. While he knew that being a gentleman wasn't all he had once believed, he didn't know what would be left of his life if he renounced all claims to gentility.

"Everything I cook here turns out better than it did at home," Sadie said, tasting the sauce herself and adding a sprinkle of something green. "Partly it's the range. But I think it's also because things taste better when you aren't miserable."

"I see," Hartley said. Was it possible that he had been miserable until now? He didn't think so. He had been frozen, insensible to both pleasure and pain. If so, presently he was thawing, and the process was as strange as sensation returning to a frostbitten limb, and it left him feeling peculiarly vulnerable.

He absently fingered the top button of his waistcoat, feeling the cool smooth ivory beneath his bare skin. His dress, his manners, his reserve—they were his only defenses, cultivated to put as much distance as possible between the world and his true self. He knew other people might think him an affected snob, but the alternative was walking around in a terrifying state of exposure. Some of those defenses he had cast aside to be with Sam; he had a grim suspicion that he'd have to cast aside yet more if they were to go on. That would mean rendering himself vulnerable in a way that he doubted he could tolerate. He didn't even know who he would be without the fortress of his house and the outward signs of wealth and status, and he doubted he'd give them up, not even for Sam.

CHAPTER NINETEEN

Hartley dressed with his typical fastidiousness, but with a different goal than usual.

"Leave off the cravat," Alf said, coming up behind him. Hartley spun away from the looking glass to face the lad. The bruise under one eye had darkened to a painful-looking wine-colored blotch, ringed with pale green. Hartley winced whenever he saw it.

"Why in heaven's name would I go out without a cravat?"

"Because it's past ten and you have on your oldest breeches and a pair of boots I haven't gotten to polishing yet. And I don't know where you got that coat but I'm selling it at the stalls tomorrow and keeping the money myself. You don't look like a man who's up to any good, and men who are interested in late-night crimes against nature don't need to wear cravats. Also, you might spare me the trouble of pressing and starching them."

"I wasn't aware that I'm ever up to any good." Hartley brushed some lint off the sleeve of the coat he had borrowed from Will. At least he hoped it was merely lint. "And I'm not engaging in crimes against nature this evening." He had in mind an entirely different kind of criminal venture.

"Now I really am worried," Alf said.

Hartley nearly told him, but he didn't want to risk the boy deciding to come along. Sadie was nearing the point where Hartley didn't like to leave her alone, even though Kate had assured him that babies didn't arrive on the scene without ample warning. He unwound the neckcloth and rolled it neatly before putting it back in the drawer. "Nothing to worry about," he said. "I need to run an errand to retrieve something that's mine."

"Sounds like breaking and entering."

Hartley waved a dismissive hand. He had given Philpott a week and still had not heard a word from the solicitor. Hartley decided he had been more than generous, and would now search the solicitor's chambers. He hadn't quite worked through the details of how this might work, but he was willing to learn as he went.

"Do you have a pistol?" Alf asked. "A knife?" Hartley shook his head. "A stocking filled with rocks? Anything?"

"I'm breaking into an empty building, not holding up carriages on the Ratcliffe Highway," Hartley said quellingly. "I don't need to be armed."

"Right, because people take kindly to their homes being broken into. They'll step aside and let you have your way. Robbing people is famously easy."

"I said empty. And it's not a home. Rather a place of business. And I'm not robbing it, so much as restoring objects to my possession." He needed his painting in the same way he had needed to give Sadie that silver cup. It was a matter of justice. Not revenge, not petty spite. It was his, and he meant to have it. When he thought of that painting, even the fact of its existence, he thought of himself as a vulnerable idiot of a boy. "Look, I mean to do this, so leave off."

Alf was silent for a moment. "I think this may not be an area of your expertise, mate."

"Be that as it may, it's none of your concern."

"Leave me some money so I can bring you supper at New-gate."

"Piss off."

Alf did piss off, leaving Hartley to fuss over his cuffs and find a hat that covered his hair as thoroughly as possible. Having yellow hair was a powerful detriment to a life of crime, he was realizing.

He pulled his hat low on his forehead and went out into the mews behind his house.

Sam cleared his throat and knew a small satisfaction when Hartley startled and then spun to face him. He had been waiting in the shadows since Alf fetched him, hoping the boy had been wrong about Hartley's intentions.

It had been a long day of dealing with shiftless chimney sweeps, that sodding bastard of a constable, an entire delivery of porter that had gone sour, and a surprise visit from the landlord, who had cheerfully mentioned that with all the work Sam had done, he could probably let the premises to a new tenant for a tidy sum. By the time Sam closed the Bell for the night, he felt the weight of every burden he had taken on. But when he heard pounding on the door, he opened it anyway. There he found Alf sweating and out of breath, saying that Hartley was about to do something foolish. Sam hadn't even paused to deliberate; he simply turned the key in the lock and followed Alf to Mayfair.

"What are you doing here?" Hartley asked.

"Alf told me you were up to no good."

"And you came to stop me?"

Any hope Sam had that Alf might have been wrong vanished with Hartley's words. "Depends on what you're planning to do."

"I'm going to Easterbrook's solicitor's office to search for those paintings." His chin was tilted up, as if he really thought his plan was above reproach.

"Why didn't you tell me? I thought we were in this together."

"No, I told you I'd send word if I found Kate's painting, not that I'd bring you along on every felony I commit." He pulled the cap off his head and ran his hand through his hair. "I'm not putting you in harm's way again, and that's final."

The brisk certainty in his voice touched Sam—he suspected Hartley cared about him, but he hadn't ever said so. Hearing the man say he didn't want to expose Sam to danger was the closest they had gotten to overt declarations. It struck Sam that this wasn't enough, and that he was selling himself short to settle for something so paltry. "But you'll put yourself in harm's way, will you? With no regard at all for the feelings of people who don't want to see you arrested or clubbed on the head as a trespasser?" he demanded. "Why?"

"Why?" Hartley repeated, incredulous. "Is that really something you need to ask? I thought you understood. You were the one who came to me looking for Kate's portrait in the first place."

The faint moonlight slanted across Hartley's face. He looked young and vulnerable. Sam could have gone to him, gathered him close, and confessed that he understood futile anger as well as anyone on earth. But that wouldn't do either of them any good, so he shoved his hands in his pockets and stayed where he was. "You could get those paintings. Hell, you could burn the solicitor's building to the ground, and it still wouldn't undo what happened to you. The old man is dead, and you can't—"

"I know that," Hartley spat. "I'm not stupid. I know I can't have a proper revenge, I know I can't undo what was done, but this is all I can have, so it's what I'm going after."

Sam felt a desperate helplessness pooling in his gut. He didn't know if he had the words to explain himself to Hartley, and doubted that it would do any good anyway, but he had to try. "I care about your safety. I care about you. Doesn't that count for anything? I won't be able to sleep tonight if I'm imagining you shot dead or in a prison cell."

"People face dangerous situations every day," Hartley had the nerve to say.

"Some people have no choice, Hartley." He thought of how he had encouraged Davey to take part in a game he knew could be his death. He couldn't let someone else walk right into danger. "But you're choosing this. Life is hard enough, and here you are borrowing trouble."

Hartley fell silent. "The fact that you don't see my reason is . . . disappointing." His voice was small, his arms crossed over his chest.

Sam stepped closer. "I understand why, Hart. I just wish you cared for yourself as much as I do. I wish you cared for anything as much as I care for you."

Hartley looked up at him and for a moment Sam thought he'd close the gap, fall into Sam's arms. Anything. Instead he shook his head and went back inside, closing the door behind him. At least that meant he wasn't going off to get himself arrested tonight. Sam waited in the cold and the dark until his feet went numb in his boots, then turned homeward.

Hartley was aware that he wasn't being entirely rational. Some vital knack for self-preservation had gotten knocked loose from his brain now that he couldn't hide, now that the option of secrecy and safety had been taken away from him. He heard Sam's words, knew Sam was correct, and at the same time knew he was going to break into Philpott's office to search for those paintings. Not tonight, but soon. And this time he'd make sure Sam didn't find out.

The sensible thing would be to put on his dressing gown, have something warm to eat, go to bed at a reasonable hour, and maybe see if when he woke the next morning he felt better. But he didn't think he could stand his own company tonight. Alf was out and Sadie had gone to bed early. So he changed his clothes and went back outside, this time heading north and east, avoiding both the Bell and Philpott's offices, and went to a part of the city he usually had no reason to visit. As he walked, the streets narrowed and the symmetrical facades of Mayfair gave way to a ramshackle hodgepodge of houses that seemed at risk of falling into one another. Lean dogs and hungry children peered out from the shadows. He climbed a rickety wooden staircase that seemed to be stuck to the outside of a narrow building with nothing more than years of grime.

"If you won't come stay with me," he said when Will answered the door, "at least tell me why you won't let me give you enough money to hire a better set of rooms."

"There's nothing wrong with my lodgings." Will opened the door wider, letting Hartley in.

It wasn't horrible. In fact, it wasn't that much shabbier than the house where they had grown up. Chipped plaster, bits of damp on the ceiling and walls, the pervasive smell of vague unwholesomeness. "Certainly. If you're a mouse, that is. I daresay all manner of vermin are quite comfortable here."

Will didn't answer. He had a lot of practice ignoring Hartley's minor tantrums. "I'll put on my coat and we'll go get a pint."

"It just doesn't seem fair that you're living like this while I'm living in comparative luxury."

A rare smile spread across Will's face. "We'll make a radical of you yet, Hart."

"Ha. I mean because you're my brother I don't feel right about your living like this. I have more than I need, and I want to share it." Strictly speaking, this wasn't true: when he had sold off the silver epergnes and jewel-encrusted snuff boxes that littered the Brook Street house, he had been left with enough capital to invest in projects that interested him—first a pottery in Staffordshire, then a series of canals. But lately he had been toying with the idea of cashing out those investments and doing something else. He hadn't only been bluffing when he told Philpott that he had a good deal of money and nothing to do with it. Perhaps he could use it to help Will.

"I don't want your money." Will proceeded to shake some dust off a coat.

Hartley's spine stiffened. "I see."

Will looked at him for a long moment, one sleeve in his coat and one out of it. "Because I don't believe in having more than I need, not because of how you got your money, you gudgeon. You shagged some fellow to help your family. Nothing wrong with that as far as I care. For some reason he left you his house. Those aren't connected."

Hartley goggled at him. "Of course they're connected. Everybody knows that. Why else would he have left it to me?"

"Maybe to punish the person who would have gotten it otherwise? Maybe to embarrass you both?" Hartley must have looked as shocked as he felt. "You hadn't thought of that, had you?" Will asked. "Easterbrook rarely bothered to pay his bills. Do you really think he'd leave you an entire house to you as compensation?"

"Why would he have wanted to punish Martin?" Hartley knew why Easterbrook would have wanted to embarrass Hartley himself. But Martin was his son and heir.

"Because he didn't care much for Martin." Will was now fully, if unsatisfactorily, dressed, and he took the single step required to cross the cramped room and open the door. "You do remember that, don't you?" When Hartley didn't answer, he raised an eyebrow. "You don't, do you?"

"I don't remember him being a fond parent," Hartley said slowly.

Will snorted. "You and Ben were so busy thinking about money and schooling and leaks in the roof, you missed everything else."

Hartley decided not to point out that Ben had kept them warm and fed when nobody else could be bothered, and that money, education, and functional roofs were matters well worth considering. "I see," he said gravely. It was oddly thrilling to think that maybe the house wasn't something he had acquired through greed but rather had foisted on him due to an old man's ill will. The house had always seemed to have meaning set into its mortar, but now that significance had shifted. Will's words had shaken the cobwebs loose from a certain corner of his mind, something to do with the paintings, and assets, and blackmail, but he couldn't quite put it all together now. "Have you seen Martin?" he asked when they had descended the stairs and reached the street.

Will shoved his hands into his pockets. "Not since the summer. Ben wrote that Martin planned to go to the Continent, and I haven't heard anything since." They turned into a lane. "I feel certain he's dead."

Hartley startled, not from the news—he would not be shedding any tears over Martin Easterbrook, dead or alive—

but from the grief in his brother's voice. "Why do you think he's dead?"

"Because if he were alive he wouldn't have left me without a word. He'd know I'd worry myself half mad. Every day that passes I become more convinced that he must have died."

Hartley tentatively squeezed his brother's arm. When they got to the public house, Hartley ordered two pints and paid for them before Will could put any money on the bar.

It had been dark in Will's rooms, and it was only marginally brighter at the table they sat at, but now Hartley could see the shadows under his brother's eyes, the weariness in his face. He was habitually disheveled, but tonight he was more unkempt than usual. He hadn't shaved in the last fortnight and the less said about his hair the better. Will periodically went into what Hartley thought of as a decline and Ben called an episode. He didn't sleep, barely ate, forgot to write whatever he was meant to for those horrid publications, and was forced to seek even more dismal lodgings than before. During one terrifying period the year before, he had turned to opium to calm whatever trouble roiled inside him.

Hartley tamped down a surge of panic. "Have you been eating?" he asked, noticing that Will's coat was now ill fitting in a new and troubling way. Hartley knew his brother had his reasons for these episodes; Will had served in the navy under an infamously cruel captain, and while he hadn't volunteered any information, Hartley read the report of a fellow officer's court martial, and gathered that the conditions on board ship had been grim in the extreme.

"Yes," Will said, looking thoughtful, as if trying to recollect his last meal, or what meals even were. "I do eat. From time to time."

"Right. Do they have supper here?"

Will gave a ghost of a smile. "If they did, you wouldn't want to eat it, and neither would I."

Glancing around, Hartley had to agree. This place stank of stale beer and had more damp than Will's lodgings. "You really ought to go to the Bell. They have excellent pork pie." For a moment, he considered taking Will there presently, but it was too late for them to have any supper left. "I'm sorry about Martin." Hartley had already reconciled himself to the probability that Martin was merely a prig, not a villain. Hartley could accept his brother's friendship with a prig. "I do hope he isn't dead." That ought to have been a ludicrously inadequate sentiment, but Will nodded solemnly, so Hartley thought that perhaps he hadn't missed the mark.

"Hart, I'm grieving him, but I don't have a body to bury." His voice cracked on the last words.

"He may be well," Hartley offered weakly.

"And if he's alive, then what I'm grieving is a friendship that isn't what I thought it was."

Hartley drew in a sharp breath at this acknowledgment. "If you see him . . ." Hartley paused in disbelief that he was going to say this. "If you see him and he needs anything, can you pretend to have saved up—really anybody who looks at you will believe that you don't spend much—and then quietly take some of my money to give him? I mean, don't tell him it's from me. You can say you stole it from the prime minister or some Tory lord."

"I don't lie to Martin, but if he's alive I might take you up on your offer. Uh, thanks, Hart. Decent of you."

Hartley waved this away. "I know you don't like coming to my house, but I have a very good cook who is bored of cooking only for me. I happen to know she has a massive gourd and a brace of partridges, and probably some other things besides that she's planning to cook for tomorrow's supper. It's a lot for one person, but if I don't sit down for supper, she and Alf won't eat anything themselves."

Will stared at him for a moment. "Very well," he said finally. "I'll oblige your cook by eating her supper."

"Oh, also we have to eat in the kitchen because almost all my servants quit and I don't like to make too much work."

Will opened his mouth and then shut it again. "I was going to ask if you wanted to come with me to the next meeting of the Hampden Club, but perhaps you'd like to be the speaker."

"Shut up, you. I'll have nothing to do with your radicals." But Hartley couldn't stop himself from smiling.

Chapter Twenty

Hartley returned home to find Sadie in the kitchen, surrounded by about twenty pans of various sizes, two cloth-covered lumps of what he supposed was rising dough, and cuts of meat in assorted stages of preparation. The kitchen looked like a mess hall.

"Is anything amiss?" he ventured.

"No," she bit out. A few strands of dark hair were coming down from her cap and her apron was askew. This was the first time since the night of her arrival that he had seen her even slightly disordered.

"Where's Alf?" He had specifically told Alf not to leave Sadie alone.

"Gone to get Mistress Bradley."

"Miss . . ." It took him a moment to understand that Mistress Bradley meant Kate. "Is it . . . um . . ." He gestured to Sadie's stomach. He had never gestured to anyone's midsection as often as he had since Sadie entered his household and it filled him with dread rather than relief that the reason for this delicacy was about to make its appearance.

She nodded curtly and resumed stirring what appeared to be a blancmange.

"Are you quite certain this is the time to prepare dinner?"

"Mr. Sedgwick," she snipped. "I started these dishes earlier in the day with the hope that you and Alf might not starve during my lying in. If you'd rather I abandon my efforts and take to my bed, I can arrange for that."

"Ah, no. Carry on," he said quickly. "Thank you. Perhaps you'll let me stir that pot while you attend to the goose?"

She turned away and gripped the edge of the table while Hartley looked on helplessly, then resumed plucking the goose. Hartley stirred the pot fervently.

"Can I get you anything?" Hartley asked after the third iteration of this pattern of table-gripping followed by furious goose-plucking. Sadie shook her head.

When Kate arrived with Alf in tow, Hartley fully expected her to take control of the situation. Instead, she watched Sadie for about half a minute, then gathered a basket of parsnips to peel. When Alf saw this, he whimpered. "You're not going to do anything?" he asked.

"How old are you?" Kate asked.

"Eighteen this summer." Hartley rather thought Alf meant this coming summer, but refrained from mentioning this.

"You can tell me how to do my job when you're thirty and you've helped deliver over two hundred babies." That got a choked laugh from Sadie. "Meanwhile, go get a cask of stout brown ale, the darker the better."

Hartley fished some coins out of his purse to give Alf for the purchase, then resumed stirring the pot. An hour later, the motley array of pots and dishes had transformed itself into the beginnings of a minor feast, Hartley had learned that chopping a turnip involved taking one's life into one's own hands, and Sadie was still puttering about in the kitchen.

"I think we're about done," Kate said with an air of finality.

"There's the washing up." Sadie's hands were wrapped tightly around a heavy wooden spoon and her voice was choked. She looked very, very young.

"Alf can wash up when he gets back," Hartley suggested.

"Or you can do it now," Kate chirped, then put an arm around Sadie's waist and led her to her bedchamber.

Before Hartley had finished the dishes, Alf returned, rolling a cask of ale before him. He looked half sick with nerves. Hartley wasn't sure what Kate intended the ale for, but looking at Alf, he reasoned some of it could be spared toward putting the lad's mind at ease. "It doesn't have a tap on it," Hartley said, walking around the cask.

"They don't come with taps, mate," Alf said patiently. "You have to put them in."

"I know they don't come that way," Hartley said, slightly indignant. "I just assumed that in London ale was sold with taps already on the barrel." As he said the words, he realized why he had made that error. So did Alf, evidently.

"That's because you've had a servant since you came here."

"I'm aware of that," he bit out.

"A whole house full of servants, even. You know your floors don't sweep themselves, either, right?"

Hartley, who at the moment was elbow deep in dishwater, knew that Alf was taking the piss rather than accusing him of being too fine for work. "I'm also aware that there isn't another employer in London who would put up with this kind of insubordination," he managed.

"Nah, you like it. You were always on edge when the house was filled with proper servants. You like this better."

With all the force of an epiphany, Hartley realized that Alf was right. He did like this better. He was happier doing the marketing and helping Sadie in the kitchen than he was sitting in state upstairs and being waited on. He enjoyed the company of Alf and Sadie more than that of anyone he had met before his disgrace. This was likely some perversity of his own nature. But he also knew that he was beginning to view his few years of life as a gentleman as an aberration from the norm, a strange holiday in the land of the rich and idle. Doing the washing up felt like coming home.

A sound came from Sadie's bedroom. Hartley and Alf locked alarmed gazes. "At the moment I don't care if I have to pry that cask open with my hands, but we're each having a pint. Now," he commanded.

Alf nodded, his eyes wide, then rummaged around in the still room before emerging with a tap.

"Ought we to go upstairs?" Hartley asked dubiously. "To give them some privacy?"

"If you're asking me, you must really be lost."

"Well, obviously I'm lost, Alfred," Hartley said tartly. "I

hardly know what the protocol is when one's housekeeper is experiencing a blessed event and one is drinking copiously in the kitchen with one's valet."

"Who are you calling a valet?" Alf's speech was slightly slurred.

"Frankly I don't know what to call you."

"I told your friend Sam that I'd like work at the Bell."

Hartley stilled. "Is that what you want?"

"No offense but I'm bored off my arse here. And you're going to need to decide whether you're running a proper establishment—" those were Sadie's words, Hartley guessed "—or if you want the likes of me sewing on your buttons."

Hartley had already started to suspect he couldn't go on indefinitely with this odd living arrangement. It was one thing for a man to live in lodgings and have a very bad servant, but to live in a grand house that was half shut up and almost entirely unstaffed was peculiar indeed. It would ultimately draw more attention than he wished. But Hartley doubted Alf was concerned with keeping up appearances, and wondered what had gotten the boy thinking about this. "Why do I need to decide?" he asked.

"It might make life easier for certain people who are used to life being a bit more settled."

"Are you one of those people?" Hartley asked skeptically.

Alf shot him a weary smile that made him look far older than his years. "No, mate."

"And I don't suppose we're talking about Sadie, either."

Alf shook his head.

"What does Sam care what kind of house I keep?"

"It's not about your house. But for a regular person like him to take up with a rich man looks a certain way."

"I beg your—He's never said anything of the sort to me," Hartley protested. "You don't know what you're talking about."

"Maybe not. But here you are with your house and your cravats, gold coins falling out of your pockets—"

"Alfred, you are drunk." He snatched the cup of ale away from the boy.

"Look, all I'm saying is that if I were to take up with a person, I'd want them to be my equal. Otherwise one person holds all the cards and it might start to seem more like the sort of thing I did at the docks and you did upstairs."

Hartley sucked in a breath. He had to bear in mind that Alf was very young, and was likely letting his own experience color his judgment. "I should never have let you drink half this much," Hartley managed, feeling his cheeks flame. "It seems the wildest flight of fancy on your part to imagine that any of this piddle has occurred to Sam. He's a decent-minded person."

"Oh mate." Alf shook his head. "You have a bad case of it."

"If he any reservations along those lines, he hasn't said a single word about it."

"What could he say about it? Oh Mr. Sedgwick, please renounce all your worldly goods so we can live in beautiful and noble squalor together." He said this last sentence in a slightly mincing tone that Hartley suspected was supposed to be an imitation of his own accents.

"Utterly foxed," Hartley muttered. But still, he suspected Alf was partly right, in that a person of Hartley's class could hardly manage a lasting friendship with a person of a different background, let alone something more than a friendship. This, he told himself, was a point of merely theoretical interest: Sam surely was not looking for anything more complicated or enduring than their current arrangement. Hartley was perpetually struck with amazement that Sam wanted him around at all.

The night dragged interminably. Hartley filled Alf's cup until the lad fell asleep in his chair, then proceeded to clean the kitchen. When the pots were scoured and the surfaces wiped, he was left with nothing to do, so he cleaned it all again. Muffled noises were coming from Sadie's bedchamber and none of them sounded in the least promising.

"Don't leave her," Hartley said the second time Kate entered the kitchen in search of clean linens and broth for Sadie. "If you need something, shout for me and I'll get it. Just don't leave her."

Kate tilted her head. "She's strong, you know."

"I do know. But she shouldn't be alone. She ought to have her mother or her sister." Not a confused employer and a snoring boy. "She deserves better."

"Maybe you need to get rid of your idea of better. Your boots are better than mine, but they won't fit my feet. So to hell with better. Your boots and your 'better' can both go fuck themselves. Now, if you'll excuse me, I'm busy, and she's busy—" she gestured at Sadie's room "—and sodding everyone but you is busy. Go to sleep. There'll be plenty of work that needs to be done tomorrow, and right now there's nobody in this house that's fit to do it."

Hartley was not going to be able to sleep and he saw little point in even making the attempt. How could anyone sleep under these conditions? Sadie might die. Her baby might never live. It was appalling that this was how people came into being and Hartley had a mind to lodge a complaint, or, since that was not possible, to weep onto someone's shoulder.

Hartley checked that Alf was safely arranged on his chair, grabbed his topcoat, and headed outdoors. He didn't even need to think about where he was going; there was only one possibility, late though it was. If the windows above the Bell were dark, he'd go back home, he decided. But there was a flicker of lamplight inside, and when he knocked on the door it wasn't long before he heard footsteps.

Sam was sweeping bits of crumbled brick and soot from the floor around the hearth when he heard a quiet tapping on the door.

"The hell?" Nick asked. "It's gone midnight. There's somebody at the door every night these days. It's no better than running a cathouse."

"Might be Kate," Sam pointed out. He swept the soot into a tidy pile and was about to dump it into the dustbin when he heard Hartley's voice.

"Is Sam in?"

"Yeah, he's in. Don't know where else he'd be at this hour," Nick said. "But he's about to go to bed and so am I, so—"

"It's fine, Nick," Sam said, approaching the door. "This is Kate's friend, Hartley."

"That's right," Nick said, realization dawning. He held the door open for Hartley to enter, then shut it against the chill of the night. "She said she was going to your . . . who is she, now?"

"My friend," Hartley said. "Sadie is my friend." There was a moment of empty silence as it seemed to occur to Hartley that he needed to explain why he was here at such an hour. Sam wracked his brain to come up with an excuse, but he wasn't cut out for deceit. Inspiration struck Hartley first. "Kate sent me for a cask of ale," he said, and Sam wouldn't have known it for a lie if he hadn't sent Alf home with a full cask of their best porter only a few hours ago. But it was as good an excuse as any.

"I'll get it sorted," Sam started to say, but they were interrupted by a loud, echoing clatter that began deep within the bowels of the building and culminated in a crash and puff of soot.

"That's another one," Sam said with a sigh. "And I just finished sweeping up."

"Makes three tonight," Nick said.

"We'll get the sweep in again tomorrow, I suppose."

"Wait. You've had three bricks fall from the chimney tonight?" Hartley asked. "That's not a good sign." Nick shot Sam a glance because that's exactly what Nick had been saying all day, only Sam wouldn't listen.

In the near darkness, Sam regarded Hartley levelly before turning to his brother. "I've got this, Nick. There's nothing more we can do tonight. Why don't you go to Kate's rooms so you'll be there when she gets home?"

Hartley shifted awkwardly while Nick took a coat off the hook near the door and disappeared outside.

"What's this really about?" Sam asked. "You have me worried."

"I'm really sorry," Hartley said. "I was careless. I wanted to see you, but I didn't think anybody other than you would open the door. It was reckless, which was just the thing you were scolding me about the other day and I'm so sorry." His words came out in a rush and ended on a half sob.

"Shh." Sam came near but didn't touch the other man. "What's the matter?"

"Sadie's having the baby and I'm worried sick." Hartley's brow was furrowed with worry, and by the light of the guttering candle, his eyes shone. He usually did such a thorough job of tucking all his feelings out of sight that Sam was startled by the sight of him in distress.

"Has Kate said anything about it not going well?"

"No, no, nothing like that. I just—I don't want anything to happen to Sadie. Sam, I really shouldn't have come. Now your brother will know and if anyone saw me come here they'll know too." He stepped close enough for Sam to hear when his breath hitched. Sam opened his arms in invitation, and Hartley tucked his head under Sam's chin, wrapping his arms around Sam's neck.

"You can always come to me," Sam spoke into Hartley's hair, his arms around the other man's back, holding him close.

"No, I can't. It's not safe. I must have been half mad."

Sam guessed that Hartley had started to worry about Sadie

and then the worry started to gather speed like a cart rolling downhill. This didn't have to do with him, but with Hartley being out of practice in feeling things and caring for people. "Hart, when I told you I wanted you to stay safe, I meant not to get yourself hurt or arrested. There's nothing wrong with coming here. People come here all hours of the night and day."

"You don't let them in at this hour."

"I can let in whoever I want."

"If anybody knew me, they'd wonder about you, and you don't need that. Your brother, Sam. How long do you think it'll take him to figure out why I came to you? Or what about that constable you told me about?"

Sam's heart thudded at the idea of Merton seeing Hartley leaving the Bell in the middle of the night, long past closing. "Nick bought your line about the ale," Sam said, because it was the only answer he could make.

Hartley pulled away, letting the cold air slide between their bodies. "Eventually he'll figure it out."

"No, he won't. I'm careful. And even if he did, he wouldn't say anything, even to me." Nick wasn't nosy, he didn't ask questions. But what if he did find out? Sam couldn't quite imagine a world in which Nick knew that Sam went to bed with men, even less one where Nick knew Sam went to bed with a rich, dandified gentleman.

Hartley gave a wintry smile, as if he knew Sam was conceding the point. "I see how it will go," he said. "You're such a bad liar, you know. He'd start to wonder. And you'd be ashamed of me."

"I would never—"

Hartley held up a finger. "Not of me, per se. But of the need to keep a secret. It would weigh on you, because you're an honest man, and you're close to your brother. And I would resent you, because I'd envy that you have the option of secrecy."

Sam was about to protest when he was interrupted by the sound of another brick clattering into the hearth. They both stood wordless for a moment, listening to a peculiar creaking coming from above.

"Sam," Hartley said. "I don't think this chimney is safe. We really ought to get out of here."

The sweep had assured him that the bricks that had fallen were old, not part of the chimney stack. Sam had no idea what that meant. But since the alternative was to believe that the chimney was unsound, and about to topple down and destroy the Bell, he had chosen to believe the sweep. But this time there was a sound like a groaning, deep from within the walls of the Bell. And with it came an echoing clatter, then something was falling from above. The next thing he knew, Hartley wasn't in his arms, but on the floor.

He scooped Hartley up in his arms, dimly aware that this was the first time he had held his lover so close. The next moments were a vague rush of hollered orders. "The chimney is collapsing," he shouted into the empty street. A head poked through an upper story window, and then the street was filled with people in nightcaps and hastily donned clothes who either wanted to be clear of the buildings adjoining the Bell or who wanted to watch the spectacle of a building being destroyed.

"I need a doctor," he shouted. In the moonlight he could see that there was blood on Hartley's head, but that he wasn't out cold. His eyelids fluttered and his mouth moved slightly, as if he were trying to talk. Sam knew well what serious blows to the head looked like, and this wasn't one. But it was still bad, and it was his fault.

It took less time than Sam might have imagined for a building to be destroyed. Until there was no more noise from the Bell, no more clattering bricks, no more heaving groans, he held Hartley close; half his attention was on what used to be the Bell, the other half on the man in his arms. When everything was silent except the voices of the people in the street, he could almost convince himself that it was safe to return, that he had imagined the falling bricks. If it weren't for the weight of the man in his arms reminding him of the seriousness of the danger, he might have gone back inside.

"Now, what's going on here?" said a sneering voice.

Sam looked away from Hartley's to see Constable Merton.

"The chimney is collapsing, and this man was hit by a falling brick." There was blood on Hartley's forehead, just a trickle but enough to stain his hair dark.

"At one in the morning? You ought to have closed hours ago." He held his lantern up to examine Hartley's face. "He doesn't look like the sort of man to be prowling about after hours in taverns like yours."

Sam could not believe he had to explain this when what he really needed was to bring Hartley to a medical man. "He came after hours to get a cask of ale for a laboring mother. The midwife sent him."

"Christ in heaven. He has a baby on the way?" Sam didn't correct the man, and stayed silent as the constable peered into Hartley's bloodstained face. "Put this gentleman down," Merton said. "If he comes to and sees that he's being manhandled by the likes of you, he'll faint from terror."

Sam gritted his teeth but put Hartley down on the cold pavement. What Hartley needed was warmth and care, not this.

"Are you certain he wasn't injured in a fight?"

Sam gaped. "Do you think he looks like a prizefighter? Look at him, man."

There was another ominous clunking from inside the Bell, followed by a broken window. Sam was surprised there was anything left to break.

"I suppose not," Merton said, leaning over Hartley once again with his lantern. "So you can be on your way," he said with a shooing gesture in Sam's direction. Sam shouldn't have been surprised. Hartley made a sound and tried to sit up, but the constable firmly shoved him back onto the pavement. "Stay there, young man," Merton said.

Hartley's eyes flew open at the contact.

"Don't worry . . . Mr. Sedgwick . . . sir," Sam managed. "You got hit by a falling brick, but this copper will take care of you."

With unfocused eyes, Hartley regarded the constable, and then shook his head. "No," he repeated, but this time with plain fear in his eyes.

Merton took hold of Hartley's chin and turned his head to either side. Hartley whimpered.

"You mustn't touch him," Sam said. "He doesn't—" Sam didn't know what to say that wouldn't expose them both to the constable's suspicion, so he shoved his hands in his pockets and looked on helplessly.

Merton was about fifty or sixty, with gray hair. He was broad shouldered and somewhat portly, but the way Hartley was looking at him one might have thought the constable was an ax-wielding giant. With an indrawn breath, Sam realized that this was probably what Hartley's godfather had looked like.

It ought to have been a harder decision. He ought to have given serious thought before abducting a man from under a constable's eye. But either he took Hartley with him now or he left him to whatever terror he was reliving. Really, there was no choice.

"I need to take this man to his home. It's a matter of urgency." That was all he said before scooping Hartley up.

They were in a pitch-dark alley, the constable's shouted protestations ringing in his ears before Sam fully registered that Hartley was awake.

"Thank you," Hartley said.

"Damn it, Hart," Sam said. They were in a narrow space between two buildings, hidden from the street. Sam waited for the sound of running footsteps, tried to imagine what he'd tell the constable this time.

"You can put me down," Hartley said. "I think I was only dazed."

Sam gently lowered Hartley onto his feet. But instead of stepping away, Hartley burrowed his head into Sam's coat, and Sam didn't know what to say. "Oh Sam," he said after a moment. "I am so sorry." He wrapped his slender arms around Sam, tucking his head under Sam's chin, their bodies fitting together as well as Sam had always known they would.

The Bell was crumbling, Sam had exposed both of them to suspicion, but all Sam could think about was that Hartley was safe and in his arms.

Chapter Twenty-one

When Hartley opened his eyes, all he could see was a sliver of light making its way through the gap in his bedroom curtains. He squeezed his eyes shut, because even that strip of brightness made his head hurt. He didn't remember having gotten drunk last night, but from the pounding in his head and the heaviness of his limbs, he was extravagantly hungover. In fact, he remembered nothing at all about last night. He struggled to piece the previous evening together. He had gone out with Will, but only drank half a pint of weak ale. Then he had come home to find Sadie cooking.

Sadie. He sat up straight.

"No, no, you don't want to do that, mate," said a voice that seemed to come from a shadowy corner of the room. The voice was absolutely correct. Hartley did not want to be sitting up. He did not want to be awake, or possibly even alive, for that matter. Gingerly, he lay back and with some effort turned his head to see Alf seated on a chair in the corner.

"How is Sadie?" Hartley asked, and the sound of his own voice made him wince in pain.

"She's doing well. So is the baby. A little girl."

"Oh, thank God." Hartley felt a rush of relief. "Thank God," he repeated, and it was the closest thing to a prayer that he had managed in years.

"She's downstairs, fast asleep. Kate's gone home but she'll be back later."

The mention of Kate stirred something in Hartley's memory. He had gone to the Bell. He dimly remembered something loud, and then—

"Where is Sam?"

"He brought you here early this morning. Said you were injured in a chimney collapse."

"The chimney at the Bell," Hartley said, remembering the sound of falling bricks, followed by darkness. No, not entirely darkness, but dreamy confusion punctuated by fear. His godfather had been there, somehow, which was impossible. Except he remembered Sam rescuing him from Easterbrook's hands. Doubtless he had been deluded from the blow to the head, but he'd figure that out later. For now, he needed to know about Sam. The Bell was everything to him. "Where is he now, though?"

"I don't know. He said you needed a doctor, but by then you had come around, so I cleaned you up and put you to bed. A doctor couldn't do much more, and I didn't think you'd want a stranger pawing at you."

"Quite right. Good thinking. Thank you. I hate to ask

you this, because you've been up all night, but can you please check on Sam and see if he needs anything?"

Alf was silent for a moment. "I would, if I knew where to find him."

Hartley started to shake his head, but stopped when he felt the contents of his skull lurch painfully about. "I'm certain he's returned to the Bell."

"He may have done, to see if he could get his belongings from the rubble."

Rubble. "It was destroyed, then?"

"Have you ever seen a chimney collapse? There's not much left afterward. But maybe Sam was lucky."

"I need to go to him." He got to his feet, but the room spun darkly around him. He sat back down and raised his hand to his throbbing head. There was a length of linen wrapped around his temple, and beneath it was tender with pain.

"All right, sit back down," Alf said. "I'll run over to the Bell and see if Sam's there, so long as you promise not to do anything stupid while I'm out."

Hartley agreed on the condition that Alf help him downstairs. He didn't want to be in his dark lonely room, two flights of stairs away from any other person. "Go into the top drawer of my desk," Hartley said, when they passed the library door. "And take out whatever money is in there. Give it all to Sam for repairs and tell him he can have whatever else he needs."

"I don't know if he'll take kindly to that," Alf said doubtfully.

"The Bell is his life." Hartley held himself up against the doorframe. "I only want to help him have that."

"Maybe you ought to tell him so yourself."

Hartley shook his head. It felt like it was filled with sludge where his brains ought to have been. "I can't do that. It's better if he stays away from me." The events of last night were slotting into place, and he remembered stray words from a man he thought was a constable. Hartley had been terrified of the man, having gotten him mixed up with his godfather. Sam had risked his own safety by bringing him home, and Hartley knew that he needed to return the favor by not exposing Sam to any more danger.

It wasn't until late that afternoon, when the crowd of gawkers had thinned a bit, that Sam ventured to reenter the Bell. It hadn't been a complete chimney collapse, and for that he ought to be grateful, several people cheerfully assured him. And he was grateful: a chimney had collapsed on Shoe Lane a few years earlier, and five people had died, not to mention the building being destroyed. But, surveying the ruins of the taproom, Sam reasoned it might as well have been destroyed. He'd never manage to repair the building. He'd certainly never reopen the Bell.

Everything he had worked for was gone, and he wouldn't get it back. The Bell had been his life, his home, the center of all his hopes. When he had buried Davey and stepped away from the ring for the final time, he had gone directly to the Bell. Between him and his father, they had seen ten lifetimes' worth of blood and sin and evil. He had hoped to use the Bell to balance the scale in the other direction, even if all his work amounted to only a pebble against the mountains of wrong that had been done. Without the Bell, he didn't even know who he was or what he was for.

"It's not that bad," Nick said, coming in from the kitchen.

Despite himself, Sam almost smiled at his brother's un-flagging optimism. "Three walls and a roof good enough for you?"

"Nah, it's got four walls in there, only a little hole in one of them." The kitchen had originally belonged to one of the neighboring buildings, so it was set off to the side of the Bell and had been spared the bulk of the damage. "And the stove still works, so I'll go on making pies just as I did before you bought the Bell. And if you help, we can sell them as fast as I can make them. That'll do for a bit."

It would do, and for more than a bit. A person could make a living selling pies, which is precisely what Sam's mother had done. She had gone to markets, fairs, hangings, all the usual places. "All right, then," Sam said, not wanting to crush his brother's hopeful mood. "And will you sleep in the kitchen?" Even Nick would have to acknowledge that the upper floors weren't safe.

"About that," Nick said. "Kate agreed to have the banns read starting this Sunday. So I might as well go on staying with her."

Sam managed a smile. "I'm glad. Good for both of you."

"Don't make a fuss in front of Kate. She'll have my hide."

Nick left, promising to return in the morning after doing

the marketing. Sam had just enough good sense not to attempt to climb the stairs to see whether any of his belongings were salvageable, but not nearly enough sense to find someplace more suitable to spend the night, so he bedded down in the cold kitchen. After a while, Daisy appeared and curled around his feet, and Sam let himself drop into an uneasy sleep.

When he opened his eyes, a faint light was coming through the broken window. It was late enough in the year that this dimness could mean dawn, dusk, or anything in between. The clock had been destroyed by a falling brick, so time hardly existed at all, although the emptiness of his stomach argued that it had been a good long while since he had eaten. A sound came from the courtyard. Muffled swearing, as if someone had stubbed a toe on one of the stones and bricks that now dotted the ground behind the Bell. Sam hoped whoever it was broke a bone. Then Sam registered that there was no good reason for anyone to be behind the Bell. Somebody had probably decided to help themselves to the ale, or the contents of the till, or whatever else they could carry off. Sam grabbed a fire iron and stepped into the darkness.

He didn't see the man right away, only a shifting in the shadows. He gripped the iron harder. Then his eyes adjusted to the dark and he could pick out a slight silhouette.

"I hope that's you, Sam," said a voice from the darkness. "Otherwise I suppose I'm about to get myself murdered."

"Alf?" He lowered the iron. "What are you doing here? Is it Hartley?" he added, a sick queasiness seizing his insides.

"He's fine. I left him sitting by the fire, holding Sadie's baby, of all things."

Hartley was safe. That, at least, was something.

Alf dug into his pocket and produced a purse. "He told me to give this to you. He wants to help with repairs."

"Repairs, my arse." He gestured toward the ruined tap-room. "It's all gone." Saying it aloud was like ripping an organ out of his chest. "And I don't want his money." The Bell had been his. It was the shape and size of his character, not the charity project of a man in a fancy coat nor a favor to bestow on a lover. Hartley's money—mixed up as it was with his pain and shame—was all this situation needed to get worse. If Sam took this money from Hartley, it would bring all of that confusion into their friendship. It would change everything between them, change what had already been a precariously unbalanced partnership and make it completely unstable.

At the sound of a knock on the front door, Hartley assumed somebody had the wrong address, so he ignored it. When, five minutes later, there was a knock on the back door, he swore. The baby was with Sadie, at least, so he didn't have to worry about dropping her while making his unsteady way to the door.

In the doorway was an older man, portly in a rather Henry VIII sort of way. Hartley vaguely recognized the man, but couldn't quite place him.

"Ah," the man said. "I see I do have the right address. Mr. Sedgwick?"

"Yes," Hartley said, confused. "I'm Hartley Sedgwick. I'm afraid you have the advantage of me."

"Jerome Merton, constable. I've come to ask you about the events of this past Tuesday." His accent was pure cockney, but without Sam's soft edges.

"Oh, I see." If this had been the constable from the night of the chimney collapse, Hartley must have been entirely off his head to mistake him for his godfather. "I'm quite well, as you can see," Hartley said, gesturing to the bandage.

"I understand there's been a blessed event," Merton said, his beady eyes darting around the kitchen. "I daresay your household has been in a bit of an uproar. No, the reason I'm here, not to put too fine a point on it, is that the circumstances of your injury were a bit unusual." He paused, as if waiting for Hartley to supply details. When Hartley remained silent, he went on. "You were carried out of a public house, quite unconscious, by a black man of a very low sort. Very dirty and rough. And at a most unusual hour. I thought you might have been attacked."

Hartley realized that this constable was the same one who habitually made trouble for Sam. He kept his voice steady. "I wasn't attacked. The chimney collapsed at the Bell and I was injured by a falling brick." Surely the constable already knew this.

"If you don't mind my asking, what were you doing roaming about town in such low company in the middle of the night?"

"I believe Mr. Fox explained that," Hartley said, hoping Sam had come up with something plausible to tell the man.

"Sam Fox said you visited his public house at that late hour for a cask of strong ale the midwife required for your wife."

Hartley let out a crack of laughter. Of all the lies, Sam had come up with the least plausible one. He was about to set the man straight—really, what else could he do, when two minutes of inquiry would inform the man that Hartley most definitely had no wife—when he heard Sadie's door open.

"That's right," she said. "The midwife specially directed him to get the strongest ale. Something about it helping the babe nurse." Hartley got to his feet and offered Sadie his chair.

"I asked around," Merton said. "I had to ask quite a few questions to find the right Mr. Sedgwick, you understand. And part of my confusion is that when I asked for a Mr. Sedgwick of your description, everyone agreed that there was no Mrs. Sedgwick."

Hartley saw Sadie go rigid. With Sadie sitting right there, he couldn't very well insist that the baby wasn't his, because that would seem to be repudiating Sadie. He remembered how Sam had reacted when he had failed to consider him a proper visitor; this would be even worse.

"Gossip is so often wrong," Sadie said in her most refined tones. "That's why I never pay any attention to it. Merton, you said your name was? I'm afraid I haven't had the pleasure of being introduced to any Mertons."

Hartley was quite in awe. So, evidently, was the constable, who twisted the brim of the hat he clutched in his meaty fingers. "I beg your pardon," Merton stammered.

"'Truly," Sadie went on, "we owe Mr. Fox a debt of gratitude, don't we darling?" She cast an appealing look up at Hartley. "He saved my baby's father." She blinked quickly, as if fighting back tears. "Mr. Fox will always have us for allies, will he not, dearest?" She gazed up at him with the most appalling sheep eyes.

"Of course," Hartley said, scrambling to think of a suitable endearment. "Of course, my, ah, pet." He placed his hand on her shoulder in a proprietary manner and kept it there until Merton stammered an apology and hurried out the door.

Chapter Twenty-two

When Sam knocked on the kitchen door it was opened by Hartley himself, holding a bundle of cloth that Sam, after a moment of confusion, identified as an infant.

Seeing Hartley holding a baby was like watching a pigeon play a fiddle. Nothing wrong with pigeons, or with fiddles, for that matter; indeed they were commonplace enough sights. But seeing them in the same place made Sam's head spin in a way he couldn't properly name. He nearly walked right out of the house to see if when he reopened the door, the occupants might have arranged themselves in a less bizarre tableau.

"They're supposed to look like this," Hartley said, misunderstanding Sam's confusion. "Kate assures me this is a fine specimen." He dubiously pulled back the shawl that wrapped the infant and peered at its wizened little face. "There isn't much of her," Hartley added. "The other day I bought a gourd bigger than this."

Sam didn't ask what Hartley was doing buying gourds. "Half a stone, I'd say."

"It doesn't seem right that a person starts out so small and fragile," Hartley said, wrapping the child more tightly in the shawl and stepping closer to the fire. "I'm afraid a mistake was made somewhere along the line."

"Yeah, somebody ought to do something about it," Sam said, smiling. This was the first time he had smiled in two days.

"Calves and lambs are much sturdier." Hartley cast a skeptical eye at the bundle in his arms. "Better looking, too, if I'm honest."

"How's Sadie?"

"Asleep." A cloud passed over Hartley's face. "Kate says she's well, but we all know things can go wrong." Sam nodded. He wasn't going to insult him by attempting easy comfort. "How are you, Sam?" Hartley asked, a furrow between his brows. Concern set oddly on him, like new boots that hadn't yet been broken in. "I've thought about you and the Bell every minute."

"I don't want to talk about it," Sam said, his voice gruff and abrupt. He had been putting one foot in front of the other for the past two days without much thought to how he felt about it. Hell, he had been plodding on that way for years, putting himself last, working himself to the bone, because that was what he wanted. Only now that he didn't have the Bell to pour himself into did he feel those years of weariness in every mote of his being.

"Sam." Hartley tipped his head in worry. "Oh Sam. Let me do something to help."

"No, no, it's not like that. I've got things under control," he said, afraid that sympathy from Hartley would reduce him to a puddle of emotion. Besides, here was Hartley, a new life in his arms, his hair rumpled and his coat wrinkled as if he hadn't bothered glancing in the looking glass, and altogether looking more peaceful than he had in the months since Sam first set eyes on him. Sam didn't want to disturb him with tales of his own hardship, didn't want to tell Hartley that the Bell was gone, and all his hopes along with it. "You look good," he said instead.

"Well, I guess fatherhood suits me." Sam must have looked as befuddled as he felt, because Hartley let out a peal of laughter. "It's your doing. Your constable came here to make trouble, and Sadie put him well in his place. He thinks she's my mistress and also quite possibly a royal princess." The baby started to stir, and Hartley tentatively patted her, probably not so differently to how he might have inspected yesterday's gourd. "I doubt he'll cause you much trouble, but maybe next time he comes into the Bell buy him a pint for me?"

For a moment he forgot there would never be a future in which that could happen. No more pints, no more Bell. "How's your head?" he asked. There was a faint purplish bruise over Hartley's left eyebrow, but the cut had already healed to a fine line.

"Not bad. Thank you again. I owe you—"

"Nothing. I would have done it for anyone." And that was true—he wouldn't have left Merton himself to be crushed by a falling chimney. "But you're not anyone," he added gruffly. "And you know it."

The next words Hartley spoke were a whisper. "When did I get so out of my depth?" Hartley held the baby against his chest, as if she were a shield that would stop Sam from seeing him or knowing what he was thinking.

"Out of your depth?" Sam repeated in confusion.

"With you, Sam Fox." He gave a sad little smile. "I've been trying to pinpoint exactly where I went wrong, when I could have walked away from you without either of us getting hurt."

For Sam, it had been earlier than he wanted to admit, maybe even before that first time Hartley went to his knees. "Do you wish you had walked away?"

Hartley let out a frustrated huff. "No, and that's the worst part. I'm glad we had this time together."

That sounded terribly final. Sam's chest tightened. "Sounds like you're about to walk away now," he said, trying and failing to keep his tone conversational.

Hartley sighed, as if his patience were running out. "We didn't get to finish our conversation the other night, so I'll ask you again, Sam. What will you do when people come to the obvious conclusion about our friendship? What will you do when your brother suspects?" He shifted the baby into the crook of one arm.

Sam wanted to deny Hartley's concerns, to once again say that there was nothing to worry about. But regardless of whether Hartley's concerns were well founded, the fact was he believed them to be true. "Why don't you let me deal with that if it happens?"

"Because I don't want you to stop being able to hide." On the last word he raised his voice, startling a faint whimper from the baby. "I can't hide anymore, and it caused me a good deal of trouble. I couldn't face that happening to you." By now the baby was fussing in earnest. "Oh hush, you. Uncle Hartley is off his head, nothing to worry yourself about."

Seeing Hartley kiss the baby's head gave Sam the sensation of his heart being filled with the most improbable butterflies. "I care about you more than I care about the rest of it."

"You don't mean—"

"Don't tell me what I mean," Sam said gently. "I know the risks, but I also know that the way I feel when I'm with you is worth it. It's one of the best things—you're one of the best things that's ever happened to me. I feel like I've been waiting for you, and I didn't even know it." He heard Hartley suck in a breath of air, and when those pale eyes looked up at him, their expression was thunderstruck. Sam brought his hand to Hartley's face, rubbing his thumb along the other man's unshaved jaw. "Can you trust me to keep loving you? No matter what?" Sam kept his voice soft and low, belying the urgency he felt.

Hartley pressed his cheek into Sam's palm. "But how would it work?"

Sam smiled at the shift from *whether* to *how*. "Can we leave that for later? I have so much to figure out." There was the Bell, his lease, and about a dozen other moving parts that he was tired of thinking about. Hartley nodded and turned his head to press a lingering kiss into Sam's hand, and the contact of lips on skin sent shivers of want and need through Sam's body. "Any chance you might put that baby down for a minute or two and, ah . . ." He jerked his chin in the direction of the stairs.

"Only a minute or two?" Hartley asked, but he was already knocking on Sadie's door.

Hartley needed this time with Sam to seal whatever unspoken promises they were making their tentative way toward. From the beginning, Hartley had been able to trust Sam with his body. Now that Sam was asking for Hartley to trust him with his heart, Hartley needed the comfort of their physical connection. Since the only words that could do justice to his feelings were buried under layers of stone and shell, he needed his body to say what his voice could not.

They climbed the stairs in record time, Hartley tugging Sam's hand and not stopping until they had the bedroom door shut behind them. Sam had never been upstairs, Hartley realized. "This is my bedroom," he said, most unnecessarily, as he gently pushed Sam toward the bed.

When Sam sat on the edge of the bed, Hartley straddled his lap. He unwound Sam's neckcloth, kissing the skin as he exposed it, his lips soft and hungry on Sam's warm skin. At first those kisses were nothing but whispers of lips across flesh, but when he sucked lightly on the underside of his

Sam's jaw, the larger man finally let out a groan. "Hartley," he rasped, his fingers entwined in Hartley's hair.

"Mmm?" Hartley hummed into Sam's skin.

"Can I unbutton your waistcoat?" Sam whispered almost solemnly.

Hartley raised his eyebrows in surprise, but he nodded. "Help yourself." With unsteady hands, Sam worked open the first of the buttons. "I have the salve in the table by the bed," Hartley said. A silver button landed with a plink on the wood floor.

"Sorry—" Sam started. "Salve?"

"I used your cock on myself the other night," Hartley whispered, and felt Sam's hands clamp on his hips.

"How did it feel?" Sam asked, his voice ragged.

"So good. I thought of you the whole time, wishing it really were your cock inside me."

Sam bucked his hips up helplessly. "Oh fuck, Hart. Jesus fuck."

"I know you would make me feel good." Hartley, still straddling Sam's lap, ground down so Sam could feel his arousal. "You'd be gentle. You'd care what I wanted." He punctuated each sentence with another thrust of his hips.

"God yes, I'd do whatever you needed. You know it."

Hartley kissed Sam's shoulder. "You'd fuck me now if I wanted you to."

Sam stilled. "Is that what you're asking for?"

"I think it is. I know it would be fine. Or, rather, even if it wasn't, I'd ask you to stop, and you would. And then it would just be something unpleasant that happened. It wouldn't have to mean anything. And you'd be with me, so I'd be safe." Sam held Hartley tight against him.

When Sam shrugged out of his coat then tugged his shirt over his head, Hartley let his gaze trail hotly over Sam's body.

"See something you like?" Sam asked.

A wicked grin spread across Hartley's face. "We're just two extraordinarily good-looking people about to fuck. I wish I had a looking glass." It was shameless bravado, and Sam must have known it, because he stifled a laugh while undoing the rest of Hartley's waistcoat buttons.

When they were both naked, Hartley climbed on top of Sam and leaned in for a kiss. He had always thought kissing intrusive and messy, but Sam's kisses started out gentle and soft. With one hand Sam cradled Hartley's head and with the other he caressed Hartley's back, and before Hartley knew it he was thrusting his hips forward in a rhythm that matched their kissing, rubbing against Sam's own erection.

"Ease off," Sam said, his voice strained. "I'll come in about half a minute if you keep going."

Hartley put some space in between them. "Would you touch me?" Hartley asked, and Sam, bless him, didn't need to be told twice. He moved his hands to Hartley's lower back and then to the curve of his arse, touching, squeezing, spreading. Now Hartley's breaths were coming fast, his movements ragged. Sam traced his fingers into Hartley's cleft, seeking out sensitive skin as he thrust his hips up.

"You want this," Sam said, almost wonderingly, as Hartley groaned and pressed back into his touch. He fumbled on the table beside the bed for the salve.

"I want *you*," Hartley clarified. "Inside me. I've hardly been able to sleep for imagining it." He took both their cocks together in his hand and stroked. "And if we can't, then we can't. We'll both be fine." Slowly, patiently, Sam worked Hartley open with slick fingers while they kissed, until Hartley was babbling and bossy. "Now, Sam. I can't wait."

"Go ahead," Sam said, his voice rough.

Hartley knelt over him and took hold of Sam's cock, positioning it against his entrance. Sam clenched his jaw and twisted his fingers in the bedsheets.

Hartley knew a moment of doubt. A cock was very different from fingers, very different from the glass prick. But he relaxed and let his body adjust.

"This all right?" Sam asked, because of course he did. Hartley smiled.

"Oh Sam. Yes." As Hartley began to move, Sam rested one hand on Hartley's hip and with the other reached over his head to grip the bedframe, his bicep bulging with the tension of holding fast. Hartley took a moment to thank whatever providence had led him to this man, and then drew Sam inside him.

"**Y**ou're a good man, Hart," Sam said as they lay on Hartley's soft bed, the covers pulled over them. Hartley made a scoffing sound. "I mean it. How many men do you think would have taken Sadie in and rocked her baby into the bargain. You really are decent, Hart." Sam put his hand up to Hartley's cheek.

"Sod off," Hartley said, but didn't pull away. His voice was ragged and his hair fanned out chaotically where his head rested on Sam's shoulder. He looked peaceful, sated, and utterly well-fucked. Sam wanted to shower him with all the praise he deserved.

"Softhearted."

"I'm responsible for both Sadie and Alf. They're not much more than children," Hartley protested. "People can get into a lot of trouble at that age."

"Like I said, decent."

Hartley wrinkled his nose. "One decent thing I could do would be to give you a sum of money to finance the Bell's repairs. Not a loan. No strings attached. Just a gift."

Sam gave his head a quick shake. "I already said I don't need it."

"Neither do I."

"I don't want your money." He heard Hartley suck in a breath and felt his body stiffen. "Not because of how you got it, you silly git." He kissed Hartley's hair.

"Then why? I tell you, it would be a trifling amount to me."

"But it wouldn't be trifling to me. If five hundred pounds—" he made up that sum, since he couldn't fathom how much it would cost to repair the Bell "—means nothing to you, but means the world to me, then I don't see how we bridge that gap."

"I'm trying to!" He propped himself up on his elbow and looked at Sam. "That's why I want to help, but nobody will let me. Will won't take my money, Alf says he'd rather work for you than for me, and I had to badger Sadie into accepting a blasted christening cup. I feel like you all know you'd be contaminated by touching anything that comes from my purse. It makes me feel so dirty, Sam, as if—"

"Hush," Sam said, smoothing his hands down Hartley's back. "It's not that. Sometimes people need to get on by themselves, to know that they're building good things with their own hands." That was what Sam had been telling himself—that the work he did at the Bell wouldn't be good enough unless he did it on its own, that accepting money would be cheapening what he thought of as service and turning it into ordinary work. But there was no shame in plain work, and maybe he needed to think his way around that over the next few days. But he couldn't think straight with Hartley so near.

"I care about you more than I know how to manage," Hartley finally said, looking up at Sam with wet eyes. "More than our circumstances will allow."

Sam's voice rumbled. "I think you care about me just the right amount."

"I want more than occasional nights, more than hushed conversations outside the pantry. I want a life with you. When one of us needs something, I want us to take for granted that the other one will help." There was a note of helplessness in his voice, and his words came in a whispered rush. "I love you, and I want to keep loving you, all the time, without your demons or mine coming in the way. But we can't have that, and even if we could—"

"Damn it, Hart. I love you too. God." He could hear his own frustration. "I don't know how we do this." When he looked down, the grim resignation he saw in Hartley's face made him doubt that they could ever see their way through. "But we will, though. Hear me? We will."

CHAPTER TWENTY-THREE

During the next week, Sadie got back on her feet and the baby thrived. Winter set in, leaving its frosty traces on morning windowpanes. The household settled into something like a rhythm. Hartley mostly fended for himself, Alf ran errands, and Sadie stayed in the kitchen. The baby either nestled in a shawl across her mother's chest or slept in a cradle Alf found in the box room. Only after several days did it occur to Hartley that this must have been Martin's cradle; he waited for some kind of distaste to set in, but it didn't happen.

Hartley found himself spending most of his time in the kitchen. At first he pretended it was because he couldn't be bothered to haul his own coal up to the library, and the kitchen was both warm and conveniently located to the food. He maintained that pretense for maybe two days before acknowledging to himself that he just wanted to hold the baby and make idle conversation with Sadie and Alf.

Sadie informed him that babies reared on the most

modern scientific principles required regular fresh air. Hartley, who was rather taken with the idea of children being raised according to any principled system whatsoever, volunteered to take the infant for an airing in the park. He ordered Alf to sell two of his waistcoats and a coat that had lately seemed a bit too fine, intending to use the proceeds to purchase the best pram money could buy.

"You that hard up?" Alf asked when Hartley handed over the garments.

"No," Hartley said. "Well, not exactly. I live within my means. If I don't have ready money, I need to either sell something or touch the capital."

Alf's gaze traveled around Hartley's bedchamber. "I suppose I never thought about someone who lives like this not having money. If Sam had taken you up on your offer to pay for the Bell's repairs, what would you have sold? I suppose it would have cost more than a few brass buttons."

Hartley busied himself in arranging his shirt studs in a drawer. "I would have sold the house."

Alf let out a low whistle. "Maybe you can sell it anyway? Just to spare Sadie the trouble of having to sprinkle salt on the windowsills to keep out the evil spirits that live in the attic."

"What kind of good would salt on the windowsills do if the evil spirits are upstairs?"

Alf shrugged. "I suggested holy water but Sadie says that's papist. About the Bell, Kate told Sadie that Sam still needs to pay rent even though it's unusable."

"That can't be right."

"I reckon landlords do a lot of things that aren't right, and even more if they have a tenant who looks like Sam."

"Sam let me think he had the repairs underway."

"He's proud, though."

Hartley was surprised to realize that he didn't feel hurt by Sam misleading him. He understood the urge to hide behind a protective screen. He just wished he could figure out how to offer a kind of help that Sam would agree to accept.

Upon receiving the pram, Hartley wrapped the baby in approximately seven shawls and took her for a walk in the park. It was the middle of the day, right when Hyde Park was busiest with the very people who had shunned him, but he was too preoccupied with worries about the infant catching cold to think overmuch about the whispers and stares of the beau monde. Indeed, the child finished the outing tucked warmly inside Hartley's coat.

When he came home, the kitchen was warm and steamy and scented with cooking. Alf chopped nuts while Sadie ground something with a mortar and pestle. The light slanted feebly through the high window, making Hartley wonder when it had last been cleaned. The house was acquiring the slight shabbiness of a well-worn coat, and he found that he didn't mind.

"Is that nutmeg?" he asked Sadie, gesturing at the contents of the mortar.

"No," Sadie said, looking up from her work only long enough to smile at Hartley and coo at the baby.

"Smells like nutmeg," Hartley said to the child he was cradling in his arms.

"It's mace," Alf said. "With nutmeg she uses that thing that looks like what a carpenter uses to smooth the wood. And why are you making such a nuisance of yourself? Go upstairs and comb your hair or something."

Hartley instinctively patted his hair and saw Sadie stifle a smile. "Oh, sod off," he told Alf.

"The boot boy next door is collecting bets on which of us is the baby's father," Alf said. "Seven to one odds it's you."

Hartley nearly choked on the piece of bread he had stolen from the chopping board. "I beg your pardon?"

"Settle down," Alf said. "The butler already told him it was bad form to gossip. But he also said that having a yellow-haired upstart—that's you—living with his mistress and the child he got on his mistress—that's Sadie and the baby—is bringing down the tone of the neighborhood. We're gentry here, Mr. Sedgwick, and we won't tolerate none of that." These last words were delivered in a tone that was clearly meant to ape the neighbor's slanderous servant.

"Unbelievable. Which neighbors? Immediately to the left? I'm going over now to give that fellow a piece of my mind."

"Does that mean punching? Because you can't go around socking other people's butlers."

"Don't care. How dare he—how *dare* he—speak of Sadie like that." He put his gloves on and adjusted his collar. "If he were a gentleman and had spoken that way about a lady—which Sadie is, of course—I could have called him out."

Sadie looked up from her nutmeg or whatever it was in order to exchange a look with Alf.

"What's that supposed to mean?" Hartley demanded. "Do we have secret glances now? Seems unfair."

"If you went around making a fuss, everyone would know for sure you had gotten that baby on Sadie," Alf pointed out.

"True," Hartley conceded. "I do wish everyone could make up their mind about which direction my dissipations take me."

"Whatever Sadie told the constable must have done wonders for your reputation. At any rate, you do remember you hollered at me for hitting someone who said ugly things about Sadie not a month ago."

"I've grown older and wiser, and I seem to recall that it was Sadie who did most of the yelling in that situation. Sadie, do you really not mind? That people think the baby is mine?"

She frowned. "It doesn't matter to me in the least. The question is whether you mind."

"Are you kidding?" Alf asked. "This is the best thing that could have happened to him."

"Be nice to Hartley," Sadie admonished.

Hartley was taken aback and more than a little gratified to hear Sadie use his first name, even though not long ago he would have considered it the height of impropriety. Probably Sadie would have, too, come to think.

"Oh, I nearly forgot," Alf said, his mouth full of a roast potato he grabbed from a pan warming by the stove. "You have a visitor waiting for you in the library."

"A visitor?" Hartley repeated, and for a mad moment thought it might be Sam.

"It's not him," Alf said quietly.

Hartley tamped down his disappointment. When Sam had left, they had agreed to take a few days to themselves. Sam needed time to sort out the Bell, he had said, but they both knew that they were at an impasse regarding what to do next. Hartley knew he couldn't go on living essentially below stairs in his own house; Sam couldn't continue sleeping in the wreckage of his old pub. It was all very fine to say that they meant to go on together, but they were at a loss as to what their first step ought to be.

Hartley opened the door to the library, where he found his older brother sitting in the chair by the fire, a newspaper open on his lap, a valise on the floor beside him. "Ben," Hartley said, shutting the door behind him. "What are you doing here?"

"I'm here to pay a visit," Ben said, lowering the newspaper and attempting to fold it. "Didn't you get my letters?"

Hartley thought of the stack of unopened letters on the table in the hall. "No," he lied.

"I hadn't heard from you in weeks. And while you don't owe me letters—you don't owe me anything, Hart—I did want to check that you were alive."

Hartley shrugged. "I'm alive," he said, holding his arms out to his sides as if to say *Behold*.

Ben frowned. "You left before we could talk about what happened."

Early that summer, when Hartley had realized that Martin Easterbrook knew the truth of Hartley's relationship with his godfather and wasn't going to balk at telling the world, Hartley had gone home to visit Ben so he wouldn't be taken by surprise by the news.

"I don't want to talk about it." He didn't think he could endure a sermon on sacrifice and personal harm endured for the greater good of the family.

"You don't need to say anything. I just wanted you to know that I'm grateful for what you did—getting that man to pay for our school fees and Will's commission—but I'm so sorry that you were in a position where that seemed like our best option."

Hartley frowned. He had long since accepted that all his efforts at establishing his brothers had backfired spectacularly. And yet, despite all this, none of their lives were tragic. Indeed, Hartley had known something with Sam that he hadn't thought he'd ever deserve. He had other things, too, more tangible assets: the house, his small income, a solicitor who seemed terribly concerned that Hartley knew something about the contents of a certain lacquered cabinet.

"Oh!" Hartley said.

"What's wrong?" Ben asked.

"Nothing," Hartley said, a plan starting to come together in his mind. "I'm just counting my blessings. How is Father?" he asked brightly, trying to change the subject, and knowing Ben would take the bait.

Ben made a sound of exasperation. "He went walking and didn't come back for three days. Drove his wife half mad with worry. We sent out a search party, but then he wandered home again. He had gotten as far as St. Johns in the Vale!" He shook his head. "And he had my dog with him."

Hartley suppressed a smile at his brother's outrage. Their father's vagueness sent Ben into a fury, but Hartley understood that Alton Sedgwick simply didn't occupy the same world that the rest of them did. He was selfish and solipsistic, but not out of any ill will toward his fellow man. He simply forgot other people existed and might have thoughts and desires of their own. Ben, who was in the habit of noticing what other people needed and going out of his way to seeing that those needs were provided for, couldn't understand that their father's selfishness wasn't personal. Hartley, who for so long had tried to ignore other people as a matter of policy and self-preservation, had once rather envied the older man's obliviousness. It was a lot easier to live with oneself when one disregarded other people's interests. Hartley doubted he'd be able to go back to his old ways, now that he had developed this habit of caring about people. He could foresee that his future was going to involve a great number of inconveniences, if he had it his way—if he could find a way forward with Sam.

"Oh, that reminds me." Ben reached into his satchel, producing a sheaf of papers. "I have letters for you. This one is particularly good. It contains four pages of creative invective against yourself from Miss Dacre. It seems you promised her and the boys a ride in your curricle but scarpered before you could deliver. She proposes three crown and a calico kitten as just compensation." Ben's face lit up with obvious affection for his captain's children. During Hartley's visit, he had been rather startled to find his older brother smitten with another man. And one had to wonder about Will. Perhaps he'd write to Percy and Lance and see if this was a hereditary quirk of the Sedgwick constitution.

"You look well," Hartley said. "Domestic bliss and apostasy suit you."

"You don't," Ben said, squinting at him. "You look like you haven't slept in weeks."

"I haven't," Hartley said. "The cook had a baby."

Ben tilted his head. "And?"

"And the baby is loud and likes to be walked back and forth in front of the cabinet clock in the front hall at the most unreasonable hours. I can't expect Sadie to do it all herself, in addition to cooking my meals, can I?"

"No," Ben said slowly. "But I daresay nearly everyone else you're likely to meet would expect precisely that, especially as it sounds that there's not a, ah, Mr. Sadie."

"Yes, ha ha, very droll. I assure you that if you're about to engage in any comedy about my becoming a radical, Will has gotten there before you. Repeatedly. Do restrain yourself. She's my friend."

"Duly noted." Ben took a sip of brandy and regarded Hartley closely over the rim of the glass. "I take it back. Maybe you do look well after all."

Sam was at the Fleet Market selling slices of pie for a penny each when he saw a familiar face: a tall trim woman with a basket in one arm and a baby in the other.

"Sadie?" he asked. "Is this your usual market?"

"It certainly is not," she said. "It took a fair amount of doing to find you, I'll have you know."

"You really wanted some of that pie, did you?" he jested.

"I do not want your pie, Mr. Fox, although it does smell very tasty. I want to know why you let Mr. Sedgwick think you were able to repair the Bell. I just walked past it and there's no sign of work being done, nor is there likely to be. Do Kate and your brother know you turned down good money?"

He hadn't told them. Kate would have thought him an utter lunatic for refusing Hartley's money, and Nick wouldn't have understood how Hartley came to offer money to Sam in the first place. "I didn't mention it."

She sniffed. "Do you realize that for him to pay for repairs to the Bell, he'd have had to sell his house?"

Sam nearly dropped his knife. "Really?"

"And you know what that place means to him, don't you? On the way here I posted a letter for him. It was addressed to an estate agent. He's been asking Alf and me questions about what parts of London we would find convenient. He thinks he's being discreet about it, too, the dear. I do believe he means to sell the house one way or the other."

Sam had been certain that Hartley would cling to his old life, to the trappings of gentility, everything that separated them.

"There's something else," she said, rummaging through her basket. From beneath a heap of potatoes she produced a box about the size of a loaf of bread, made of polished cherrywood. Holding the baby against her shoulder with one hand, she opened the lid of the box with the other, leaning close so only Sam could see the contents of the box. Inside was a bright silver cup nestled in ivory satin lining. "It's a christening cup," she said. "Hartley got it for the baby. See," she added, as if she had proven something.

"It's really lovely, Sadie," he said, because she plainly was waiting for him to say something.

"Of course it's lovely. And it cost upward of five guineas, I daresay. The point is that he got it for my baby. For *my* baby. A child with no father and no background. Five guineas. He tried to tell me that the point of it was for the child to have something to pawn if she hit hard times, which is eminently sensible but a banknote would have done just as well."

Sam nodded. The truth was that Hartley hadn't bought that bauble simply to present his housekeeper with something that could be pawned. He had chosen something fine, something that everyone who saw it would admire. Each time Sadie looked at it, she'd be reminded that somebody thought her baby was worth something.

"My point is that he's trying to do good. Maybe he hasn't quite got the hang of it yet, but he's making an effort. And if giving my baby pricey silver cups and offering you money to fix your pub is the best he can do right now, I think we ought to encourage him."

"What's that about?" Nick asked, coming to stand by Sam as Sadie left. "Somebody offered to pay to fix the Bell? And you turned them down?"

Sam couldn't meet his brother's eye. "That's hundreds of pounds, at least. I can't just take that kind of money."

"Why not?"

"You don't understand the situation," Sam said feebly. "Money changes things."

"Sam, you pillock. You give away money, not to mention food and drink, every day." Nick faced Sam, his eyes lit with a shrewdness that Sam didn't see often. It was easy to forget that Nick, for all his easy optimism and bluff good nature, was as canny as anyone needed to be. If sometimes he didn't see things, it was because he didn't think it was any of his business. "And you know what? You're right. Money does change things. You and I have been doing business side by side for years and sometimes when I'm running short you cover the balance."

"You're my brother," Sam protested.

"And when Kate and I get married, you know that money will be involved in our setting up house together, right? She makes a fair bit and guards it like a dragon sits on its hoard. That'll be something we have to deal with down the road, and she and I both know it."

"That's different," Sam said, and the words didn't have the ring of honesty even to himself.

"I'm trying to figure out who you know who has a couple hundred pounds to throw around. There's only one person I can think of, and he walks around alone with five guineas' worth of buttons, all hours of the night and day. But if you don't want to talk about it, that's fine by me, I suppose. I'll just ask this. Does this person mean you harm?" Nick asked.

"No," Sam admitted.

"Does he want something from you that you don't want to give?"

Sam's face heated. "No."

"Then if he's offering help, and you need help—and you

do, Sam—then don't you think it's a bit of a slap in the face
to refuse? You love the Bell. You did good work, work that
you believe in. If you walk away from help, I'll think you're
soft in the head."

"But—"

"You know I'm right," Nick continued. "Now go take a
walk or something. I'll finish up here."

Sam went to what used to be the Bell and headed for
the pump in the back, where he washed himself off in brac-
ingly cold water and dressed in a clean shirt. As he looked at
the wreckage of the taproom, for the first time he let himself take stock of the damage. There was no way out of this
on his own. As far as he knew, he was still on the hook for
this quarter's rent. He had enough saved for now, but soon
he'd need to ask for some of Nick's earnings. But if he went
to Hartley for help, he'd want to offer him something in
return—not to make it fair, not to make it an even trade, but
because if Hartley had been willing to give up his house for
Sam, then Sam needed to find a way to prove that he could
throw his lot in with Hartley as well.

CHAPTER TWENTY-FOUR

"I was thinking," Hartley said, patting the baby's back as Sadie toasted some bread for him, "I ought to hire a maid. It's a lot of work you're doing in addition to taking care of the baby."

She blinked at him over her shoulder. "I *am* the maid."

"Balderdash. You're the cook. And, well, it seems a dreadful imposition to ask you if you're my friend, when we both know that I pay your wages, and it isn't as if you could just tell me to bugger off, but I do think we have an understanding that is probably uncommon in most establishments." The baby made a purring sound that probably indicated indigestion. "Baby agrees."

He had been thinking about his family a fair bit these past weeks, and even more since Ben's arrival the previous day. Maybe it was the smell of milk and nappies that set him off, but every time he shut his eyes he remembered his own mother cradling one of his younger brothers. He remembered Ben hanging out the washing when he could hardly reach the line. He remembered his mother and Will's mother sewing by the fire while his father read aloud; he had always known this was a highly anomalous household arrangement, but was it any stranger than his current living situation? Whatever it was, it had been a family, and perhaps this was too.

She turned away from the fire and looked at him carefully, and it occurred to Hartley that she probably had more experience with friendship than he had. She couldn't possibly have less. "Why do you think I'd tell you to bugger off?"

"I'm not a warm person. I'm . . . difficult, perhaps." He thought of how peaceful and predictable Sam's life must have been before meeting Hartley. All of the risks in their friendship had been taken by Sam; all the work had been done by Sam. Hartley had contributed nothing beyond some brandy, a warm bed, and emotional disarray.

"Who told you that?" Sadie put the toast on a dish and loaded it with butter.

"It's hardly the sort of thing I need explained to me," Hartley said with as much dignity as he could with a mouthful of toast and an armful of wriggly infant. "Even before my disgrace and all that, I didn't precisely have friends." There were hostesses who routinely invited him at the last minute to make up numbers; there were gentlemen who nodded to him in the park. There wasn't anyone he could talk to beyond the basic civilities. "And now, other than, ah, Mr. Fox, the only people I'm close to are the people whose wages I pay, which I do think says something about the paucity of what I have to offer." Perhaps that was partly why Sam was reluctant to take his money—delicacy about not wanting Hartley to feel Sam's affections had been purchased.

"I've seen you with your brothers," Sadie pointed out.

Hartley made a dismissive noise. "They're related to me. They're required to put up with me."

"Really, Hartley. You're going to say that to me, of all people?"

"Your family is uniquely terrible."

"No, they aren't. Ask Alf about his parents. Ask Kate about her people. Not everyone starts with a family who likes them, so some of us make our own." She glanced pointedly at the baby in Hartley's arms, rolled her eyes, and turned back to the stove. "And since you're asking, the thing that makes friendship between us a bit awkward isn't that you pay my wages, but that I don't have anywhere else to go. So if you died or went to France or took rooms, I wouldn't have any recourse. Now, that doesn't bother me much because if I had married the curate, as my father wanted, and he had died, I'd have been left equally badly off. Worse, even, because at least if you left I'd have a reference."

"Perhaps we could do better than that," Hartley mused. He didn't know how, but he knew there had to be something he could do to make Sadie's situation less precarious. Alf's, too, although he supposed that being a man and not having a child, Alf had more options.

When the sun had fully risen, Hartley bundled the baby into a shawl, then wrapped her in one of his own wool mufflers, and carried her to the church to speak with the vicar about her christening. The plan was for Ben to do the talking. "They'll always listen to one of their own," Ben had said, and then proceeded to cheerfully extract a promise from the vicar about never mentioning the blank spot on the baptismal record where the child's father ought to be named. Afterward, still carrying the baby and with his brother in tow, the three of them went to Philpott's office where Ben did an admirable job of pretending that the scheme Hartley proposed to the solicitor wasn't in the least remarkable.

That night, there was a scratching at the kitchen door. Hartley was once again holding the baby, pacing back and forth from scullery to the coal cellar and back again. Infants were both whimsical and fickle, Hartley was discovering; the cabinet clock upstairs was entirely *vieux jeu*, and the baby would lay off her nighttime howlings for only as long as she was borne in state along this path. He had been walking long enough to be concerned about the state of his boots when he heard the sound from the mews. Shifting the child to his shoulder, he opened the kitchen door to see Daisy.

"Come in, you," Hartley said, stepping back and beckoning the dog inside. But the dog didn't cross the threshold. Instead he danced in a circle. "No, I will not bring cheese and bread for all your dog friends in the street. If you want supper, it'll be indoors." The dog let out a shrill bark, loud enough to make the infant stir against Hartley's shoulder. "What's the matter with you?" Hartley demanded. The dog yelped a few more times, and in the interest of not disturbing the rest of the household, Hartley made haste in finding it some crusts of bread to eat. "Greedy is what you are," Hartley told the dog while slicing him some cold ham.

"This is . . . quite a scene," said a sleepy voice from the stairs. Hartley looked up to see Ben. "You're holding your cook's baby and feeding a . . . what is that thing? A ferret?"

Hartley didn't dignify this nonsense with a response.

"Mother used to do that, pace back and forth with the baby. It must have been Percy, or maybe Lance. You look like her, you know. I stand by what I said earlier," Ben said. "You do look tired. But you also look . . . I don't want to say happy, because you plainly have a lot on your mind. But you look as if you've been living. As if you've been feeling things. Your heart seems lived in."

"That sounds disgusting, Benedict."

"Do you want to tell me about it?" asked Ben at his most vicarly.

Hartley held the baby closer. He shook his head, but managed a smile.

"I wish I were staying longer," Ben said. He meant to spend only a few nights in London before returning north. Ben had little desire ever to go further than shouting distance from his village; for him to have come this far spoke of the seriousness of his concern.

"Why?"

"The Hartley Sedgwick I saw this summer would never have been so at home in anyone's kitchen, in old clothes, with baby spittle on his shoulder. I'd like to see what you do next, because I think it's going to be wonderful."

Hartley turned so his brother wouldn't see the tears in his eyes. For the first time since he had been a child, he could see his way toward a future that was his own. Not a life his godfather had thrust onto him as revenge or recompense or some combination of the two; not a life he himself had clung to as if doubling down on a bad bet.

"Do you think you could hold this baby for a while? I have a dog to return."

It was hard to believe that this was the same lane Sam had lurked in all those weeks ago. The winter's first snow was falling, and when the sun rose London would have the temporary veneer of clean uniformity. Later, the snow would melt into greasy gray puddles, soaking through his boots and dirtying the hems of cloaks and gowns. But for a while, the streets would be smooth and white, the higgledy-piggledy array of rooftops merged together in a single expanse.

During his first hours in the mews that autumn, he had seen servants go in and out of Hartley's house, before even knowing the house was Hartley's. There had been maids and lads with their noses in the air, and Sam had decided they were all too far above his touch to ask about a dirty painting. He grinned at the memory. Little had he expected to share common cause with the master of the house. Even less could he have expected that common cause to turn into something else.

The door to Hartley's house opened, and he saw a slim figure emerge, a coat in one arm and a dog in the other.

"You'll freeze, dressed like that," Sam said.

Hartley spun to face him. He was in his shirtsleeves, a pair of dust-stained pantaloons shoved into scuffed boots. One of his braces was sliding off his shoulder, and Sam resisted the urge to put him right. "Don't tell me you came back for this troublemaker," Hartley said, indicating the dog.

"I see two troublemakers here," Sam said, stepping close.

"I missed you," Hartley said.

It had been less than a week since they had seen one another. "I missed you too. I came to tell you that I'll take your help. Whatever you're offering. But I want to do something for you too."

"Oh?" Hartley looked up curiously.

"I want to help you get your painting back."

"Really?" Hartley's eyes were a bit dazed. "You know I meant to burgle a solicitor's office?"

"Look, Hart," Sam went on, "I want to help you lay this to rest. When I met you, you were—"

"A disaster."

"Sad, I was going to say. And hurting. I think the idea of getting the paintings was the first thing that had made you happy in weeks."

"I have other things making me happy now." Hartley tipped his head back to look up at Sam, and on his jaw Sam could see the faint stubble that meant he hadn't shaved for a few days. "You're the best man I know, Sam Fox, and I love you."

"I love you too. God, I've missed you." Sam breathed in deep, inhaling the scent of whatever scent or hair soap Hartley used.

Hartley stepped into the open circle of Sam's arms. Sam hoped Hartley could feel how heavily his heart thudded, and that he knew it was for him. Sam held still as Hartley settled against him, first tucking his head beneath Sam's chin as Sam pulled his own coat around them both. Hartley went onto his toes and Sam tilted his head down, and in the split second before their lips met, Hartley's mouth curved in a smile. Their kiss was slow and patient, the kiss of people who knew they had time. Hartley kissed like he had never done it before, and maybe he hadn't. That thought touched Sam and tore at his heart at the same moment. Hartley ought to have had years of kisses, a lifetime of kisses; but at the same time Sam was all too happy to be able to claim the entirety of Hartley's kisses for himself.

Hartley broke the kiss and buried his face in Sam's coat, but Sam could tell Hartley was smiling. God, it was a rare gift to have this man in his arms. It made Sam feel like he had been given care of something unspeakably precious and fragile. Before they pulled apart, Hartley cupped Sam's jaw and gave him a wondering look that told Sam that Hartley felt the same way, and this thing between them was equally precious and dear to both of them.

"I don't need your help with the paintings," Hartley said. "I used them as a bargaining chip to get Philpott to write a letter to your landlord explaining that you need to be released from your lease. There's apparently a fair bit of precedent." He produced a sheet of paper from a pocket. "I didn't post it. It's yours to do with as you please."

Sam's mind reeled. "A bargaining chip?"

"I told him that I'd never tell anyone what was in his filthy cupboards as long as he wrote me the letter. He seemed hugely relieved."

"Isn't that blackmail?"

"I don't think so." Hartley wrinkled his brow. "Well, can't say I care if it is."

"Well, then," Sam said. "I suppose then neither do I." Hartley drew him inside the house for another kiss.

They were interrupted by what seemed to Hartley the rather pointed stomping of feet on the stairs. He pulled away from Sam, because even if Will and Ben knew exactly what Hartley was up to, Sam's privacy meant something. He didn't try to wipe the smile from his face, though.

"Sam, these are two of my brothers, Ben and Will. Ben's visiting from the frozen north. You've sort of met Will before. Ben's about to leave at dawn on the mail coach. You'll join us for a very early breakfast?" he asked, looking expectantly at Sam.

Sam nodded.

They crowded around the table in Sadie's parlor, passing dishes of ham and toast, Hartley eating with one hand because the baby slept in the crook of his other arm.

"She's to be christened next week, Sam," Sadie said. "I'm calling her Charlotte."

"That's a pretty name, Sadie," Sam said. "And she's a bonny girl."

This was the first time they had addressed one another by

their Christian names, and it made Hartley feel for a moment like everyone in this kitchen belonged to one another.

"Hartley's middle name is Charles," Ben supplied.

"I know," Sadie said pointedly.

"Does that mean Hartley's going to be the babe's godfather?" Will asked. The room fell silent.

Hartley was stunned speechless. Under the table, Sam's hand found his leg and gave it a comforting squeeze and then stayed there, warm and heavy on his thigh. "I'm hardly fit to be anybody's godfather." Sadie and Alf both looked meaningfully at the christening cup that sat on Sadie's chimneypiece and then at Hartley's coat. Hartley followed their gaze and saw that the infant had deposited some nasty sort of sputum on him.

"Are you suggesting than an infant selects its godparents by means of vomiting on them?" he asked, furiously dabbing at his coat with his handkerchief. "But if you want me to, of course I will." Perhaps after a while *godfather* would come to mean his relation to the baby, rather than Easterbrook's relation so him.

Sam and Sadie didn't even bother to conceal the satisfied glance they shared. Hartley didn't need to look in Will and Ben's direction to know they were sharing similar glances.

"I hate all of you," he announced. Hartley finished the meal in a mood of rare merriment, despite it being wretchedly early in the morning and not having had a full night's sleep in days.

Later, after Ben had left to catch the mail coach and Will

had gone with him, Sam and Hartley had the house to themselves.

"I'm sorry you had to give up on the paintings," Sam said from the zinc tub they had placed in the kitchen by the hearth. It was Sadie's morning out and Alf had made himself scarce, so Hartley felt utterly free to sit back in his chair and admire the proceedings. Sam barely fit in the tub, and his strong muscles were soapy and gleaming in the firelight.

When Sam had let it slip that he was bedding down in the back room of the Bell, Hartley had insisted that he instead stay with him. To Hartley's surprise, Sam hadn't protested. "I'm too old to sleep on the floor," he had said. "And I suppose your neighbors have been watching me come and go for months now. No harm in my sleeping here. People will just think you've gotten another servant."

But to hear Sam mention the paintings brought Hartley up short because, after making his deal with Philpott, he had felt strangely free. He was building a life that didn't depend on being seen as anything other than what he was. There would be danger, and he and Sam would always have to be discreet when they were in public. He would need to find work; with that would go his last claim to gentility, and good riddance to it. But he would be surrounded by people he cared about and who cared for him in return. Hartley had been hurt in a way that couldn't be undone or avenged: Easterbrook had done wrong and had never paid for it. But Hartley would be happy anyway. In addition to happiness, Hartley had a new feeling that was utterly foreign. It was like a new flavor he couldn't quite identify. He was looking forward to the future, eager to see what it brought. This was hope, he supposed.

Sam stood and dried himself off on a length of toweling that Hartley had left in arm's reach of the bath. "The water's getting cold. I'll have to put more on if you'll be wanting a wash."

Reluctantly, Hartley tore his gaze away from Sam long enough to fill the pot at the pump.

"It's odd to see you doing work," Sam said.

"I can boil water, Sam. I'm not a total incompetent." With a flourish, he hung the pot over the fire, as if to demonstrate his competence at water boiling. "I didn't grow up in a house where people poured me baths scented with rosewater or whatever it is you're imagining."

"I know you didn't. But I'm glad to have met your brothers, or I might not have believed it."

"Ha. I'll tell Will that you'd never take him for a gentleman. He'll be delighted."

"I meant the vicar. Benedict. His hands are rough. And he had some dirt under his nails. It made me think that you might not mind that for yourself. After you leave here, I mean."

Hartley had explained that he was selling this house and looking for a set of rooms that would accommodate him, Alf, Sadie, and the baby. Theirs was an odd arrangement, and he hadn't yet come across anything suitable. After the events of the past few months, he couldn't stow Alf away in the servants' quarters or put Sadie and Charlotte in the basement. It would feel, somehow, like a lie. And yet he didn't know what the alternative was.

"I wouldn't mind it," Hartley said. "If it meant being with you."

"I was wondering," Sam said, "if you'd like to let the rooms above a tavern. There's a place to let on Shoe Lane. There are four rooms upstairs, two in front and two in back. If you took one pair and I took the other, it wouldn't look out of the ordinary."

"Would you really want that? I don't think I'm precisely easy to be around, and I doubt my ability to be charming at all hours of the clock." *Do you know what you're getting yourself into*, was what he really wanted to ask.

"There's nobody who's charming at all hours. Come here." Sam patted his lap.

Hartley made a show of rolling his eyes but he settled comfortably in Sam's lap.

"I love you," Sam said.

"How unwise of you."

Sam chucked him on the chin. "Maybe you are a prig after all. Offer rescinded. Go find somewhere else to live."

"I love you too," he said, dropping a kiss onto Sam's forehead. "Is there room for Sadie and Alf?"

Sam's expression softened. "I made sure of it. There's a pair of rooms on the top floor. Hart, I'll be honest. I can't imagine you in rooms above a pub."

"I see that one day I'm going to have to bring you to blasted Kirkby Barton in the arse end of nowhere so you can see the cottage where I was born. You'll see that rooms above any pub are a stately pleasure dome by comparison. Let me make this equally clear to you, because I think I've failed on this score. I want to be with you, in rooms above a pub or anywhere you happen to be. A cave, a pirate ship, a desert island, doesn't matter. And while I maintain that it would have been vastly better for you to never have met me, the fact remains that you have. I love you, and I want to be with you, and if I haven't made that clear then it's because I've made a hash of everything. Frankly, if you actually plan on being such a fool as to keep me in your life, which I dearly hope you are, you'll just have to get used to my making a hash of lots of things."

Sam brought his hand to Hartley's cheek. "If that makes me a fool, then I'm glad to be a fool."

"Well, good. Glad that's settled." Hartley climbed off Sam's lap and bathed quickly, all the while conscious of Sam's gaze on him, as hotly as his own gaze had been on Sam.

Later, upstairs in bed, Hartley settled himself into the crook of Sam's arm, and within a few moments Sam's chest was falling and rising with the steadiness of a man fast asleep. Of course Sam was the kind of person who simply fell asleep. No tossing or turning or prolonged exercises in self-recrimination; no worrying about where to put his limbs in relation to his bedmate's. If Hartley hadn't been so fond of him he'd have been quite disgusted.

At some point, Hartley must have fallen asleep, however, because he could hear the clanging of pans from downstairs, which meant it was afternoon and Sadie had returned. One of Sam's huge arms was draped heavily across his chest, and he felt a rare peace of mind.

Maybe that was why, after all these years, he finally let

his thoughts drift to the room across the hall. He had hardly poked his head into his godfather's bedchamber in the years he had been living here. Hartley's memory supplied a dim vision of a large bed with dark velvet hangings, matching window curtains perpetually closed. Easterbrook had commissioned a small cabinet that was festooned with gilt and fashioned with a golden lock; it was in this exemplar of the old man's terrible taste that Hartley's portrait had been kept. Upon inheriting the house, Hartley had confirmed that the cabinet was empty, then promptly sent it to the auctioneer, along with all the pricier bits of furniture.

He pulled the quilt up to Sam's chin and slid out of bed carefully, so as not to disturb him, and hastily dressed. The door to Sir Humphrey's room creaked as Hartley nudged it open, his hand sweaty on the latch. The curtains were drawn, letting in only the faintest slivers of wintry light. Hartley had no intention of poking about this room in the dark, so he pulled the curtains open, dislodging a cloud of dust and revealing a tangle of cobwebs, some still bearing ominous-looking shadows. He thought he could hear the skittering of tiny arachnid legs over cold glass, and shuddered to think that this had been only across the corridor from where he slept.

Walking the perimeter of the room, he saw that, a piece of paneling had come loose. Some wood shavings were scattered atop the layer of dust that adorned the floorboards, suggesting that this damage was new, dating from after the departure of his servants. Around the edges of the panel were a few jagged marks. He shuddered, imagining the creature that had caused this damage. Spiders were bad enough, but mice were—he preferred not to think about mice, and the size of these marks indicated something rather more ambitious than a mouse. He'd call in the rat catcher first thing. But he didn't want to leave the panel just hanging there. He still lived here, for God's sake, and he wasn't going to tolerate bits of his house wobbling about like loose teeth. Using the toe of one bare foot, he tried to press the panel back into place.

Instead it fell off completely, landing on the floor in a cloud of dust, with a noise that seemed to echo in the quiet of the house. Behind the panel he expected to see exposed stonework or bricks or whatever the interior walls of houses such as these were made of. Instead there was a gap, a dark and shadowy emptiness.

For a moment his mind reeled backward ten years, fifteen years, until he was in an entirely different house, an entirely different wall but with a similar gap. Then, Will and Martin had tried to convince him it was a priest's hole, and when Hartley had pointed out that the Easterbrooks were not Catholic, they had insisted it must be a secret passageway leading to a medieval oubliette. That had been almost plausible, quite in keeping with what he might have expected from Easterbrooks of yore.

This was no oubliette, no passageway of any kind. At closer range, he could see that the panel had been pulled roughly off the wall, not damaged by a hungry rodent. And there were only so many reasons a panel might be pulled off a wall. Biting his lip, Hartley stuck a hand into the darkness. His fingers met something coarse and yet almost slick in places. A tube? Some kind of pipe? He pulled it out and saw that it was a rolled-up canvas.

There was no sound but the beating of his heart as he unrolled the canvas. Yes, this was one of the paintings that had once hung in the library. He remembered it well. A girl in a yellow wrap that was draped in such a way as to cover nothing of relevance. He didn't think he had ever met her. In the shadowy recesses of the wall, he could see several other rolled canvases leaning against the exposed lath and plaster, and one small painting that still remained in its gilt frame.

He reached into his pocket and found the knife he used to open letters and peel apples. Flicking it open, he knelt before the canvas. Best to get this over with. He slashed the canvas sufficiently that the girl would be unrecognizable. It took more effort than he had expected, this slicing of metal through layers of oil paint on thick canvas. His knife was a delicate thing, made for cutting nibs and trimming candles. It was hardly up to this task.

"Hartley," said a soft voice. He looked up to see Sam, wearing only his trousers, standing in the doorway. "Let me help."

"No. This is for me to do." He didn't want anyone to look at the pictures, even though he knew many of Easterbrook's London callers must have seen them. He felt, somehow, responsible for seeing this through. "But do you have a knife? This is getting dull."

Wordlessly, Sam stepped out of the room, only to return a moment later with a much more utilitarian knife than

Hartley's pretty filigree one. It felt heavy and rough in his hand, but it got the job done.

The next painting he unrolled was Kate's. He had tried not to look at the subjects' faces, because it seemed like an invasion of privacy, but he couldn't help but notice that Kate looked like she had been having a jolly time as she reclined on the artist's sofa. He really hoped she had been. He hoped all the women had a grand time, collected their money, and carried on with their lives, never sparing the paintings or Easterbrook another thought. But the painting had weighed on Kate, and he knew a furious satisfaction when he slid the knife through the rough surface of the canvas.

"That's Kate's painting done," he said when he started on the next canvas.

"Thank you," Sam murmured, leaning against the wall near the door, his arms folded across his broad chest. Hartley gave him a watery smile.

"You can go back to bed," Hartley managed. Sam only shook his head.

When he removed the next canvas, he got a good look at the gilt frame. Carved into the bevels of the frame was a pattern of laurel leaves that he surely oughtn't recognize after all this time. But of course he did, just as he recognized the bare arm painted on the exposed part of the canvas. He ought to abandon the painting he was defacing and move to that small frame. Instead he worked methodically, destroying one painting after the next, until he was kneeling in a drift of brightly colored bits of canvas, the knife handle digging painfully into his palm.

Sam hadn't known where he was when he woke up, but he knew Hartley ought to have been there. He slid his hand blindly across too-fine sheets and found only lingering warmth where Hartley's body had recently lain. When he heard what sounded like a gasp, he threw on trousers and all but ran out of the room, driven by some silly instinct to keep his lover safe, expecting to find that Hartley had tripped over a loose bit of carpet or something.

He hadn't expected this. By the looks of things, neither had Hartley. Some other time he'd ask what had prompted Hartley to kick a hole in the wall, or done whatever it was to expose the paintings' hiding place. But for now, he was just going to be here in case Hartley needed him.

He watched as Hartley unleashed an efficient hell on those canvases. They were pretty thoroughly destroyed, all except one, which stood framed, inside the wall. Hartley glanced at the one surviving canvas, and Sam followed his gaze. It was a young man, little more than a boy, lying on a sofa, not a stitch of clothes on him. Yellow hair, pale greenish-gray eyes. Sam's stomach lurched.

Hartley had never said outright that one of the paintings he wished to recover had himself as a subject, but Sam had suspected as much. Now that he saw the portrait, he knew that its revelation would have meant more than the public embarrassment of being caught without one's clothes on. Sam looked away from the canvas, but not before noticing that whatever tricks the painter had used, he had made Hartley look like a—there was no way around it—like a whore. Nothing wrong with honest whoring, but when you were that young it wasn't whoring. It was something altogether different. The bile rose in Sam's gorge, and he knelt beside Hartley.

Hartley leaned against Sam's chest, the knife dropping from his hand. Sam wrapped his arms around Hartley and felt the smaller man sink against his chest, felt the rise and fall of his breathing. Only later did Sam take the knife and slice through the one remaining canvas until nothing was left but unrecognizable scraps.

After they had built a fire and watched the remnants go up in flame, Sam looked hard at Hartley.

"You all right?" he asked.

"Oddly, yes," Hartley said. "That was . . . a lot. It felt good, though. *I* feel good. But Sam, you realize what this means?"

"That somebody went to a fair bit of trouble hiding the paintings in your own house. I can't make heads or tails of it."

"Well, there is that. But what I really want to know is what Philpott had in his cabinet."

Sam let out a whistle.

"You know what," Hartley went on, "I don't want to know. I don't care if he was conducting black masses or worshipping devils. I'm glad to be rid of him and everyone connected with the Easterbrooks. Somebody else can deal with that lot. I have my own life." He settled against Sam's chest as they watched the paintings burn.

Chapter Twenty-five

It was in the snug back parlor of the new premises that they formed a plan, Hartley making notes in his small feathery handwriting while Sam paced the dusty floor, listing what they'd need to buy and what they'd need to build. At first, Sam had only seen the ways it differed from the Bell—no polished counter, too many small rooms instead of one wide taproom, an old-fashioned sort of gallery looking down from the upper floor. But also absent was the back room: no blood stains on the floor, no ghosts of the ring. It was a bigger space, too, and there was room in the kitchens for Nick to have a helper and for Sadie's cooking range to be brought from Brook Street.

"We could do a supper from noon to four," Nick said. They were gathered around a table for the first meal Nick had prepared in the new kitchen. "Like they do at the Crown and Sugar Loaf. Three shillings six, they charge."

"I'd pay six shillings for more of this mutton," Hartley said, gesturing at his empty dish.

"You would," said Kate.

"And there are those parlors upstairs for ladies who might not want to be seen in a public house," Sadie pointed out. "Or for people who want to meet privately."

"Much nicer than the setup at the Cross Keys," Alf chimed in from where he leaned against the chimneypiece, baby Charlotte in his arms.

Sam was about to remark that they weren't running a molly house, when Hartley cleared his throat. "Safer too."

Nick didn't say anything, and Sam might have supposed that his brother had no idea what Alf and Hartley were talking about, but then Nick raised an eyebrow at Kate, and Sam realized his brother had to know. And it was fine—Nick hadn't been angry or disgusted, he had simply raised an eyebrow and shot his wife a knowing glance. Sam thought he might have been underestimating his brother. After all, Nick had once said he'd gladly help Sam dispose of a body; perhaps accepting a love affair was not more to ask than covering up a murder.

Later, when Nick and Kate had gone home to their rooms, Sadie had gone upstairs to put the baby to bed, and Alf had gone out, Sam and Hartley were left alone in the empty barroom.

"I met with a new solicitor," Hartley said. "After all is said and done, I'll have about two thousand pounds left."

"Oh?"

"And I don't want it. I want to stand on my own feet. I've given five hundred pounds to Sadie, because it's the sum she would have had as a dowry—an entirely inadequate dowry, I might add. Also, I signed the deed to the Brook Street house over to Ben, so he'll get the proceeds from the sale."

Sam nearly choked on his beer.

"It's not that dramatic," Hartley went on. "If I know Ben, he'll spend the majority of it on urchins and stray animals, but he'll keep the rest safe for a rainy day. So that means if Will or I ever fall on hard times, we'll at least have that recourse. I know I said I wanted to stand on my own two feet, and you likely think being able to run to my brother is cheating, but—"

Sam held up his hand. "I don't think it's cheating. I'd want you even if you were swathed in furs." That was no more than the truth, but Sam was grateful Hartley had given up some of his wealth and status to join him on a more equal footing.

Over the next fortnight, Sam realized that the new tavern was getting fixed up so quickly because somebody was greasing the wheels.

"How much did you pay that glazier?" Sam asked Hartley. "When I talked to him, he said he couldn't be bothered until Thursday next. But when I came in this morning, I find I have three new windows."

Hartley had been attempting to hang a picture, but he let the hammer fall to his side. He gave Sam a smile that might have looked sly if not for the plaster dust on the tip of his nose. "I didn't pay him anything at all. If you want to know more you're going to have to talk to Kate. And that's all I'm going to say on that subject." He closed his lips tightly and mimed turning a key in a lock.

"I'll have the truth out of you later," Sam muttered.

"I'll bet you will."

Sam stepped out onto the street, ducking under a ladder that was propped against the side of the building. A freshly painted sign swung above the entrance. Instead of a picture of a bell, it bore a bright orange fox. *The Fox*, it read. And stenciled on the door were the words:

The Fox
Public House
Samuel Fox, Publican

It still felt both silly and more than a little prideful to name the place after himself, but his brother and Hartley had insisted that he was the main draw.

He found Nick in the kitchen beside the old Bell, packing tankards and dishes into a battered old crate. "What's this about the glazier?" Sam asked. He spotted the peeling paint on the wall and thought of something else. "And the paper hanger and plasterers."

Nick looked up from the crate. "Kate," he called. "What day is it?"

Kate appeared from the back room, where she was packing up tankards and dishes and anything that could be salvaged and moved to the Fox. "The twentieth of December."

"You owe me three bob," Nick said.

Kate looked at Sam. "Blast. I had bet you wouldn't figure it out until Christmas."

"Figure what out?"

"Kate's running a racket," Nick said. "She's got all the regulars pitching in whenever your back is turned."

"It's not a racket," Kate protested. "Not really, at least. But everybody wants the Bell—or the Fox, rather—to be up and running as soon as possible. The King's Arms over in Popingjay Court has a nasty barman who pinches girls, and the Bull's Head in Gough Square serves watered-down ale. But really, people miss one another. That's what we all liked about the Bell, seeing one another, and seeing you."

Sam felt his face heat. "That's all very nice, but it doesn't explain about the workmen."

"Well, I was at a lying in for the glazier's sister-in-law. Her husband is a paper hanger, and they've all been living together in a pair of rooms because last summer the brother-in-law fell off a ladder, broke his leg, and has been out of work since. So I told the glazier that we'd find work for his brother-in-law if he took care of the windows first thing."

"And the plasterer?"

"Alfie did it, along with some help from Johnny Newton. Johnny was looking for work down at the wharves, which I suppose is a step up from picking pockets or whatever it was he was doing before. But his mother wanted him out of harm's way, so he plastered and whitewashed the entire ground floor."

"How come I didn't see any of this?"

"It was meant to be a surprise," Kate said. "Hartley kept you out of the way."

"Three bob, Mrs. Fox," Nick said.

She fished around in her pocket and slapped some coins onto the table. "That's two and six. I'll make up the balance in trade." Then Kate laughed at her own joke while Nick stammered and Sam pretended not to understand, but as he walked back to the Fox he caught himself whistling.

Empty of furnishings, the house on Brook Street seemed to have lost some of its power. The kitchen was stark and lacking without the big iron range, which Hartley had hired a man to cart off to the Fox. The shiny copper pots and pans were in crates by the door, along with the few belongings Hartley had packed up. He had been surprised by how little he wanted to take with him: a few changes of clothes, some fine linen sheets, a looking glass, a few odds and ends. Everything else had already been sent to the auctioneer.

He had been prepared to spend the rest of his life in this house, among objects that had belonged to a life he hadn't chosen. Now, a few weeks before his twenty-fourth birthday, he had a chance to start fresh, a chance to live a life that meant something, a chance to let go of everything this house had once meant to him. Stripped to the floorboards, though, it was just a house. Nothing but bricks and wood and plaster. Memories didn't live in a place, but in a person, and Hartley, now that he had a future, was at peace with his own past. Alf had said that the house was haunted, but it had been his own mind that was beset by dark spirits.

As if to prove him wrong, there came a thumping sound from the attic. Hartley supposed some enterprising squirrels had decided to winter in one of the old box rooms. He decided to inspect the situation for himself, partly to prove to himself that he was above any base superstition.

He rarely had cause to go to the attics, especially in the dead of winter. Dark and dusty places were in general not Hartley's idea of fun, even less so when they were almost certainly crawling with vermin. So he was feeling rather put upon when he pushed open the door. Chasing squirrels out of his property was not what he had planned to do this afternoon.

Later, he'd wonder if he had known all along what he'd find in the attic, if he had known from the moment he had found the paintings behind the loose piece of paneling. But at that instant, when he saw the man standing in the center of the space, his first thought was that Alf had been correct in supposing the attic haunted. For here was a spirit of a man with shaggy hair and a great unkempt beard. Then his eyes adjusted and he saw that it was Martin Easterbrook.

His first thought was to wish that he had Sam with him. His second thought was that he ought to flee. Martin didn't look like he was in fighting form, and surely Hartley could reach the street before him. He could pretend he had never seen Martin. He could leave the new occupants to deal with Martin as they might.

But then he took in the full extent of Martin's haggard appearance, his sallow complexion, the bloodstained handkerchief in his hand, his thinness. He again wished he had Sam with him; not to keep him safe, because it was plain Martin posed no threat to anyone, but because Sam would know the right thing to do.

Hartley didn't know whether Martin had been behind the gossip that had gotten him cast out of society. Perhaps it had been Philpott. Or perhaps somebody from his godfather's old set had spoken up. At the moment it didn't matter.

"You're not going to ask what I'm doing here?" Martin asked. He looked terrible. Hartley supposed living in unheated attics was not generally beneficial to one's health, but Martin looked positively sickly. Hartley found that he was very nearly concerned.

"It's quite clear what you're doing here," Hartley said, gesturing at their surroundings. There was a pallet bed, a few candle stubs, and a pile of apple cores. "I daresay you have nowhere else to go, or at least that's what you've told yourself. You will need to seek other accommodations, but we'll discuss that in a moment. First, I'm going to need you to come with me."

Martin didn't respond. He only coughed into a dirty handkerchief.

Hartley sighed. "For God's sake, take this." He handed Martin his own handkerchief.

They went out the front door and Hartley hailed a hackney. When he gave the driver the address, Martin startled, as if he wanted to jump out of the carriage. "Don't do it," Hartley said coolly. "I don't think you'd survive the fall." Hartley paid the driver and they set off down a series of insalubrious lanes and climbed a rickety staircase. At first there was no answer to Hartley's knock, but then he heard footsteps. Will answered the door and turned so pale that Hartley regretted not breaking the news to his brother more gently.

"I thought you were dead," Will said, and proceeded to punch Martin solidly in the jaw.

All three of them stood in shocked silence for a moment, Martin rubbing his jaw, Will looking between his fist and Martin as if unsure how they had connected, and Hartley edging between them to prevent any further fisticuffs, as if he even knew how. Then Hartley cleared his throat. "Well. Didn't anticipate that. Martin, I can't believe I'm about to do this, but here's five quid if you want to find someplace to stay that doesn't put you into proximity with a man who means you harm." He dug into his coin purse and picked out five pound coins. When he held his hand out to Martin, the other man waved him away, so he slid the coins into the outer pocket of Martin's exceedingly dirty coat.

When Hartley went downstairs, the hackney had already left, and there was no chance of finding another in this quarter. He thought he ought to feel more than he did after seeing Martin, but as he walked back to the Fox he felt only pity for Martin and compassion for Will. The events of the past felt remote, not quite irrelevant but not important either. The snow was falling again, and soon he would be in his new home, starting his new life, with the man he loved.

It was snowing, so the flagstone floors of the Fox were growing slippery despite everyone's best efforts to stomp their boots at the door. But somebody was playing a fiddle and the smell of roasting meat filled the taproom, making the pub feel like an island of warmth and merriment in the middle of a winter storm.

Hartley was at his customary table, a stack of papers and an inkwell before him. He absently rocked Charlotte's cradle with one foot.

"When do you think he'll be done?" Alf asked.

"He's only been working on it for a month," Sam pointed out.

"Yeah, but how long can it take to write a play? It only takes two hours to act it out."

"I wouldn't mention that to Hartley, if I were you," Sam said, and handed Alf a tray of drinks to bring around. Then he poured a cup of coffee and brought it to Hartley's table along with a roll.

"Thank you," Hartley said, slipping a morsel of the roll under the table to Daisy.

"How's our evil count?"

"Insufferable." Hartley glanced up with a light in his eye. He was looking slightly scruffy these days, having disposed of his finest garments and adopted a style that he probably thought more suited to a working man. Sam didn't have the heart to tell him otherwise. "He's being very dastardly indeed. I think it'll be entirely amusing."

When Hartley had said that he meant to stand on his own two feet, Sam hadn't thought he had anything particular in mind, but it turned out that Hartley had meant to write a play. It was a rare treat, watching Hartley work, watching him find his footing. He had thought Hartley set such store by being a gentleman, but he seemed to enjoy his scribbling. Perhaps idleness, like pricey clothes, was another aspect of gentlemanliness he was glad to be shot of.

Sam took in the sight of him, ink-stained fingers, unkempt hair, a waistcoat the same pale grayish green as his eyes. "All lined up right and tight," Sam said. "Not a single button out of line." They both knew that Sam already was aware of this, since he had watched Hartley put on that very waistcoat a few hours earlier.

If there had been a bit more light, Sam bet he would have seen the pink rise in Hartley's cheeks. It was a gift, knowing someone this well, seeing them day after day and living side by side. And to know that there were years ahead of them, that he'd get to see lines form around those pale eyes and gray streak that yellow hair, made him feel—well, it made him feel the way he hoped people felt when they came to the Fox and got whatever they needed. Warm, safe, and hopeful.

When people came together, in pairs, and families, and communities, it was a kind of commonplace magic that warded off the dark and cold of the outside world. He hadn't ever thought he'd be on the receiving end of that sort of miracle, had thought it was reserved for people with fewer burdens and cleaner consciences.

"Later," he said, his voice low and intent. "Later, I'm going to show you how glad I am that I found you in that alley."

"Sam Fox," Hartley answered, laying down his pen and looking up at him with an expression that was equal parts outrage and affection. "You show me that every day, every minute. I'm the one ought to be showing you how grateful I am. If I hadn't met you, I'd be alone in the dark, counting my shirt studs or something."

Sam leaned over the table on the pretense of wiping away a drop of candle wax. "I'm sure we can figure out a way to properly express our gratitude," he murmured.

Hartley's answering smile was fierce and joyful. "I bet we can."

The next exhilarating romance in
Cat Sebastian's Regency Impostors series,

A DUKE IN DISGUISE

is on sale
November 2018

About the Author

CAT SEBASTIAN lives in a swampy part of the South with her husband, three kids, and two dogs. Before her kids were born, she practiced law and taught high school and college writing. When she isn't reading or writing, she's doing crossword puzzles, bird watching, and wondering where she put her coffee cup.

Discover great authors, exclusive offers, and more at hc.com